For Claire and Grant, with love.

DARK WINGS

For Ann—
Enjoy the read!
Best,
J Leish Jackson
August 2020

J. Leigh Jackson

~~~~~

Published by *thewordverve inc.* (www.thewordverve.com)

First Edition 2020

eBook ISBN: 978-1-948225-85-4
Paperback ISBN: 978-1-948225-86-1
Library of Congress Control No.: 2020912502

Cover design by George Arnold
www.hspubinc.com

Interior book design by Bob Houston eBook Formatting
http://facebook.com/eBookFormatting/info

Prologue

"Your husband has dragged you into a world of trouble...and it may not be over. You have to understand this, please!"

She bit her lip and shook her head, but said nothing, staring defiantly at him with her piercing green eyes. They sat across from each other at her kitchen table, sipping coffee as they had done so many times over the last three years. Discussing her husband—missing or dead, she still wasn't sure. And she fought with every fiber of her being to no longer care.

He almost lost himself in her gaze, but he snapped back to the reason for his last-ditch effort to keep her in Sleepy Hollow. "Please hear me out."

"I already have. You're going to tell me that it's time I accept everything we learned about Will and his actions. That he's a bad guy, that he set me up to take the fall. Same old story."

"Yes. I mean, no. I'm not here to rehash all of that."

"Then what?" She raised her eyebrows as if challenging him to prove her assumption wrong.

"I'm just..." He paused, took a breath. "I need you to *listen* to me. *Hear* me. Whether you want to believe it or not, Will's actions have put you in danger. Indefinitely."

"So I'm supposed to live in fear forever?" She threw her hands in the air.

"No, of course not. But you have to realize—"

"It sounds exactly like what you mean. It's been almost a year since they officially declared him dead. You were there. And now that I signed the cease-and-desist documents from those Orwellian government agents, promising not to look into it anymore...I'm just done." She shrugged. "I've given up. What's worse is I feel like I've abandoned him, okay? For God's sake, I let the military bury an empty casket. I've done enough, don't you think? *We've* done enough." Her voice cracked like the tension in the air.

He stared at the table, tracing an imaginary line with his finger. He knew how gut-wrenching all of that had been for her. It had been the same for him in some ways. Will had been his best friend. "You didn't abandon him. He chose..." He held back that line of thinking. "We searched for three years." His voice barely reached the level of a whisper.

"Okay, here we go again. Do you know why I can't believe all of those horrible things about Will? Because if I do, that means my entire marriage was a sham—that Will never loved me." A tear fell down her cheek. She pushed it away angrily. "He was my husband, your friend. You knew him as well as I did. Why is it so easy for you to make him the villain?"

He looked at her, the woman he had grown to love, and pleaded with his eyes as he leaned across the table toward her. "You know I don't want to believe those things either, but the evidence speaks for itself. He implicated you. I cannot forgive him for that. You need to accept that none of this is my doing or your doing. We tried to clear his name. I wish he'd never done any of it. The last thing on earth I'm trying to do is hurt you." He reached for her hand. She pulled away.

"Well, it doesn't matter now. I'm taking my life back, and the one thing I *can* control is getting out of this limbo. I can't stay here and do that." She grew more unsettled. "I have to move on."

Her last words struck him like a knife. "You're missing the point. I get that you need to reset—moving away from here seems like the answer. But it's not that simple. The cartel won't stop keeping tabs just because you move. You are running toward a fairy tale, a dream in your head. You have to deal with reality."

"Don't you see? That's exactly what I'm doing. I'm taking charge, ending the nightmare."

He knew how stubborn she could be, so he tried a different

approach. "Then let me go with you. I will make sure you're safe."

Her eyes filled with tears. "I have to do this on my own—at least for now."

"This is—" He caught himself before he uttered something he shouldn't. Instead he said, "This is unnecessary." He pushed the mug away. "What about the feds? They aren't going to let you just disappear, either. You can't outrun what has happened, what *could* happen if the cartel finds you. And..." He choked on the words he wanted to say.

"And?"

"What about us?" He felt his heart breaking.

"I don't know. I'm just so confused by all of this. I need to figure out who I am first." She touched his hand. "I just need time. You know how much I care about you. But, please, care about me enough to give me time."

~ 1 ~

Porter Leighton

Two days had passed, and I hadn't seen Jack, which definitely didn't feel good—or normal, for that matter. Jack, an army pilot like my husband, had been my steadfast confidant and protector as we'd looked long and hard for resolution to the multitude of questions surrounding my husband's disappearance.

Even when I hired the private firm that discreetly and illegally rescued Americans from foreign enemies, Jack hadn't called me crazy or tried to talk me out of it. Instead, he had tried to help by funneling to me as much information as he could without getting himself in a load of trouble with the military. What we didn't realize at the time was that the search would become all-consuming and yield no real answers, at least none that I wanted to acknowledge. And that's where Jack and I stood now—with a wedge between us built out of fragments of what appeared to be a brutal truth that my husband, Willhem H. Stone, had died a traitor to his country. And to me.

I could feel tears building from the torrent of mixed emotions that overwhelmed me as I thought of leaving Jack.

"No. I'm not doing this now. I need to keep busy." I resumed packing, tossing several photographs into the cardboard box, when one in particular caught my attention—Will standing in front of the plane he'd flown that day, February 13, 2000, the day of the crash.

"Will, what happened?"

I felt as if my very essence carried the imprint of that day when a sense of order, of harmony, ceased to exist and life had shifted from living to desperately coping with the disquiet in my soul. Fainthearted, I spoke aloud F. Scott Fitzgerald's haunting words as if defining my own life in one sentence, "So we beat on, boats against the current, borne back ceaselessly into the past."

And with those words, my past absorbed the present, and I began to relive that heart-wrenching day...

Jack's voice tense on the phone: "Are you okay?"

I could not see his face, but I tasted the bitter fear that covered the void at the end of his words, which quickly transformed into one of those foreboding pauses that makes the hair stand up and gives one too much time to play out worst-case scenarios.

"Jack. What's wrong?"

"Porter. I'm not on a secure line, so I need you to listen carefully. The raven flew this morning and did not return. It did not land. It fell. But there's still hope."

"Jack! No!" I remembered screaming and how my blood had run cold.

I knew Jack used the code words only to keep the Colombia spies that monitored the phone lines from identifying any keywords. The message to me couldn't have been clearer: Will's plane had gone down deep in the Colombian jungle in FARC territory during an intelligence mission.

I begged Jack to find him. He promised he'd do everything he could and had warned me not to watch the news or listen to the military officers that would be at my door soon.

In that moment when the line went dead, the emptiness that ensued never left me. It still imprisoned me, even now.

But none of that mattered anymore because some government higher-ups had put the kibosh on my search, which in turn illuminated the fact that nothing I had done had amounted to any more than a futile dance between hope and truth.

And I had reached my limit.

So, now I planned to take advantage of the bittersweet circumstance fate had dropped in my lap.

Right around the time of Will's disappearance, my great-aunt Lila Leighton, my last living family member, passed away suddenly in her sleep. Small in stature with steely blue eyes and a European sense of style in her clothing, she had built quite an empire for herself. This, in turn, left me with an overwhelming inheritance and a fully furnished, historic home in Turnberry, Virginia, that she had never moved into—neither of which I had the energy or desire to address at the time. I left the estate in the hands of the family lawyer, until recently.

Come Monday morning, which will be two months past my twenty-ninth birthday, my two border collies, Gatsby and Ripley, and I would pile in the SUV amongst a few boxes and head to what I hoped would be a bright future.

Stubbornly, I refused to think about how lonely I'd be without Jack. Yet his worries about the cartel still following me niggled at the back of my brain. "Stop worrying. It's been three years!" I clearly had nothing to give those criminals—or the feds. No. This would all be for the best, so I pressed on with the task at hand, even though it crushed my very soul to leave him.

He, too, would have to move on now. From Will Stone's disappearance. And from me, at least for a little while.

I wonder how he'll do.

~ 2 ~

Jack Wade

Monday morning had come fast with little sleep behind it, and Jack had been ready to roll since 6 a.m.

Today was the day. He'd given her space to cool off, and he hoped she had. Hoped she had changed her mind.

His strong hand, the same hand that had held hers so many times, reached for the coffee. Without a second thought, Jack poured the creamer in the bottom of the cup, then the coffee and a sprinkle of cinnamon. He stared at the cup, realizing he'd just made the coffee exactly the way Porter made hers. He took his coffee black.

Jack walked toward the back deck overlooking the Hudson River. His house reflected the perfect juxtaposition, rustic yet sophisticated. He'd purchased the place hoping that he and Porter would live there together someday. His mind drifted back to the day they'd met with the realtor. The day after he'd left the military for good. Jack had barely spent a dime his entire career and had saved up quite a bit. He'd never even touched the trust from his grandfather's farm, an inheritance that had been his since the age of fifteen. Jack had always wanted to build his own life, earn his own way in the world.

Before Porter, Jack lived on the edge. Whatever the military mission, no matter how dangerous, he was game. No thought, just action. But once he became close to her, life changed. He cared about his future. He would actually long to be home. Time with her became his priority—his new normal.

Jack rinsed his cup and took a last look around. He'd be back in a few days, after he assessed the situation in Porter's new town. Sadly, something already seemed different. He sensed a new hollowness to this place, or maybe it came from him. Either way, he refused to give up hope for their future together.

~~~

A few hours later, Jack parked his motorcycle, the one he'd bought just yesterday, and stood at a distance watching as she drove away. His heart pounded with disbelief.

"She's really leaving." He said the words under his breath, and his head dropped. He'd planned to talk to her again, to try and convince her to stay, to let him come along, to do anything but leave what they had together. "Damn it."

Jack looked to the sky. The air felt crisp, but the clouds hung gloomily overhead. It was the kind of morning he would have gotten up early and taken doughnuts to Porter's for breakfast so that they could linger, cozy inside. For almost three years, the two of them had been inseparable as they searched first for his best friend, her husband, and then ultimately searched simply for the truth, the why.

Jack thought about the necklace—the dark wings. The one Will had carried on all of his missions and had joked about as being a silly gift from his wife. But after learning the story behind the wings at the funeral, he suspected that Will had, in fact, grasped the magnitude of her gift all along. Jack easily recalled her words, "Fly with dark wings into the shadows, my love; they will keep you safe until you fly back into the light to me."

Replaying everything, he came to the usual verdict—that Will Stone had indeed become a traitor to his country and had died in the process. Just like the government had said. End of story. No shifting of the puzzle pieces, no matter how clever, made them fit any other way. It hadn't been easy for Jack to accept either, but he wasn't one to keep fooling himself.

Painfully, the reality of Will's betrayal had started to shine through pretty early in the search, the motivation for his fall from grace—that age-old vice called greed. But Porter had wanted to prove everyone wrong. Porter wanted to clear Will's name. So, Jack had acquiesced, offered to help. Ultimately, the futile search simply led him to the same conclusion about Will. But Porter just couldn't accept it then, and still couldn't. Reluctantly, Jack had stepped back and given her some space. Apparently, not enough space. She'd left, just like she said she would.

However, Jack Wade wasn't one to give up so easily. Besides, he had made a promise to that bastard of a husband of hers that he'd take care of her if something ever happened to him. The feds had her under surveillance, at least there in Sleepy Hollow. The Colombia drug cartel knew of her, too—whom she'd been married to, that she had looked high and low for Will. The icing on the cake? Jack feared that her research might have exposed some of the cartel's operations to the wrong people. All thanks to her stubbornness, her insistence, her poking the bear.

Porter leaving Sleepy Hollow may be for the best, all things considered, but not alone. So, big on keeping promises, Jack vowed not to let this one slip.

Those dark wings won't let you down this time.

~ 3 ~

"Take a deep breath, Porter. Take a deep breath." I whispered to myself, but the trembling inside my chest made it hard to do. I gripped the steering wheel like my life depended on it, and I supposed it rather did. Prying my fingers away in a desperate attempt to beat the anxiety, I rolled the window down, letting the chilly air smack me in the face. A wake-up call was what I'd been hoping for, something to reinforce my decision, embolden me. Was I really leaving?

I pushed my foot harder against the pedal to quicken the pace: no turning back now.

I needed to outrun the echoes. I sighed, "Everything about this place reminds me of something."

I looked at the gray sky—dreary, just like that blustery day in February 2002, when the military officers had once again shown up at my door to give me the news that Will had been reclassified from missing to deceased.

I had glared at the officers because I knew that no bodies had been recovered. Definitely not my husband's. "How can you say someone's dead when there's no body?"

I recollected biting my tongue and failing. I'd snapped at the uniform-clad messengers, "My husband's plane crash-landed in the Columbian jungle, and you people didn't go rescue him. I've spent countless hours and thousands of dollars doing *your* jobs." Fury dripped from my words that day as I fought to compose myself. *Lest I rip their throats out.*

The well-trained notification officers didn't miss a step and offered—or more accurately, had demanded—that I call a friend, next of kin, someone before they left.

I'd called Jack.

I sighed at the memory. Yes, leaving this tarnished place felt right, but leaving Jack? That wasn't going to be easy.

~ 4 ~

After the sting of Porter driving away faded, Jack hopped on his motorcycle. He'd been practical and prepared himself for the possibility that she would actually go through with it and leave. He just didn't believe it until he saw it. Armed with a full tank of gas and a bag packed with a few things to tide him over, he planned to follow soon enough. Right now, he needed a moment to gather his thoughts, and his heart too, as it seemed those aspects were less prepared. Plus, he wanted to put a little distance between the two of them on the road. No need for a confrontation today.

He pulled into the parking lot of O'Malley's and headed inside.

"Guinness, please."

The bartender nodded. "Here you go."

"Thanks, man." Jack took a long swig then wiped his mouth with the back of his hand.

"How's it going? Where's your usual co-conspirator," the bartender joked.

"Away." His stoic face said it all. He didn't want to talk about Porter.

"Hey, buddy, you okay?"

Jack looked up to make eye contact briefly, "Maybe."

The bartender finally took the cue, patted the counter, and said. "I'm headed to the back for my break. I'll be back in a few. If you need anything, my nephew can help you out."

Jack nodded and sat for a few more minutes. Then he up and left, his glass of Irish stout still half full. Alcohol wasn't what he needed right now.

He needed Porter. For her to understand. For her to believe. In him. In them. Or at least the possibility.

He walked down the street toward the flower shop and stopped to look in the window. Jack couldn't help but smirk at the memory that flooded his mind. He'd given Porter a dozen white roses on Valentine's Day two years ago, having spotted them at a roadside stand. He'd bought the flowers on a whim...well, sort of.

Her delight had been clear, and he'd immediately decided that she would have white roses at the end of every week. And he hadn't missed a Friday since.

He headed back to his bike and mumbled, "And I won't miss one now."

Time to ride.

~ 5 ~

Driving, driving, thinking, overthinking.

Panicking. What have I done? It hadn't even been an hour, and I already missed Jack. I should have said goodbye, but I just didn't want to risk another argument—or risk changing my mind. "Still, not okay, Porter," I scolded myself.

Instinctively, I looked in the rearview mirror.

Were they following me—the feds? The cartel? I wasn't so worried about the feds really—they at least wouldn't bring violence. But the cartel? Fear flashed down my spine. Had the feds actually served to keep the cartel at bay? The doubt over my choice to go it alone mounted.

Not now, Porter.

Then I thought about Will. Him being in the outskirts of the Colombian jungle, where bomb blasts served as constant background noise, and if he had survived the crash, how the threat of kidnapping for ransom lurked around every corner. "I'm sorry." My heart broke for the millionth time, as I thought of how he never made it out of that hell and back to the United States.

The crippling effect of my mixed emotions made me want to pull the car over and cry. I feared my vision would soon become too blurry for driving. But stopping was not an option.

Let the panic flow through you.

I held on, trying yet another mind trick from my arsenal. I imagined holding my toughest yoga pose and wanting to quit but knowing that glory only came from withstanding the challenge—conquering. I forced myself to breathe through the shaking that came deep from the core of my body.

I can do this.

I had managed panic attacks for three years. I knew what worked and what didn't, and I knew that more times than not, nothing worked.

"Ride out the waves," I said aloud. "Everything is okay in this moment."

I kept driving.

~ 6 ~

A couple hours later, I turned into the boundaries of my new town, Turnberry. Main Street looked just like a Norman Rockwell painting. The sights immediately lifted my spirits, and I breathed a sigh of relief to have arrived at such a beautiful place. The buildings stood in rows, some touching and some with small alleys between. The vibrant awnings adorning the entrances to stores and businesses gleamed. People bustled about with shopping bags, some with dogs on leashes and some pushing baby carriages. I relished in the potential that contentment waited for me in this deliberate little town that sat on the imaginary line once dividing the North from the South.

A small bakery caught my eye, tucked between a bookstore and a florist. I quickly pulled into a metered spot right out front. I sat back against the seat and closed my eyes, my hands still gripping the very top of the steering wheel a little too tightly. I didn't let go—fearful that the anxious tremor still plagued me.

Fortunately, the rustling of my dogs brought me closer to a feeling of normalcy. I began the ritual of blocking my emotions, pushing against that pit in my stomach and swallowing the lump in my throat. I reached deep inside myself and put on the mask of confidence I had learned to wear so well. Slowly, I released my grip. My fingers felt stiff and looked splotchy white, but my hands remained steady. *I'm okay.*

I fumbled with my keys and managed to grab some coins from the center console for the meter. Stepping out, I lifted my face to the sky, and let the sun hit me.

"Be back in a minute, boys," I said as I cracked the windows to let the cool breeze in for the dogs.

The bakery door had *Tess's Pastry Shop* painted in a white, swirly font reminiscent of icing on a birthday cake. The inside of the shop sparkled in the perfect colors of pale pink and white—straight out of a movie. As the warmth of the humid air from the ovens and the scrumptious aroma of fresh pastry surrounded me, I felt like Audrey Hepburn in *Roman Holiday*, finding joy in the discovery of "the little things." I hoped this proved to be only the beginning of doing just that.

A friendly young man behind the counter wearing a white apron greeted me. "Hello. Welcome!"

I smiled. "Hi. What a beautiful shop this is."

"Thank you. The owners just recently had it painted."

"It's perfection. I feel like I've stepped back in time." I stood silent for just a moment, absorbing the energy of this adorable bakery.

The young man looked at me. He seemed at a loss for words, waiting for me to finish looking around. Then, he gently broke our silence. "How can I help you?"

"Oh!" I giggled, which surprised me. "I'd love a bag of your house blend coffee and some donuts."

A young woman, who looked about my age, stood nearby pouring creamer into her cup.

I leaned closer to the glass to pick out what I wanted.

"You have to try the blueberry one," the woman said in a cheerful voice.

I looked over, smiled. "I think I will. Thanks."

I glanced up at the young man, "Could I have few napkins and a couple of those little to-go creamers, please? I'm trying to stall a grocery trip."

"You must be new in town or just visiting, maybe?" the woman asked.

I hesitated, but only for a second. I needed to get over my suspicious nature. New town, new home, new friends, new beginnings. "Actually, I just drove in. I'm moving here."

The woman waved her plump hands in the air. "Oh, wonderful! I'm Patsy. I work at the library just a couple blocks from here." She nodded at the case full of goodies and giggled. "Unfortunately."

I nodded and laughed. "I get it. I'm Porter. Nice to meet you."

The young man from behind the counter handed over the pink-

and-white shopping bag. I thanked him and turned back to Patsy. "It was a pleasure meeting you."

"You too. Enjoy your first day in town. I'm sure I'll see you around. Stop by the library sometime. I can give you a rundown of Turnberry. But don't get your hopes up, Main Street is kind of it."

And that was just wanted I wanted to hear.

We said our goodbyes and I strolled back to the car with a wide grin on my face.

After climbing into the driver's seat, I looked at the dogs in the rearview mirror.

"Okay, boys, almost home."

At least, I wanted it to be home. So far, so good.

~ 7 ~

Joe and Max

From across the street, two undercover agents watched as Porter got back into her car. One of them started to get out.

"Max, where the hell are you going?" Joe asked as his partner unlatched his seat belt.

"To get donuts." The youthful Max, not particularly attractive, but blessed with a thick, dark head of hair—something Joe had lost long ago—hopped out of the car.

"Ummm, no. We need to follow her," Joe said.

Max rolled his eyes. "We know exactly where she's going, and I'm starving. Besides, we've been trailing her for months. She's not looking for him anymore."

Joe sighed and rubbed his chin—one of several he sported. "Fine, but hurry up."

With a quick wave, Max headed across the street.

Joe yelled out after him, "Grab a powdered jelly-filled for me and a coffee, would ya?"

~ 8 ~

Jack had driven over ninety miles per hour to make up time on the road and catch up with Porter. He cursed himself for not having left just a bit sooner, for wallowing. Not his style. But he was here now, in Turnberry. The moment he hit Main Street, he caught sight of what he'd hoped he wouldn't see. An obvious (to him, at least) government-issued SUV parked on the other side of the street from Porter's car, which was in front of a bakery—they indeed had tracked her from Sleepy Hollow. After Porter drove away from the shop, he pulled up behind the Feds, removed his helmet, and stowed it on his bike. He walked over to the car and banged on the hood just hard enough to startle the shorter, not so slim man he knew as Joe.

"Hey! Watch it!" Joe couldn't hide his annoyance. "What the hell?"

"You guys sleeping at the wheel? Your target just left." Jack let the sarcasm ring throughout his words.

Joe grimaced when he realized who it was. "Oh, it's you, hotshot."

"Yep. It's me. Don't you think it's time you guys throw in the towel on this one? She said she would stop looking, and she obviously has."

"You know what? Mind your own business for a change. We're just doing our jobs."

"Well, from where I stand, it looks like you're half-ass doing your jobs. Maybe I should let someone know."

"What's your problem? I could take you in for stalking. She doesn't want you around anymore, obviously. So why are *you* following her?"

Jack leaned in the window, just inches from Joe's round, red face. "Do you really want to go there with me?"

Joe saw intensity in Jack's stare—the man meant business.

"Okay, okay, calm down, military man. I think our detail is about to get pulled, anyway."

"That's what I thought." Jack walked away and headed toward the donut shop. He passed Max on the street. The agent's eyes widened when he saw him. Jack tipped an imaginary hat in his direction and continued toward the bakery without a word.

He needed to get some caffeine and then go check into the little cottage he'd rented by the river. He planned to ride over to Porter's place later in the evening, just to make sure she was okay.

I'm watching out for her, not stalking. There's a difference.

~ 9 ~

Giant canopies of grand trees divided the freshly manicured, rolling hills of green lawns that led up to the stately old homes of faded brick and stone—some red, some yellow, some pale white, all trimmed in soft whites, light grays, and even pale blues. I peered out the car window, driving down the cracked asphalt street that bowed in the middle, its edges sinking low next to the curbs.

Up ahead, I saw it. The house. I recognized it immediately from the photos that I had been studying for weeks, letting my mind fill in where they ended.

"Perfect. Walking distance to downtown and the river. Isn't it fantastic?" I spoke aloud, as if the dogs could understand me and possibly offer their opinions.

My heart fluttered a bit. It almost felt like meeting an old flame after years of being apart.

I slowed the car just in front of the house and took a deep breath as I reveled in the picturesque home sitting atop a small, emerald-green hill—number 1221, the Mitchell family estate. Actually, it was now my home, the Leighton estate, just me and my dogs.

"Welcome home." I almost breathed the words instead of speaking them.

My heart ached with the hope that this would be the place I found peace.

For a moment, I caught my reflection in the windshield. My blond hair, pulled back from my face, and my large, black sunglasses created a glamorous façade that stared back at me. Yes, I looked basically the same as I did before everything had happened, but my soul didn't match anymore. The spark that had been there from childhood had long since faded from my eyes. I had the eyes of the broken, eyes that betrayed my smile and that tempted others to ask what was wrong.

Looking up at the house, I noticed that white drapes covered all the windows, upstairs and down. The front, although somewhat of a flat façade, looked attractive with its gray stone accents, whitish trim, and paned windows. Two white columns stood sentry on either side of the leaded-glass front door, and lighted stone pillars flanked the sides of the front walkway, as if waiting to greet the 1920s aristocrats that had once gathered here with their martinis and sparkling dresses—at least in my imagination. *This beautiful piece of history may just be the remedy to forgetting my own smoldering one.*

There were two other buildings both on the left side of the property. A guesthouse, partially covered in blooming wisteria, sat close to the street. It shared part of the driveway with the stone garage that occupied an area quite a ways back, close to the wood line behind the main house. The garage sported two large, mahogany doors that surely once housed the fancy cars of the illustrious flapper era. I grinned as I imagined turning the little guesthouse into a writing studio.

The restless dogs yelped and wagged their tails, beating the back of the seat like a drum. I opened the hatchback, and the two beasts made a beeline to the back yard.

Excited to take that first step into my new home, I fumbled with an antique brass key that sported a large silver tag with an M monogrammed in the center. *I'll definitely need to get a new monogram with my initial L.* I unlocked the back door and stepped inside.

The stuffiness of the air caught me off guard. I quickly flipped on the light. I'd had the electricity, internet, water, and gas set up in my name weeks ago, so that everything would be in working order upon arrival. I found that I now stood in a well-outfitted laundry room, which at some point most likely had been a service entry.

The dogs barreled past me, leaving little doggie footprints on the black and white marble floor.

I smirked. It was starting to feel like home already.

First thing in the morning, I planned to open the windows to let the whole place fill with fresh air and loads of sunlight. However, at the moment, I longed for sleep.

I'd packed my favorite soft pillow, something familiar—although I wasn't entirely sure anything would make me sleep soundly the first night in this old house. The line from *The Wizard of Oz* popped into my head, but in a more appropriate version for my life: "Ghosts, thieves, and government spies, Oh my!"

My laughter startled not only me, but the dogs as well. The silence needed to be wrestled out of there.

I felt that Leighton family sardonic wit rising to the surface.

I wish my only fear in this life revolved around seeing ghosts.

~ 10 ~

Joe had been driving slowly while Max searched for the address 1221. Suddenly, he slammed on the brakes.

"Dang it, Joe." Max blotted the splash of coffee on his shirt

"It's her car. There." Joe pointed.

"Yep. I see it. She's arrived at her new house. Let me send an alert." Max's sarcasm rang clear. He crumpled his napkin and gave up on his coffee stain.

Joe ignored him and looked around, left then right. "This is a residential street. Parking here for days on end...we'll stand out like a sore thumb. There isn't a single car parked on this street. Everyone has long driveways and garages."

"Yeah, this isn't New York," Max scoffed. "A blacked-out SUV isn't going to blend well."

Joe had a faraway look for a moment, then he said, "I'm sending in a request that this surveillance mission be pulled."

"No kidding. I've been bored out of my mind for weeks."

"Nothing is happening here tonight. Let's go to the motel." Joe took his foot off the brake and started to drive again.

Max gave a quick nod and then pointed straight ahead. "Besides, we can count on lover boy to keep an eye on things."

Jack had just driven up on his motorcycle.

They watched as Jack took a path around the far side of the guesthouse.

Max frowned and looked at Joe. "What the hell's he doing now?"

Joe shrugged. "No idea. I think they're on the fritz."

"So, he's what, like spying on her or something?"

"I don't know. It's strange, but let's not make it our business."

Max nodded.

"Let's go. I need a drink." Joe pressed on the gas.

~ 11 ~

Jack parked his bike behind a line of tall shrubs lining the far side of Porter's garage. He didn't want to scare her on her first night by lurking around. Instead, he sat on the ground in the shadows under the eaves of the garage. From that angle, he could see the neighbor's house across the street more than he could see Porter's. He noticed one light on in the neighbor's home and what seemed to be a small figure peering in his direction.

Jack wasn't too concerned. Nosy neighbors. The least of his worries. He planned to win Porter back sooner rather than later. He wanted to be the one to ease her mind, pamper her to no end, and most importantly, keep her safe from those who may do her harm. And there were plenty of those out there, thanks to her stubborn insistence on "finding out the truth."

As he sat, wanting to go knock on the door and try to work things out with her, his mind began to justify her leaving—temporarily, he hoped. Jack understood that Porter needed to get away, finally get a break from it all for her mental and physical well-being. But, damn, it wasn't going to be easy. Protecting her, watching for any signs of danger, yet keeping her at arm's length would be a challenge he couldn't quite fathom yet.

Pulled from his thoughts, Jack heard a door open. He sat silently, listening for the direction of the noise. Porter had come out the back door. He needed to move quickly. He darted to the other side of the hedge. He listened as she unlocked her car and presumably took some more of her belongings into the house. He felt sick to his stomach—this was wrong.

Jack started to go to her, but knew now was far from the right time. Patience was something he knew well—though he had to admit, it was wearing thin.

~ **12** ~

"What was that?" My heart pounded.

The sound of an engine starting, revving, and then pulling away. A car? A motorcycle? Was someone in my driveway? In front of the house? I looked out the front window at the road. Nothing. I put my hand on my heart and fought to control my breathing. I realized I was overreacting. The jumpiness I'd felt for so long would take a while to ease up. This town couldn't be safer, and I gave myself permission to stop worrying.

Still, there were a few moments where I'd thought I had seen the blacked-out SUV following me on the road to Turnberry. I threw up my hands in defeat. *Who cares, really?* That SUV had become a constant fixture in New York—those same two agents always staring. I remembered countless times I had waved at them just to see their heads turn away or drop down in rapid succession. It had become almost a game for a while. Me waving, them hurriedly looking away, and then me smirking. Until even that had lost its luster. Then their presence had just become annoying.

I took one last look up and down the street. No black SUVs or any other suspicious-looking rides. Loosening my grip on the curtain to allow it to fall back into place, I hesitated. There across the street, I saw a light in the window straight across from mine, and someone stood looking at me as I looked back. The distance kept me from seeing details.

Then, just like that, the person closed the drapes, and the window went dark. I stood for a moment longer.

"How strange." I began the rationalization. *Well, you did just move in. A curious neighbor seems pretty normal.*

I took in a deep breath and said my mantra: "Everything is okay." Except that I didn't feel as sure of myself without Jack to lean on. *No. I'm not going there now.*

I spoke aloud again. "Everything is okay. Stop looking back, Porter."

~ 13 ~

Rose Blanchard

The tiny, elderly woman let the curtains fall as she quickly stepped away from the window. The young lady across the street had seen her, most certainly. Not that Rose Blanchard cared much about that—she'd given up on caring two hoots about what anyone thought of her. The course of her life had taken a turn that it should never have, and she couldn't do a darn thing about that now. At seventy-seven years old, it almost seemed pointless to fuss over things of the past. But she did anyway.

And she watched the neighborhood goings-on like a hawk.

She thought about the house she lived in, a far less stately one than the estate across the street. Hers was a simple, red brick house with a black slate roof that sagged a bit in the middle. There was only so much upkeep she could do. She shuffled over to her tattered lounger, the small hump on her back giving her that eternally hunched-over look. Something she'd inherited from her mother.

She sat down and let her mind continue its whirring process—because thinking about other people's business pretty much consumed her time anymore—pushing some stray gray hairs away from her face. Her hair had been gray so long that she could hardly remember the silky, chestnut locks she had spent hours brushing every night of her youth.

Rose had lived on Waterford Street for decades, and nothing happened on the street that she did not see. Tonight, she had seen a petite, young woman with shoulder-length, blond hair pulled back very neatly, dressed in tailored khakis and a pastel-blue spring sweater, unloading luggage into the Mitchell estate. With this young woman were two black-and-white, very hairy dogs that seemed to have more energy than was necessary for any domestic animal. The young woman couldn't be any older than thirty, if that.

"Time will tell." Rose felt a tinge of anxiety. Restless, she got back up and peered out the window again.

Rose could not stop watching as lights slowly popped on in the windows, one after another, as the visitor presumably explored the abode. Every once in a while, Rose could see the shadow of a person walk past one of the semi-sheer white drapes, blocking a streak of light from that particular window for only a moment.

For the past four years, since her neighbor had died, there had not been anyone over there except the estate gardener. However, last week there had been a white van parked in the driveway for a few hours. Rose assumed the gas or electric companies were checking on things as a formality. The cleaning team that showed up later had been harder to explain away, but at the time she thought maybe the cleaning was a standard follow-up to the utility workers having been inside and tracking in dirt.

There had never been a For Sale sign on the property. Had it sold? Or rented?

Frustrated, Rose went back to her chair. She startled a bit at the sound of an engine roaring and thought about getting up once again for a peek. But she didn't. She felt tired, and she'd already seen more outside her window today than she had in a long, long time.

"I'll just have to go over there first thing in the morning and see what's going on," Rose said out loud, even though she and her cat were the only ones in the old house.

~ 14 ~

"Brrrr." Even though I had fiddled with the thermostat last night and finally figured out how to turn on the heat, the house seemed cold this morning. I yawned and stretched, but I still felt exhausted from the long drive and a restless night's sleep. I had stirred with every tiny sound. Reluctantly, I crawled out of bed and dressed in yoga pants and a long-sleeved tee.

At least I'd had a cleaning company come in before my arrival—a big step, and hopefully not one I would regret. Only a few months ago, I never would have trusted that the house wasn't bugged before my arrival. In my house in Sleepy Hollow, the government had ultimately gained access to my phones and files that contained all the search data I'd done regarding my husband's disappearance and possible involvement with a drug-smuggling operation. But I didn't need to worry about that anymore; I wasn't searching anymore. *There's nothing to find.*

I slipped on my socks and the only shoes I could find at the moment and took off down the stairs with the two dogs almost tripping me as they ran past.

I let them outside and stood at the door, taking in the large, grassy back yard lined with trees. The cold, misty morning air seemed to energize the dogs. I stood with my arms crossed enjoying their antics as they jumped around and played in the moist grass.

"Come on, boys. Gatsby! Ripley!" My voice echoed in the early morning calm.

The dogs ignored me and ran to the front of the house.

As I rounded the corner, I saw it: the black SUV. My heart sank.

"No, no, no!" Without contemplation, I stomped toward the

vehicle.

The younger agent saw me. The SUV took off.

"Cowards!" I yelled at the top of my lungs.

The government had made a deal with me. I continued to play by their rules—by throwing in the proverbial towel, permanently. They needed to do the same and call off those goons.

I corralled the dogs back inside the house and went straight to the first box I'd unloaded last night. My fingers rapidly flipped through the files.

There...the file titled *Schultz and Associates*, my legal team.

"Thanks, Will."

I never thought I'd need to hire a criminal defense lawyer. Unfortunately, Will had used my name to cover his smuggling activities. Except the government hadn't been fully convinced that it was a cover. They actually suspected *me*.

My private investigators had gone into overdrive trying to clear me. Jack had taken me to the interview with the feds—interrogation, really—but I had to go into the room without him. Only my lawyer could go with me.

Schultz had said right off the bat, "Porter, don't answer any questions without my go-ahead. You have not been arrested or formally charged. You are not obligated to give answers."

I remembered feeling so completely numb. I was in shock, though I didn't realize it at the time.

Schultz had said, "The charges they are trying to pin on you are bad. That storage facility, the money, it looks bad, real bad. Without a deal, I don't know where this leads." The look of concern on my lawyer's face had been clearly visible as he spoke to me.

The whole time, I had felt like the process was happening to someone else.

The agreement stated that if I stopped my independent search and handed over all of the information I had obtained, the government would remove all surveillance on me and dismiss me as a person of interest.

Feeling backed into a corner, I had taken the deal.

I left that day expecting a sense of freedom, release. Something like that, anyway. It was over, after all, and I could move on with my life. Right?

Wrong.

The guilt hadn't abated, and even now I still wrestled with the feeling that I had walked away too soon.

Therefore, if the government expected me to hold up my end of the bargain, then they needed to do the same. I knew Schultz wouldn't be at the office this early, so I called his private number. Playing his role as my lawyer to a tee, he calmly listened to my diatribe and told me not to worry. The investigation would close—it wasn't unusual for the government to stall a bit.

He said that the move to Turnberry should go a long way in demonstrating that I was out of the investigating business.

Yet, behold the ever-present SUV. In Turnberry!

"What more do they want from me?" I raised my voice and threw the file on the kitchen table, continuing to vent my frustration on poor Schultz. "I gave up on my husband." *On Jack.* I didn't say that part out loud. "On everything, so I could finally be free!"

And I was determined to do just that. Be free to live—and maybe even love—fully again.

Schulz didn't have much to say after that, so I let him off the hook, literally and figuratively. I had to believe things were going to work out.

~ 15 ~

From across the street, Rose watched as the young woman walked briskly toward the street and that black SUV.

Who hosts guests this early? Rose looked at her watch—barely 7 a.m. on a Tuesday morning. When she glanced back up, the SUV sped off, and the young woman's face wore an expression of anger. She even shouted something at the SUV.

Rose looked down at her black cat, Inky, as it wrapped itself around her legs, purring loudly.

"So strange, don't you think, Inky Girl?" Then she went back to the window. "Well, since she's obviously up..."

Rose shuffled to the kitchen and started packing some muffins to take to the new neighbor or visitor or whatever she was.

Rose had questions.

~ 16 ~

Just as I had pried the tape from the doughnut box, the doorbell rang.

Immediately, I thought about how many mornings since my husband's disappearance that Jack had rung my doorbell and surprised me with doughnuts. He'd love these.

Approaching the front door, I thought how maybe I should have my pilot's knife with me.

I heard Jack in my head, "It's not if, it's when. You are preparing for the when." If he had told me once, he had told me a million times that the cartel struck when you least expected it. I knew he meant it, but I also felt it was a bit over the top. I hadn't cared about the cartel back then. I just wanted to find Will. According to Jack, the cartel cared about the information they believed I had gathered, though. *But all of that should be in the past. I'm no longer involved.*

Cautiously, I peeked through the peephole.

Okay, number one, someone that short and, number two, someone that gray probably did not pose a threat.

My shoulders relaxed, and my mind calmed—those two idiot agents had definitely ignited the flames of my paranoia this morning.

Before I could even say, "Hello," the tiny old lady sang out, "Good morning. My name is Rose Blanchard. I live right across the street." She pointed briefly at her house and then pushed toward me a small basket steaming with the aroma of fresh-baked pastries.

"Nice to meet you, Miss Blanchard. I'm Porter, Porter Leighton."

"You can call me Rose, honey." We both smiled.

Invite her in for a cup of coffee. I really didn't want to. Not showered and still riled from my call with Schultz, I reluctantly asked, "Would you like to come in for a cup of coffee?"

Unfortunately, she said yes.

Into the kitchen we went. I rinsed out a couple of coffee mugs from the cupboard. "My apologies, Rose. I haven't really settled in yet." *Hint, hint.*

Rose cleared her throat and said, "So, are you visiting for a while?"

I turned to her. "What? Oh, no. I live here now. I'm your new neighbor. Sooooo, much to do." *Hint, hint.*

Rose just stood there. *Darn it.*

I let my gaze fall on the pile of little vanilla-flavored creamers, paper plates and slightly crumpled napkins that the doughnut shop had given me yesterday. Rose must have noticed.

"Honey, I don't need anything except coffee in my cup, and I don't care what kind of plate I use as long as it is clean. And, as for real plates, they are overrated, anyway. Who wants to wash dishes while still trying to get settled in a new home? I use paper plates more often than my real ones, and I don't even have an excuse, except for pure laziness."

Rose stared for a moment at the pink box. "I see you found Tess's, the best pastry shop around. People come from all over to buy cakes for weddings, birthdays...anything really."

"Yes. It is a lovely shop. I'm sure I'll get to know it well." I managed to get one sentence in before Rose started talking again.

"So what brings you to Turnberry?"

"Timing, and I had an opportunity to move here."

"Porter, forgive me if I seem a little prying, but I had no idea this home was even for sale, let alone about to welcome a new resident."

"Rose, no need for apologies. Actually, yes, it is a bit confusing. You see, the home never made it to the public market. My aunt Lila owned the home, and...well, she passed away. Long story short, she left it to me. Actually, I have owned this home for three years, but was preoccupied and could not even come to visit before moving here."

"So you moved here...sight unseen?" Rose truly looked perplexed.

"Yes. Well, yes and no. Actually, the estate manager came and took a few pictures for me, but other than those few images, I wasn't sure what I was getting into by moving here."

"I'm sorry, but who is Lila? I have lived across the street for a very long time and knew the Mitchells very well. But, somehow, I never met a Lila. Unless my memory is failing me."

"Oh, no, you wouldn't have. Lila was my aunt, unrelated to the Mitchells. She purchased the estate in a private sale three years ago. In fact, she bought everything—the house, its contents." I stopped there. No need to tell this stranger that my aunt also somehow acquired the family's robust financial assets in the deal as well. I'd said too much already.

"Really, I just can't believe that I never knew the house across the street from me went to auction or private sale or whatever the case— anyway, that it sold."

"Yes. Well, my aunt liked to be discreet. I'm sure the transaction happened quickly and barely even made a ripple around town."

"Your aunt...she must have been a wealthy woman."

The question seemed uncouth and, frankly, made me uncomfortable. *How should I answer this?* I tried to skip the "wealthy" detail altogether and did my best to answer in an appropriate way. "Well, she was a savvy businesswoman when it came to real estate matters, especially."

Good enough. Rose looked at me a little strangely but seemed to accept the answer.

The truth: my aunt could have been described as both wealthy and eccentric. She had loved homes and bought properties like other people bought designer handbags and shoes.

"You must be an adventurous soul. I cannot imagine moving to a brand-new town all alone." Rose paused. "Pardon me, but where did you say you moved from?"

"Oh, I don't think I said. I moved from New York."

"New York City? Well, how different it must be here. You must feel like the world has just about stopped spinning."

I didn't bother to explain that I had lived in Sleepy Hollow, a quaint little bedroom town outside the city, resting on the shores of the Hudson River. In fact, the glittering lights of the city across the river had been my solace. I used to stare from my window and find comfort in the anonymity of it all. A million people with a million problems different from my own, but still the lights of the city twinkled and flashed in the peaceful beauty of distance.

But I lied to Rose to keep the conversation shallow. "No, I wanted to escape the hustle and bustle. I like it here."

"So, you will be staying permanently, then?" Rose actually looked anxious.

Another probing question. "Uh, that is the plan, yes. This is home now."

A strange darkness filled Rose's pale blue eyes. I hadn't been enjoying this intrusion or visit or whatever it was in the least bit—and even less so after that last question. And I did not feel warm and fuzzy toward Ms. Nosy Pants, either. Maybe our energies naturally repelled like the wrong ends of magnets. *I wish she'd go home.*

And just like that, as if reading my thoughts, Rose switched gears. "You know, we can do the coffee another time. You have lots to do, I'm sure. I just wanted to say hello. If you need anything, let me know. I tucked my phone number inside the basket of muffins."

I couldn't believe the level of relief I felt just then. It was huge. "Thank you, Rose. It was very nice of you to stop by, and I'm sure the muffins will be delicious."

"My mother's recipe. Fresh blueberries from my yard, too."

With that, I walked her to the front door and waved goodbye.

~ 17 ~

A week had passed since Porter moved to Turnberry. Jack had stayed four days to make sure she was okay. He had come back to New York to check on his house and grab more clothing to take back to the river cottage he had rented in Turnberry for the month. This all felt awkward—being in the shadows, especially.

Out of frustration, he flicked the florist card he had been holding onto the dining table. He had scheduled the first delivery of white roses for tomorrow, and the Turnberry florist had eagerly fulfilled his request to set up a recurring delivery to Porter every Friday, just like he'd done for years now. He needed her to know he hadn't given up. Porter could be mad; she could have her space, but she couldn't make him stop caring about her. Besides, Porter feeling completely alone was the last thing he wanted.

He sat by the window in his New York house looking out at the Hudson River and the miles of treetops. The view served as an empty backdrop to his thoughts as he reached for his glass of twelve-year Pappy Van Winkle scotch. The amber liquid went down smoothly. He gripped the glass more tightly as he stared at the photos of the crash site he had pulled out when he arrived home. He assessed the position of the plane. It had landed in a clearing, and the hull of the plane and wings were intact. The landing gear was trashed, but it took a damn good pilot to land a plane that size in the jungle like that.

Will may have been a bastard, but he was undoubtedly a talented pilot. Porter deserved a better husband, but the army had the best airman out there—that was fact.

Jack ran one scenario after another through his head, following combat procedures. The outcome always played out the same. The

FARC had the advantage; the Colombian revolutionaries were a guerilla army that knew the lay of the land—in this case a dense and brutal jungle—better than anyone. Unless one of the US soldiers had made it out of there unseen and through miles of harsh enemy territory with next to zero supplies, the reality pointed to them all either ending up captured or killed, or both.

Jack tossed the pictures aside. He leaned back as his foot found the edge of the coffee table. His flannel shirt tightened slightly across his muscular frame. His jaw clinched as he pushed back against the anger he felt toward Will. Jack knew that money, or the lack thereof, could make people do bad things—but to betray one's country for money, set up one's own wife? It didn't make sense.

Porter had been financially secure even before her aunt Lila's inheritance. It had to be something more. Greed seemed the logical suspect on the surface, but could it have been for something other than money? Jack knew the things that typically drove men: power, money and love. He just couldn't figure out which of those drove Will's betrayal. He needed to pinpoint and expose Will's motivation in order to convince Porter to let this all go. Without that, Porter may never fully feel like she deserved to move on—and, selfishly, Jack wanted her to move on with him.

Jack thought of all the times Will had commented on how Jack wouldn't understand because he had his granddaddy's fortune in his back pocket. Jack never thought of it that way. His grandfather had worked his entire life on the family's farm. Jack had worked like a dog on that farm since the age of four. Going into the military had been a calling for Jack, a duty to serve the country that had given so much to his family for generations. Greed didn't drive Jack. He wanted to serve his country with honor, he wanted to find love that lasted forever, and he wanted little ones to raise on his family's land. He thought how many times he would have easily traded fortune for the love that his friend had in Porter. He would have given everything—and still would—for a chance at forever with her.

If he could prove beyond a shadow of a doubt what Will had done and set Porter free of her loyalty to that traitor, once and for all, maybe he would get that chance. He just needed an actual plan.

~ 18 ~

Max and Joe drove past Porter's house around dinnertime.

"I don't see her car," Max said.

"Could be in the garage. It's dinnertime, though. Maybe she went out," Joe replied.

"What do you think she does in there all day anyway?"

Joe stared at Max like he was a weirdo.

"No. I mean, it's a big place," Max said. "Seems lonely. That's all." He fidgeted a bit.

Joe looked away. "Don't know, don't care."

Max sighed. "Jeez, what's got you bent?"

"I'm missing my daughter's graduation from medical school for this shitty job."

"When is it? I can cover this alone."

Joe shook his head. "No. It's not just the job. I don't want to see Sue. She'll make a big stink about how, when we were still married, I was never there for any of them. Why do I show up for the big things when I wasn't there for the everyday things? The whole rigmarole."

"Sorry, man. That's tough."

The two sat in silence as Joe drove past Porter's again, from the opposite direction. Just as they were getting close to the driveway, Max saw the narrow, dirt, car path on the far side of the guesthouse that Jack had used that first day they'd arrived.

Max pointed and said, "Hey, pull in there."

"Where?"

"There. The dirt path next to the little cottage."

Joe came to a stop on the far side of the cottage. The men got out to stretch their legs.

"Hey, I think we may have found our spot. Porter can't see us from the big house," Max said.

"Yeah, and that nosy old lady can't either." Joe frowned as he looked in that direction. "What's up with her—always looking out that window? Reminds me of that old black-and-white movie. You know, the one where the guy's mom is in the window."

"*Psycho*." Max rolled his eyes. "You're not wrong, though."

~ 19 ~

As I waited for my to-go order at the pizza place, I watched a young couple at a nearby table. My heart ached at the sight of their delight in simply being together.

I wondered if I would ever feel that way again...or if I had ever really felt it with my husband. When I was young and first married to Will, I truly believed he was the one. Unfortunately, time put a mirror on my mistake. The cracks in our relationship had been there all along. After everything that happened, I finally realized that I had never been his primary focus. Something had always taken priority. During our marriage, I chalked it up to his type-A personality and to his being young and ambitious. How many times had I heard Will say, "Porter, not now," "in a minute," or "I'm busy"? My affections hadn't always been appreciated, and for some reason, I had accepted it.

The truth hit me that I felt "it" with Jack, but I had never let myself be freed from the lingering possibility that I could still be married to Will—was he actually dead? Had declaring him dead freed me from my vows? But no matter how I tried, I couldn't deny my love for Jack. We had a connection that I had never experienced before, even with Will, which unnerved me. I just didn't know how to rework all the information in my brain to make it okay.

Jack had told me so many times that I needed to accept that I'd lost my husband and that my marriage was over the moment Will had put me at risk—regardless of whether he was dead or alive. There were times when I thought I could do that, times when I tried so hard, weeks when I had succeeded in letting go, in feeling happy with Jack, in just living for the now. And the memories of those times still remained, fused deep in my heart. Still, I knew eventually I had to face the doubts hiding inside my soul. Even if Will had done all those things, as his wife didn't I owe it to him to hear his side? Jack didn't think so. I could not understand that. Even worse, the guilt I carried from stopping the search had proven unbearable, and the "not knowing" what really happened was crippling. Everything felt heavy and confused.

I often told Jack, "Isn't what I did betrayal, too?" I stopped looking in order to save myself. He would have never stop looking for me if the roles were reversed, right?"

And Jack would say, "Nothing you have done can be judged by anyone. Porter, he did this. It is entirely his fault. You never should have been in the situation to begin with."

"Miss? Miss?" The server's voice pulled me from my own thoughts. "Here's your order."

"Oh, yes. Thank you."

I took one last look at the beaming young couple and left for home with a pit in my stomach.

~ 20 ~

Rose got to her window just in time to see Porter pull into the driveway. Shortly thereafter, the downstairs front, left window illuminated at Porter's house.

She's in the study.

Rose watched a few minutes more as Porter's shadow moved across the area, blocking the light here and there. Then the movement stopped.

She craned her neck to try to see in the direction of Porter's guest cottage. She had seen the black SUV pull into the service driveway hours ago. As far as she could tell, it had not left, but she didn't have a clear view from her house.

"Who are those guys?" Rose muttered. She didn't like that they were always watching.

Grabbing her binoculars from the windowsill, she zeroed in as best she could. She thought she saw someone running into the wood line at the back of Porter's property.

"What? Why would those guys be going into the woods?"

Annoyed at the whole situation, she closed her curtains for the night. She had a lot to think about now that the Mitchell house no longer stood empty.

~~~

"Hey, Joe. Did you see that?" Max leaned out the open window of the SUV, trying to get a better angle of what he thought he'd just seen.

"See what?" Joe looked up from his book and toward Porter's house.

"Someone, a man, I think. Hightailing it toward the back of the house."

"No. Are you sure?"

Max stayed quiet for a moment, still watching. "Yes. I'm sure."

"Probably just the jilted boyfriend. He's been hanging around." Joe went back to reading his book.

Max didn't answer. He thumbed through his notes. "No. I have it here. He's in New York since yesterday at least."

"The drive is only four and a half hours. He could have easily gotten here tonight," Joe replied.

Max turned and nudged his partner to get his full attention. "Then where's his bike? We're in his parking spot."

Joe laid the book down, shaking his head. "Fine. Let's check it out."

They left the SUV and walked around the far side of the garage so they could have a view of the backyard over the shrub line.

"Is that a dog barking? It's inside, though," Max said, then he made a shush gesture with his hand.

After a moment, Joe said, "Yeah. Maybe you saw Porter. Maybe she took the trash out or something."

"Maybe. No. I don't know." Max's eyes continued to scan the yard.

"Come on. There's no one here." Joe started walking back to the car.

"I really thought I saw someone."

"Yeah, yeah." Joe walked back to the SUV. Max lingered a bit and then followed, turning to look back a couple times.

~ 21 ~

As I sat in the study sipping a glass of Caymus cabernet and chewing on a slice of pizza, I stared at Jack's wooden cigar box that I had placed on the coffee table almost a week ago. Knowing what was inside, I eventually found the courage to open it. The hinges of the box squeaked a little, like a door to the past. There in the box, the bent white envelope called out to me. As I opened it, the photos of the plane crash spilled out onto the table, and with them, the memories flooded my mind.

I had acquired the FARC photos in a cantina in South America—paid over five grand for them—and now here they sat, tattered and useless. I knew I should have given these to the government, but Jack had given them copies instead at my insistence. The informant who had given these to us had dirty, nervous hands. He had the envelope with the photographs tucked into the waist of his pants under his poncho-like shirt. Jack had verified the authenticity of the plane right away by checking the serial number in the picture with the plane Will had flown that day. But I knew immediately that the photographs were real...because what I had seen in the last two pictures ripped out a piece of my heart.

There in front of me in a close-up photo, I saw the black-metal, raven-wing necklace that Will always carried in his pocket. The necklace forgotten, lying there on the seat where he would have been sitting—the pilot's seat streaked with just a smidgeon of blood. I remembered feeling as if I was going to faint when I saw that photo for the first time, how Jack's hand had grabbed mine under the table at that cantina and how he had looked straight into my eyes, giving me the strength to keep going. We were so close to the truth at that moment. Then, just like that, it all had been ripped out from under us. That was when the US military strong-armed us out of the investigation. Even now, I felt heaviness in my heart. This photo alone made me think Will really could have survived.

I remembered that during the first year of the search, Jack and I had been full of hope and naivety about Will's involvement in the smuggling. Information poured in from the investigative firm weekly, and the fact remained that my husband had been an excellent pilot, one of the best, in fact. No question he had crash-landed the twin-engine plane with full engine failure inside the thickest part of the jungle with minimal damage to the cabin, leaving both pilot seats and the cockpit intact. The biggest concern had been the large amount of blood staining the copilot's seat. The captain's seat, where Will had sat, however, only had a smear of dark red as if someone's bloody hand had touched the edge; it really looked as if there could have been a survivor.

The back of the plane, crafted for intelligence-gathering, had suffered more damage than the front, but the equipment had been destroyed in a manner consistent with that of US military tactics, which implied that the intelligence soldiers in the back may have survived as well. Although the military did not like that I had a private team searching for my husband, they took no action against it in the beginning. Unfortunately, Jack had fallen under a different set of rules since he was a military officer at the time of the crash. Because of his relationship with my husband and me, the US Army had honorably discharged Jack a few months after the crash. I believed that also had been a way to restrict his access to classified information that we had yet to discover. The information that I sometimes wished I had never found.

The dogs started barking, startling me back to the present.

I'd forgotten to let them outside when I got home a little while ago. Reluctantly, I put my glass down on the coffee table.

"Okay, okay. I'll be right there."

~ 22 ~

The blasts in the background shook the ground and the shacks of the small shantytown, where Jack waited patiently for his contact. He had booked a flight late last night for this morning. Maybe one last encounter with the informant could get him the proof he needed to convince Porter to let go of her loyalty to Will. They had been so close to the truth when Porter had to sign those papers to stop. "She signed. Not me," Jack muttered to himself.

He planned on being back in New York by the next morning to get his bike and then head to the river cottage in Turnberry. He didn't want to spend more time than necessary away from Porter.

"Uno cerveza."

Jack didn't know much Spanish, but he knew how to order a beer. Officers always had interpreters with them. He would have to wing it now without that military perk. The bartender opened the bottle, stuck a lime on the rim, and placed the ice-cold, dripping bottle on the counter in front of him.

"Gracias."

Jack put cash on the bar and walked to a table to wait. He leaned back in his chair until it touched the wall behind him, stretching out one of his legs next to the table. His jeans and boots were covered in dust. His rolled-up shirtsleeves clung to the damp sweat on his already sunburned arms. He scanned the cantina from behind his sunglasses. Jack had been here so many times before—undercover. This place wasn't somewhere he thought he'd be again as a civilian. He could feel his weapon at the small of his back and the KA-BAR knife stiff in his right boot.

Jack watched as the sloppy, overweight informant entered the bar.

He was shifty and not to be trusted. Waiting for the guy to notice him, Jack did an internal eye-roll and shifted his mouth off center a bit with a quiet disdain—he could have shot the guy twice over by now. Finally, the man made his way over to the table, and Jack stayed in his relaxed position on purpose as a posturing of power. The informant reached into his pocket.

Jack spoke calmly but firmly as he discreetly moved his weapon to his lap: "Whoa, whoa, muchacho, are you trying to lose a hand? Don't go rummaging in your pockets like that."

The guy stopped and lifted his hands slowly in front of him, looking around nervously as he did so.

"How about you sit down first?" Jack motioned to the chair next to him.

The informant sat.

Jack took off his glasses, made eye contact with the guy, and then looked down at his own lap. The informant followed Jack's gaze landing on his hand that held the pistol, which was pointed directly at the informant under the cover of the table. Jack met the informant's eyes with a glance that made it clear he wasn't going to play any games.

"Now, slowly get whatever you have out of your pocket and pass it to me."

The informant nodded and in a thick accent said, "No problem, señor."

Jack took the crumbled envelope, and while maintaining eye contact off and on, he peeked inside.

The envelope contained a slip of paper, a few American coins, a money clip with the initials WHS, and a tattered photograph of a man...well, his profile anyway. The man in the photo had a scruffy beard and tanned skin, but looked healthy, not like someone being held in a FARC prison camp. Could it be? Will? Jack couldn't be a hundred percent sure, but his gut told him it was. His heart pounded—he was angry.

The handwriting on the paper more than resembled Porter's and read, "You hold my heart in your heart." Jack knew she would write something like that.

The money clip definitely had Will's initials. Willem H. Stone. And

Jack recognized it.

"Where did you get these items?" Jack's piercing stare caused the mole to shift in his chair.

"Mi boss, señor. You need pay now."

Jack stared directly into the informant's eyes. "Okay, I see how this is going to go. I'll pay you when you give me something I can work with, so now you need to answer a few questions. Where did your boss get these?"

"No se, señor," the guy said, his voice shaking slightly.

"Maybe you better try a little harder to remember. Did you get these from the pilot? Did the pilot survive?" Jack patted his shirt pocket that held the envelope of money.

The informant looked at Jack, his eyes big and his brow sweating. "Por favor, señor. I make delivery."

Jack decided to take a stab in the dark that Will had survived. "Where is he?"

The mole shifted again, started to stand. "No se."

"This again. I'm losing patience, amigo." Jack leaned closer to the man and lowered his voice in a menacing tone. "I'm going to ask one more time nicely. And don't tell me that you don't know again. Comprendo? Is the pilot alive or dead ... muerto?"

"Señor, por favor."

"Alive or muerto? Alive or dead?" Jack's voice had risen, and heads turned to stare in their direction.

"No se, no se. Un pilot. I see him once, but he leave. My boss, he know him." The mole looked around, clearly paranoid that someone had heard him.

Jack fumed. "Who is your boss?"

Sweat dripped down the informant's face, and he began twisting his hands together, which meant Jack had hit a nerve.

Just then, a commotion at the bar ensued. Jack didn't want to get caught up in this ruckus. Besides, he had what he needed for now: decent confirmation that Will had survived.

Tossing half the money across the table, Jack said, "You'll get the other half when you put me in touch with your boss or this man." He tapped the photo.

The shifty informant readily took the half payment and the opportunity to scurry out the door.

Jack said to himself in a low voice, "If you are alive, Will, and I find you, I'll—" He stopped there.

~ 23 ~

Three weeks in and almost at the end of March, I finally unpacked the last few boxes. The whole time, I had fought with my memories—things that weren't good for my healing or my present state of mind, including standing and staring at the white roses that had been delivered every Friday for years, as if nothing had changed.

Jack. I smiled as I thought of him. My anger from our last conversation had long since faded. *I miss you.* My lips mouthed the words as I touched a delicate petal that had fallen onto the polished surface of the hallway table.

No matter how much I tried not to, I couldn't help but imagine Jack's face and the way it felt when we stood too close, the heat that was constantly building between us. How I wanted him to lean in, kiss me. How I would imagine his touch in my mind, even when he was standing right in front of me. How our eyes would lock, and time would seem to stand still. How guilty I felt about all of those feelings. I couldn't just allow myself to live a brand-new life with Jack, knowing how it all started. Or could I?

Time to get out of this house. In a blur, I jumped in the car to go grocery shopping.

After parking and feeding the meter, I entered the natural foods market on Main and browsed the shelves, happy to be doing something other than rehashing the past.

"Hello, Miss. Do you need any help? Those beets are fantastic, by the way."

I looked over to see a pleasant-looking man in his fifties, short of stature and wearing a loud Hawaiian shirt and black-rimmed glasses. I almost expected him to be holding an exotic cocktail with a little umbrella.

I couldn't help but return his warm smile. "Oh, hi. Thanks. I'll give them a try. Yes, actually, I'm looking for almond butter and ground turmeric, but these beets caught my eye." I realized it sounded like I wanted to mix the two first things together. I stumbled over my words, trying to get them out quickly to clarify. "Not to use together."

We both laughed.

"You never know ... there may be a recipe there. My name is Stan. My dad and I own this place. He's retired now, though."

"I'm Porter. Nice to meet you, Stan."

"Follow me. The almond butter is right this way. You'll have choices to make, though—crunchy, smooth, salted, unsalted." He winked.

"Thanks for your help," I said, grinning as I followed him.

"No problem." He pointed just a couple feet down the aisle. "The turmeric is there, on the left, near the end. Let me know if you need anything else."

I finished gathering fresh fruits, vegetables, and a variety of my favorite snacks, including the very necessary dark-chocolate almonds. Stan met me at the register.

"Did you find everything okay?"

"Yes. Thanks again."

"So, are you visiting our little town?" His eyes sparkled a bit as he asked.

I smiled. "Actually, I just moved here."

"Oh, a newbie. Well, welcome." He looked at me again for a second, as if sizing me up in some way, and blurted out, "Do you like art?"

"Well, yes, I love art."

My wife and I have a little art studio just off of Main, down by Long Street. If you're interested, you should stop in. Some of the pieces are quite interesting."

"I will definitely stop by. Thanks for letting me know."

"Great. Tell Peg—that's my wife—that I sent you." Stan handed me a business card with a beautiful painting of a white stallion on the front.

"Did you or your wife paint this?" I asked while staring at the majestic creature on the card.

When I looked up, I noticed he was blushing. "I did," he said.

"It's beautiful. You're clearly very talented."

"Just passionate about painting." Stan looked down at his feet.

Humble. I like that.

He added, "A few of my pieces are on display at the gallery." He finished packing the paper grocery bag. "Well, Porter, enjoy the beets."

"See you soon—either here or at the gallery." We said our goodbyes, and I found myself smiling all the way home.

As I pulled into my driveway, I noticed the SUV was nowhere to be found.

Good.

I also noticed that Rose stood in her front garden, looking in my direction.

I'll take the dogs out back.

~ 24 ~

Jack grabbed his bag and secured it on his motorcycle. He needed to get back to Turnberry to check on Porter. Had it really been almost a month since she left? As he drove, he thought about how he would approach Porter. Should he show up at her doorstep? Should he run into her in town? No. With Porter, it was always better to just be upfront and direct. If he wanted to see her, he needed to knock on her door and see her. Properly. She didn't like games.

The time flew, and Jack arrived in Turnberry just after lunchtime. He decided to drive by Porter's before heading to the river cottage.

He pulled up to the side of her guesthouse, and parked just behind the hedge. When he turned off his bike, he heard something just inside the wood line. Jack's movements slowed as he zeroed in on the rustling sound in the foliage.

He walked stealthily in that direction, toward the garage. Looking around, he didn't see anything or anyone. But he'd definitely heard something.

Just then, the back door of Porter's house opened, and there she was, carrying two empty boxes. Jack used every ounce of his willpower not to run to her and blurt out what he had discovered via the informant—that Will had survived the crash. But Jack knew he couldn't do either of those things, especially the part about Will. That news had to be relayed delicately.

No, he couldn't rush this. He didn't want to blow it. Most of all, he didn't want to set Porter back. She'd come a long way with her healing, and information like that could trigger all kinds of anxiety. So, Jack curbed his desires and waited for Porter to go back inside. Feeling partly defeated and partly victorious, Jack got on his motorcycle and drove away.

~~~

Rose stood in her window across the street, watching in disbelief. How many people were watching Porter? "I hope she's not one of those witness protection cases."

~ 25 ~

I looked out the window. No SUV. Perhaps Schultz had been right, and it had finally happened—the surveillance had been lifted.

My stomach growled. I checked the clock. A little past seven. I showered and dressed. On the way out the front door, I grabbed my jacket from the foyer coat closet. The first thing I saw when I stepped outside was Rose, staring at me through her window. Almost like she'd been waiting for me to leave. *How early does she start her surveillance?* I started to wave like I used to do to the government goons, but before I could raise my hand the curtain closed, as if she hadn't wanted to be seen. I shrugged it off.

I drove toward a diner called Hatch. Stan's wife, Peg, had told me about it when I had visited the art gallery a couple days ago.

The building sported white siding and large, black-paned cottage windows. Jack and I loved to eat at quaint places like this. We called them "one in the world" places. In fact, this place reminded me of a diner Jack and I had gone to in Georgia, where we'd met up with someone claiming to have information about Will's copilot from the day of the crash. The informant turned out to be a disappointment, but the trip itself had brought Jack and me closer.

As I reminisced, my heart ached a little, and I could almost feel the touch of Jack's hand on my own—the way he would steady me.

I swung open the door to the diner, and the smell of fresh-baked biscuits hit me full-on. My stomach responded with a loud growl, and I made my way straight for the counter.

"Coffee with cream, please," I said to the smiling waiter as I situated my purse strap on the back of the stool.

"You got it. Welcome to Hatch."

"Thank you so much." I returned the smile and then swiveled on my seat, taking in the rustic yet sophisticated atmosphere. Finally, I looked over the menu, debating over a couple of scrumptious-sounding options.

The waiter reappeared with a coffee pot in hand and poured some of the steaming brew into a mug. "Are you ready for me to take your order?"

"Oh, yes. Thank you. I think I'll try the smashed avocado and toast. Wheat, please." Not many places offered this dish—I had discovered it years ago on a trip to Australia with Will. One of many vacations we took where he filled up his time and left me to venture out alone. I had spent several mornings at the café in Sydney by myself. I shook off the lonely feeling that had begun to creep in.

Curious, I looked around some more and noticed an older man with silver hair and a short, well-groomed beard to match enter the diner. The man, probably mid-sixties, sat on the stool one down from mine. His clothing looked like he'd just stepped out of an ad featuring the English countryside, even down to his rugged boots. *What a stylish man.*

He caught me eyeing him and said, "Hello, there, young lady."

"Hello." The corners of my mouth turned up a bit in a shy grin.

He looked at me curiously for a second or two. "I haven't seen you around here before, and I know pretty much everyone in this town." His voice sounded calm, peppered with a natural intelligence.

A lady wearing a crisp apron with her hair neatly pulled back, probably a decade younger than the man, called out from behind the counter, "Yep. And everyone knows you, too, Cecil." Then she looked to me, "Watch out for this one. He's the real-life embodiment of the town archives."

Cecil laughed. "I could start by sharing your history."

The lady focused on me, playfully ignoring Cecil. "I'm Mrs. Tillman. My husband and I own this place." Then she looked at Cecil. "I can introduce myself, thank you."

Grinning, I said, "Hi to both of you. I'm Porter. Just moved here to Turnberry."

"Ah, a new resident. Ready to leave yet?" Cecil teased.

Mrs. Tillman shook her head but couldn't conceal the smirk forming on her lips. "Ignore him, please."

I said to Cecil, "Well, you're not getting rid of me that easily. Actually, I love it so far."

"Well, I've lived in Turnberry for close to forty years." He pointed at Mrs. Tillman. "And she and her husband have been here for centuries."

"Very funny," Mrs. Tillman called out.

Cecil continued. "Before that, I still lived in Virginia, but farther south. I was born in Petersburg. It's nicer here." He winked. "You'll be just fine. Lots of friendly, kind people."

I nodded in agreement.

The waiter approached and said, "Good morning, Mr. Bogg."

"Hello, young man. Good to see you. I'll have my usual."

"You got it." He jotted down the memorized order as he walked away.

"I'm new to Virginia as well," I blurted out. I realized then that I may be more starved for conversation than for food. "I lived in New York, but I'm not actually from there."

Like a true gentleman, he took my rambling in stride, his kind demeanor unwavering. He reminded me of my dad. "So, what brought you here?" His question felt matter-of-fact, not prying like Rose's.

I paused for a moment and watched him sipping his coffee. My extended silence didn't seem to bother him. Things were naturally comfortable between us.

"I...well, I just thought it was time for a change." I hesitated with my reply, but again, it was not an uncomfortable pause. "Actually, my life has been a little complicated for a few years. I needed a fresh start."

Did I really just say that? Something about him felt safe, like I could trust him.

He looked at me in the way a father would look at a child—not with judgment, but with concern backed by an understanding that only those with life experience, with wisdom, could offer. "I think we should back up a bit, I should have introduced myself properly. My name is Cecil Bogg. It's a pleasure to meet you." He extended his hand.

I sat straighter, shaking his hand and appreciating his penchant for simple decorum. "It is nice to meet you too, Cecil. I'm Porter Leighton."

It felt good to use my maiden name, the one I used before everything had happened, before I became someone I didn't recognize.

"Porter. I like that name. Don't hear it very often. Now, you said you just moved here. To which part of town?"

"I just moved into a house on Waterford Street. I like it. It's quiet and somewhat close to the river."

"That's a nice street. Historic homes, stately. Yes, quiet. Large yards, attractive flower gardens. I know it well."

I nodded. He was right—it was one of the nicest residential streets in town.

Then he paused with a hand to his chin, thinking about something, apparently. I waited. He turned to me with a raised eyebrow and said, "Come to think of it, I didn't see any homes for sale on Waterford Street recently, and I only know of one that isn't occupied."

"No, well, you wouldn't have seen a For Sale sign. I actually inherited the house. It belonged to my aunt."

"Who was your aunt?"

"Well, her name was Lila Leighton, but she never lived in Turnberry. She bought the estate through a private sale several years ago. It was a kind of hobby for her. Buying properties, that is."

"Extravagant hobby, but I like it. Which house is yours?"

I smiled at his elegant response, very different from Rose's wealthy-aunt comment. "It's the old Mitchell estate. The house on the hill near the corner."

"Yes." He nodded as if he had already guessed the house, but something in his eyes looked far away as he said, "Ah, the Mitchells."

Staring at the steaming plate in front of me, I wanted to dig in. Lucky for me, Cecil felt the same about his own dish. He reached unapologetically for his fork and knife and cut into the thick slice of country ham, smothered by an over-easy egg, and savored the first bite.

Cecil and I shared all kinds of everyday tidbits, from planting gardens and flowers to organic honey to red versus white wine. Cecil informed me which streets made for the best walks around town—he had a dog that he adored as much as I did mine. In fact, we lived only a couple of streets away from each other.

"Let's meet Wednesday morning for a walk with the dogs," I suggested.

Cecil agreed readily.

I felt like I'd known him my whole life—a kindred soul.

Our conversation flowed long after we had finished eating. Cecil told me how his own daughter Elizabeth had gone to school with Graham Mitchell's granddaughter, Lauren, and how Elizabeth had even lived at my home when it belonged to Lauren. I couldn't wait to pick his brain further about the history of the property and its inhabitants. I didn't have to wait long; I didn't even have to nudge. His eyes were a soft blue, a little foggy, and he looked off into the distance as he spoke.

"The Mitchells come from a long line of bankers. Graham had the house built around 1910, I believe. Graham, along with his wife Sophie, moved into the home to raise a family, two kids—a boy and a girl. Unfortunately, Sophie died while the kids were still relatively young, and then the daughter passed away not too many years later—in her young twenties, I believe. To make a long story short, in the 1960s, after Graham's death, his son William, his wife Catherine, and their young daughter moved back into the house so that William could take over running the family bank. Fast forward thirty or so years to when their daughter, Lauren, the only child, inherited everything after she lost her mother and father in the span of five years. It took a toll. So, my daughter Elizabeth moved into the house with Lauren as a sort of tenant. Both of them worked at the university at the time. My daughter wanted a bit of independence, and Lauren wanted a housemate—two birds, one stone.

"And Lauren? What happened to her?"

"Well, she passed away of an autoimmune disease close to four years ago now. Her health just continued to fail. Very sad. Hit my own daughter hard to lose her friend like that." Cecil stared at his coffee for a moment. "My wife's passing, and then my daughter's friend. It was too much for her. She said she needed to go out in the world. So, she found another professor position, far away at Trinity College in Dublin.

Met a nice local pub owner, married him, and now has a little baby girl." He smiled halfheartedly. I could tell how much he missed her. "She invited me to go with her. But I'm set in my ways. I couldn't leave this town, not at my age." Cecil winked. "I've been here too long. My roots run deep." He chuckled a bit.

"Lauren's death preceded my aunt Lila's purchase of the home by about a year," I said. "So, that's why it was available. How old was she? Lauren, I mean...when she died."

Cecil thought for a moment, as if calculating her age. "Well, let's see, she must have been about thirty-four or so, too young. She was about ten years older than my own daughter. Just heartbreaking."

Cecil paid for both our meals, so I insisted on leaving the tip.

"I had such a great time talking to you," I said. "See you Wednesday, right?"

"Bright and early!" He waved and headed toward the door.

26

Rose watched as Porter left. *It's now or never.* She needed to get over to Porter's house and try the Mitchell's safe one more time, before Porter found it. Her mother had given her the combination years ago, but only part of the numbers remained on the torn scrap of paper, making the last two numbers a mystery. Today, she would try a few more combinations with different ending numbers. Eventually, she'd get it right; it was just a matter of elimination and patience. And time— something which, before Porter's arrival, Rose had plenty of.

She crossed the street to Porter's house, making a beeline for the guest cottage. She unlocked the old door handle with the keys she'd had for as long as she could remember and entered the cottage.

She struggled with the trap door and made sure to pin it open securely. She descended the cool stone steps and entered the tunnel to the main house. It had been many years since she had used this entrance into the house. She hoped the door at the other end wasn't blocked.

When she reached the end of the tunnel, she pushed hard on the small door that led to the basement of the big house. The door opened easily, surprising her and causing her to stumble slightly. Regaining her balance, she moved the beam of her flashlight around to find the light fixture. And with a gentle tug, the basement room illuminated.

The room looked just as she remembered it—the vault on one side and the far wall having a false panel to the main part of the basement. She pressed on the panel, but it didn't budge. Instead, she heard loud cracking and clanking noises coming from the other side. Rose covered her ears, immediately regretting the clatter she had caused. Then the door released and flew open followed by brooms and a rake falling onto the floor. Walking into the basement she listened for any sign that her noise had been detected. It hadn't. She climbed the stairs to the front hallway, reaching into her pocket to feel for the dog treats that she'd brought just in case. But she wouldn't need them; she could hear the dogs whining from behind the closed door to the kitchen. She took a deep breath, walked toward the foyer, and pressed her hands on the wall just below the main staircase of the house, and this panel opened easily without an avalanche, unlike in the basement. Rose entered the small room under the stairs and went to work on trying combinations.

Over a half an hour passed with no luck. She needed to get back home. Frustrated, she left the way she had come, through the basement, trying her best to lean the garden tools back against the wall neatly so as not to leave any evidence of her visit.

Crossing the street to her house, Rose heard a car idling. She turned her head and noticed the black SUV near Porter's driveway.

~~~

"Hey, Max. Take a look at that." Joe pointed as they slowly drove toward the guesthouse.

Max looked toward the far side of Porter's property. There at the front of the cottage stood the tiny old gal from across the street, locking the door and then leaving toward her own house. "Well, she takes 'nosy neighbor' to a whole new level."

Joe nodded. "You're not kidding."

"Should we stop her and talk to her?" Max asked with a hint of eagerness behind his question.

"Nope." Joe's matter-of-fact tone left no room for debate. "For all we know, Porter asked her to take care of something in there. Besides, Porter is home. Look—her car is in the driveway."

The two sipped on sodas.

"I can't believe this. I thought we were done with this case." Max's frustration showed.

"Well, you can thank lover boy for making that trip to Colombia last week. He's got everyone stirred up again thinking the search is back on."

Max sat for a moment, silent. Then, "Joe, let me ask you this. If your girlfriend's traitor husband was missing in a jungle halfway across the world, would you look for him?"

Joe gave Max a sideways look. "Probably not."

"Me neither."

Joe parked in their usual spot with a decent vantage point.

27

After breakfast with Cecil at Hatch, I had stopped to pick up a few groceries, spoke with Stan, and agreed to meet him and Peg for dinner next week. *I'm starting to feel like I belong here.*

I rinsed the fruit I had bought then remembered the extra kitchen towels I'd brought with me were still upstairs.

Walking down the dimly lit hallway, I noticed interesting architectural details everywhere. I paused to admire the moldings in the foyer, and...

Wait. What is that? On the wall just below the staircase, there appeared to be an unevenness in the wainscoting pattern.

I ran my hand across the wall and pressed down directly on the visible seam. *Pop.* The creak of old wood broke the silence, and the wall jarred open, exposing what I deemed to be a secret doorway. Leaning into the pitch blackness of the opening beneath the stairway, I strained to see inside. The musty air made its way to my nostrils, and I sneezed abruptly.

My mind raced with intrigue as I thought of my aunt and how she always talked about old mansions and the secrets they often chose to share with new occupants.

"You were right, Aunt Lila."

I hurried back to the kitchen, sifted through a couple drawers, fumbling through extension cords, a light bulb, some votive candles, until I spotted a small flashlight. I then remembered dumping the box labeled "junk drawer" from my New York home directly into this one, now christened the "new junk drawer."

As I gripped the small government-issued flashlight, I thought of Jack. It had belonged to him. As much as I tried to pretend that I didn't,

I did: I missed that man.

With a sigh, I checked to see if the flashlight worked as I walked back toward the staircase. To my delight, the beam was strong.

I opened the secret door and waved the light around the small space in front of me. More like a closet than an actual room. Stepping inside one foot at a time, I lifted the flashlight and directed the beam straight ahead of me, revealing a large, black, metallic safe with claw-foot legs. I tried to twist the handle, which was next to a built-in combination lock. It didn't budge.

"Darn it," I muttered.

I tried again, this time pulling straight out, but no luck.

Reluctantly, I surmised that this intriguing little Nancy Drew-esque mystery would have to wait for another day. Maybe I would find a combination somewhere in the house, but that would take some real snooping, some real "getting to know" the place. It reminded me of the proverbial needle in the haystack. Still, my curiosity was stirred.

This old house has a secret. That's what makes old houses so much fun.

I turned on my heels and faced the hallway. "That's it for today. Party's over for now."

Of course, I didn't listen to myself. Over near the corner, under the highest part of the steps, hung a bulb with a string dangling from the fixture. I pulled it—and the darkness disappeared.

In the dim light, I noticed shallow shelves on the wall next to me, some still stocked with old mason jars. I smiled, remembering how Aunt Lila used to make boysenberry preserves every year. I used to sterilize the jars with her in a big stainless-steel pot that I wished I still had. My fingers would be stained purple for days after picking the little stems off the berries. The memory made me giggle.

Then, the satire of this whole room hit me. What had the previous owners thought? *"Oh, I'll store my homemade preserves right here next to my secret safe."* I laughed. Obviously, they couldn't have sent just anyone in here to retrieve the jam. Or maybe the recipe was so exceptional that they had stored it in this safe. I imagined a guest saying, *"I'll grab the strawberry jam for you. Where do you keep it?"* And, the owner replying, *"I could tell you, but I'd have to kill you."*

With that, I clicked off the light and closed the secret closet, going about my day and grinning from time to time as I thought about the little adventure under the staircase.

Hours later, right before nightfall, I let the dogs out by the side entry that faced the guest cottage, and as I stood in the driveway just in front of the garage, I contemplated the things Cecil had told me about the house. How interesting that the family had owned First Turnberry Bank on Main Street. I had noticed a large bank made of stone. That had to be it.

Maybe the safe had something to do with the bank. So, a banking family had a hidden safe under the staircase in their home. Of course. But I still wanted to see inside.

Suddenly, I felt the hairs on the back of my neck prickle. I had a feeling of being watched, so much so that I slowly turned my head to look back over my shoulder. I saw that Rose's lights were on, but I didn't see her—part of me hoped she was standing there at the window, staring at me because if it wasn't her, then... What was giving me the creeps?

Wait.

I squinted. Did I just see something moving at the edge of the woods? A person? I really didn't know. I second-guessed myself, but I still felt a surge of anxiety run down my spine. My heart pounded, and my mind raced. *Do I run inside? Do I call the police? Do I play it calm?* Then I wondered if maybe it had been those government idiots. I decided to wait in the backyard for a few more seconds, listening for any footsteps or noises. Nothing. Although I didn't see anyone, I still felt as if I wasn't alone. I stood quietly listening.

Suddenly, I heard a loud rustling and what sounded like a person running through the brush; I literally jumped in the air. Both dogs bristled, and Gatsby started to bark. Then, as if hunting, they crouched and moved slowly toward the rustling sound before diving straight into the underbrush. Hoping they could hear me over their barking, I called them back. More barking. I called again, louder. I didn't need them getting lost this time of night. For a moment, I thought I heard another voice.

Finally, the dogs came back, breathless, and Ripley was chewing on something. I grabbed at his mouth, and what looked like chewing gum fell out, wrapper and all. "Where did you get this?" I asked as if the dog could actually answer me. *Strange.* I felt the familiar tingling in my hands and the heat of anxiety. *Was someone out there—did someone use gum as a dog treat to distract them?* I knew if I didn't stop myself, my mind would go to places that weren't good. So I hurried the dogs inside to the "safety."

Later, as I sat in the study trying to read, I replayed what I thought I had seen and heard. A man.

It's gonna be a long night.

~~~

Rose quickly peeked out of the window to see Porter standing awkwardly in her driveway. Before Porter turned around, Rose moved away from the window.

That could have been close earlier. As Rose sat down to watch TV, she wondered if she shut off the light in the basement. The last thing she needed was for Porter to find that tunnel entrance and block it. That would be the end to her safety net for access into the house. Rose didn't know for sure if Porter changed the locks to the house, but probably not, since the guesthouse key had still worked.

In the morning, Rose still worried about the light. She'd been watching and waiting for an opportunity to go over there and check, but Porter had been home all day so far. Rose was getting antsier by the minute. *I just have to go. I'll be quick and quiet. She'll never know—as long as she doesn't see me going in or coming out of the cottage.*

~ 28 ~

On Friday, I found myself in the basement. I had time to spare and a house to explore, after all. Besides, I had been wanting to glance through some of the old paintings stored down there. Today seemed like the perfect opportunity. Peg told me to take photos, and she'd let me know if I had anything of value that she could sell for me at the gallery.

The first few paintings consisted of dark portraits. As I leaned back the largest frame, I was taken aback at the contrast from this one to the others. It looked like it was more recently done, and it was...*ugly*. With my face twisted in disgust, I snapped a picture with my camera for Peg. I even felt a shiver in my spine when I did so, focusing on the image. Why paint such a bleak portrait—if that's what it even was? A grim woman standing next to a distorted stained-glass window—it all reminded me of a horrible Picasso rendition. The comparison to Picasso would have been otherwise ridiculous except that everything was grossly out of proportion and broken into random fragments. I doubted the painting had any value, but I'd leave that assessment to the expert.

Patting the dust from the front of my pants, I noticed a service entrance on the back wall as well as several large windows, all covered on the outside by thick ivy. That must have been why so many tools were stored down here—easy access to the outside. I figured this side of the house opened to the lower level of the back yard under the screened porch, a place I hadn't ventured yet. *I really need to walk the property soon.* I looked around, taking in the wall of deep, concrete sinks and hanging racks as well as the unpainted, weathered, wood-plank door on the far end.

I opened the door and immediately grimaced. "Ewww." It was a stark, awful-looking bathroom. The shower in the middle had just a concrete edge to keep the water contained. A tilted metal ring that once held a shower curtain hung lopsided from the ceiling. In the corner, sat a white porcelain toilet and tiny white sink with a patina-covered mirror hanging from a nail above it.

Then it hit me. This had been the bathroom for the help. I shut the door quickly, closing the portal to the remnants of a different time; a strange, elusive time.

About to head upstairs, I flipped the main light switch off, leaving only the stairs illuminated.

Except...

There. Near the lawn equipment, a small shard of light was coming from the wood-plank wall.

I moved in that direction, and in an instant, the light was gone. I heard a loud creak coming from behind the wall, followed by a shuffling that seemed to fade quickly into the distance.

"What in the world?" I said under my breath.

The panic began to set in, starting with a rush of adrenaline that led to me feeling faint. My hands shook, and I wanted to run. My mind raced. *It sounded too big to be a mouse. And what about the light?* I could hear Jack's voice in my mind saying, "It's the anxiety taking over. It's not real. Things are not as bad as you are feeling right now. Breathe, just breathe."

So I did, two deep breaths. Then I walked toward where I had seen the light, my legs shaky. I noticed a small vertical crack through some of the wooden slats on the wall. I pressed on that area of the wall, and just like upstairs, it popped open. But unlike the upstairs panel, the basement wall jarred a bit too quickly, causing some of the junk leaning against the wall next to the panel to fall.

One of the shovel handles hit my shin, and I muttered a bunch of curses. I leaned over to rub the spot on my leg, and a rake fell and hit my head. "Good grief!" As I stepped back, I could just barely see through the darkness...

Another secret room?

I peered inside but couldn't see much. I grabbed the garden spade next to me on the wall and held it in one hand. Suddenly, I felt very silly. I lowered the spade and looked around. "Porter, it's an old house. It creaks, and the wiring isn't reliable." My eyes started to adjust, and I saw a light fixture with a pull string like upstairs. *Click.* The room glowed.

The estate lawyer definitely should have mentioned that the house had a problem—it was riddled with secret rooms. I sighed deeply. I had moved here to bury my own past and lower my stress, not to provoke a heart attack several times a week by discovering actual closets that held other people's proverbial skeletons.

I was standing next to a giant steel door, a vault, not unlike what one would expect in an early 1900s bank, a goliath of a safe built directly into the wall.

I looked up as I spoke, "So there are two safes in this house? Okay, Aunt Lila. I know I need distractions, but..."

I ended midsentence because there, nestled in the back of the room, my eyes fell upon a small miniature door, like something out of *The Hobbit.* I felt like a grown-up Alice in a dark Wonderland. *What next?*

Taking a deep breath and grabbing the spade once again, I tugged on the small door. To my surprise, it opened easily. The light from the outer room shone inside enough for me to see.

A tunnel? I could see only a few feet, but I could tell it curved to the left—that would be toward the front of the house, or the driveway.

It all seemed surreal to me. Yet...Wait! Were those footsteps? Not like an animal, like a person. *Maybe I'm not paranoid.*

I slammed the door fast and leaned against it, breathing rapidly. "Not good. Not good at all." If Jack were here, we'd definitely go in. But he was not, and there was no way I would go in there alone.

I stood back against the door. *Breathe, breathe.*

"Think. Think."

Okay, Underground Railroad, maybe? I remembered studying it in school. Pictures I had seen in textbooks looked a lot like this. Still, I couldn't believe it. *No. I'm definitely not going in there. It has all the makings of a bad horror movie. I won't be that girl.*

I needed to block the miniature door and fast. In the far corner of the room stood a stash of boxes. Quickly, I moved three of the heaviest boxes, two full of books and the third full of thick glass bottles—all empty—that clanked as I pushed. When I was done, I stood back with my hands on my hips, surveying my work. I'd broken out in a sweat and was struggling to catch my breath. No doubt, it had to do not only with the manual labor, but also the adrenaline rush.

Feeling less exposed to whatever I had heard in the tunnel, I stared for a moment at the vault before leaving the secret room altogether. As futile as it seemed, I pushed garden tools under the secret panel as doorstops to try and secure it from the basement side. A pathetic attempt, but it was all I had the energy for at the moment.

As I stood in the upstairs hallway, I stared at the dead bolt on the basement door. I had at first thought it overkill. Until now.

I turned the lock.

I thought about the footsteps in the woods and now the footsteps in the tunnel. I knew I hadn't imagined either, and I also knew how paranoid and crazy that sounded. Fighting the lump in my throat, I said, "Whoever is out there, just get it over with. Kill me. Torture me. Kidnap me. Rob me. I don't care anymore. Just do it already." My voice sounded small as I spoke to no one, to myself.

I thought about calling Jack—for the umpteenth time since I'd left—and actually went so far as to pull my cell phone from my pocket.

I headed for the kitchen, ready to dial, biting my cheek the whole time. But I placed the phone on the table, stepping back.

No. Rescue yourself, Porter, for once.

~ 29 ~

As I waited to meet Cecil for our Wednesday walk, I flipped through the morning paper, yawned, sipped my coffee, yawned again, and replayed the basement saga. Where did the tunnel let out? I shook my head in disbelief. The other night seemed like a weird dream, my own real-life *Twilight Zone* episode.

On the bright side, I had at least one friend in this town expecting to see me, because if someone had jumped out of that crazy tunnel and given me a heart attack, I could have been there for months without being missed. I laughed aloud. It sure beat crying.

I stared at the paper again. Most days, the *Turnberry Herald* read like a country club newsletter with stories about who won the local golf or tennis tournament, or which business owner donated what to the community. So far, I had seen no local crime stories—but no complaint there, especially since the zero-crime thing worked in my favor as I attempted to convince myself that no one was in my basement or woods.

As I tossed the paper aside, the Living section slid out of the middle fold. There, placed front and center, was a picture of a vault just like the one in my basement, exactly like it.

Stunned, I read the title aloud. "Turnberry's Rich Prohibition History."

I examined the photograph. "That's my basement."

I read further and looked closely at the caption, but there was nothing about where the photo had been taken. But I knew. Without a doubt. Still, I muttered, "This can't be."

I shook my head in disbelief. I didn't want my house in the paper—anonymous or not. I placed the paper back on the table and looked at the clock.

Time to meet Cecil.

"Great. I won't be distracted at all during the walk today." The sarcasm rang thick in my voice. "The punches just aren't going to stop, are they? On top of it, Now, I'm talking to myself. Good thing I live alone."

I put on my lightweight jacket to combat the late March chill still in the air and grabbed the leashes for the dogs. *Off to meet Cecil.*

I waved at Rose, who donned a large straw hat and seemed quite focused on tending to her budding spring garden. She nodded in my direction. Okay—gardening did not qualify as spying, but I still felt her watching me, and I smiled a little knowing that she was trying so hard to figure out my comings and goings.

Cecil was walking up the street and called out to Rose by name and waved. Rose looked annoyed at the continued interruptions as she threw up an unenthusiastic wave back. Cecil crossed the street and walked up the sidewalk toward me with his older blue merle Aussie. "Good morning."

Yep, he still looked like he stepped out of a catalog. "Good morning," I called back.

"My old bones are loosening up this morning with the sun shining and keeping up with old Blue here," he said as he approached. "How have you been, Porter?"

"Well, it has been interesting." I raised an eyebrow and looked toward Rose.

Cecil tilted his head. "Hmm. Update me." Then he said, "Rose has been grumpy as long as I can remember. Don't take it personally."

"Oh that. Yes." I laughed politely and quickly changed the direction of our conversation. "The good news, I'm pretty much settled in and have rearranged some things for the better." Then I gave him a side-glance.

"I hope there isn't bad news."

"Okay then...in other news, I had, well, let's just call it an adventure in my basement." I smirked at him.

He nodded in an *oh really* kind of way. "Is that so?"

"Yep. And, Cecil, I know we just met, but I really need a sanity check. I didn't want to put this on you, but..."

"Nonsense. What's going on?"

"Well, I think something is a little strange with my house. I mean, like maybe the previous owners were a bit clandestine or maybe just overly eccentric." I went on to tell him about the basement light and how that led to discovering the vault. I ended the dissertation with the statement, "Or I could just be paranoid."

I paused, wondering if I should tell him the rest—about the tunnel, the other safe, the rustling in the woods, the story of my traitor husband, the SUV, the cartel, the man I probably should not have left, Jack. Would that be overstepping?

Yes, of course it's overstepping. I'm probably already overstepping.

Before I could say anything else, Cecil said, "You know that old house of yours and the Mitchell family...well, they have quite a history. More than what I told you before."

"Really? You must tell me, Cecil. Please." I knew my voice couldn't hide my desperation for some reasonable explanations, anything to explain what I'd been seeing and hearing.

"Well, I'll tell you what I know, but I think it would be worth your while to spend some time in the library archives downtown." He grinned. "I used to work at the paper and have some of the old articles myself, but I don't have any organization to them and wouldn't even know which pile to begin looking in."

"Give me a little something, Cecil," I pleaded. "Come on..."

"Well, I'll start at the beginning." He paused and looked around. "You know how I told you that Mr. Mitchell, Graham...well, his wife died young. The official story was she had cancer. However, the rumor mill at the time carried a different tale. Rumors circulated, those of a more nefarious sort, that someone murdered Sophie. You see, that night, the biggest crime to ever hit Turnberry occurred: a jewel heist from the crown Sophie had donated to the Historical Society for display. And rumors flew that somehow the thief, or her husband, or her husband's mistress, had killed her."

For a moment, I couldn't speak. My heart dropped a little. "Why on earth?"

"First off, I don't want to scare you. It's century-old gossip. Even if it had happened, it was a long time before you were even born. Believe it or not, before I was born."

"Trust me, Cecil. I can handle it—ancient history, right?" I said this in a way that made clear I had heard much worse in my life.

"You see, it was rumored that Graham hadn't been home when Sophie died, that he had been with his mistress, who also had a young daughter." Cecil paused before saying the name, "Rose."

I gasped. "Do you mean Rose Blanchard? My neighbor?"

Cecil looked at me, nodding, his lips pursed. "Yes. It's long suspected that Rose is Graham's daughter."

"I don't know what to say. Did everyone know?"

"I'm not sure. What I do know is that things were different back then. Family secrets, indiscretions, weren't discussed openly. So, my educated guess is it was one of those things that everyone knew, but no one acknowledged. After a while, it became less and less known as the older generations slowly dissipated and took the secret to their graves."

"Does Rose know?"

Cecil sighed. "That, Porter, I could not say."

"Well, if she does, that could explain partly why she's always watching my house."

He laughed. "She's always been nosey, though."

I thought for a moment. "You know, I kind of feel bad. Maybe Rose wanted my house? Assuming she is the last rightful Mitchell heir."

Cecil stopped walking and looked at me. "Don't feel bad. You didn't know any of this. Your aunt bought the house free and clear of any obligation to Rose. And Rose has never officially pursued any birthright that she may or may not have as far as I know. The secrets of this town are not your burdens to bear. Don't ever carry anyone else's baggage, you hear me?"

Taken aback a little by the firmness of his words, I wondered if they were really meant for me or, instead, for himself or maybe for his daughter. I knew deep down the truth in what Cecil had said, but the situation remained that I already carried baggage—a lot, and a little post-inheritance guilt added on didn't matter all that much.

As we neared my street, I asked, "Speaking of ancient history, did you see the article in the paper this morning?"

"Yes." He winked. "Are you hoping to find some old bottles of bootleg elixir in your home?"

So he does know the photo is from my house. "So you know..."

Cecil cut me off midsentence. "I worked at the paper, remember?"

"Ahhh, yes."

"Have you looked in that vault yet? Anything left in there?" Cecil's eyes sparkled.

"Honestly, I don't have the combination or key. I mean, Cecil, I don't even know how to find out how to open it."

"Well, if you do figure it out, or if you want any help, I'm formally volunteering to be a lock picker and, more importantly, a moonshine taster." He waggled his eyebrows, his expression full of mirth.

I wasn't about to pass that up. "You have a deal. You'll be my first call when I'm ready. But, first, how about an extra walk next week, Wednesday *and* Friday?"

Cecil agreed, and as he strolled away with Blue, my eyes drifted to Rose's house.

~ 30 ~

Golden sunlight shone through the windows of the rented Turnberry river house, and Jack sat with pen in hand, scribbling a few sentences. He wanted to write to Porter, but he couldn't find the right words. He tossed the pen and pushed the paper out of the way.

"Dammit."

He missed her. He wanted her back. That was all there was to it.

Jack grabbed his jacket. He needed to get out of there. Get some fresh morning air.

Parking his bike in front of Turnberry Bank, he grabbed a newspaper from the street vendor and headed into Hatch for a bite. Faces turned as curious gazes followed him on his way to the counter. Attractive, eligible men were scarce in Turnberry, apparently.

The waitress wasted no time in handing him a menu and a smile.

Disregarding the onlookers, Jack put the menu down, ordered coffee, eggs, bacon, and toast. He knew Porter would have read the menu top to bottom and then ordered avocado or steel-cut oats or something he playfully referred to as "froufrou health food."

"You new in town?" the waitress asked when she delivered his food.

Jack didn't answer immediately. Finally, he said, "Huh, um, Yeah. You could say that."

Not interested in chitchat, he looked back at the paper. "Prohibition vault?" He shook his head, skimmed the article, and finished his breakfast.

On his way back to the river cottage, Jack drove by Porter's. There, next to the guesthouse, he saw the black SUV.

"What the hell?"

Jack pulled the motorcycle next to Max and Joe, who both sat slouched in the front seats. Jack removed his helmet and walked over.

Joe mumbled, "Oh great."

Frustrated and a bit condescending in his tone, Jack asked, "You boys back on the job?"

Max leaned over. "Yep, I've been meaning to send you a thank—" He abruptly stopped.

Joe had put his hand on Max's arm and gripped it firmly.

Max changed gears. "Look, we have a legit reason to be here, but what's yours?"

Jack's eyes narrowed. "Hey, Joe, muzzle your dog."

Joe said, "Listen, Jack. He's got a point."

Max said, "You really think you'll win her back by creeping around behind her house?"

"Listen, jerk," Jack fired back, "I'm no more creeping around than you are."

Max snorted derisively. "Really? You don't see us running off into the woods to hide."

"Wait. What are you talking about?"

"Look," Joe said, "we don't want to be here any more than you want us here. Just let us do our job, and in the meantime, why don't you keep your *vacations* to a minimum?"

"So, that's why you're back." Jack leaned on the edge of Joe's window casually. Max gave Joe a what-the-hell glance. "I'm just concerned, guys. Okay? That's why I'm here—'creeping around.'" Jack motioned air quotes on the last words, which made the agents scowl. "Listen, if the government thinks she's still a problem in this whole thing, then isn't it safe to assume that the cartel thinks the same thing?" He looked at Joe after he spoke, eyebrows raised.

Silence filled their space for a long moment. Joe spoke next, letting his guard down a bit. "I'd say that's a real possibility."

Each of them knew the dangers associated with the cartel. The horrendous things that happened to family members of snitches, traitors, and the like had kept each of them up nights at certain points in their careers. Women and children gained no mercy from the cartel—the monsters served brutality equally to all. Porter would be no exception.

"I can't let anything happen to her. That asshole of a husband set her up good. But I don't have to tell you two knuckleheads that."

Max looked at Joe and widened his eyes in a questioning way. Joe gave a small shake of his head as if to say, *"Don't comment."*

Instead, Joe cleared his throat and said, "Look, essentially, we're on the same side. It's just that we need you to let us do our jobs. We have to document a clear cease and desist in the search. She's been cleared of the drug-running charges—we know that jerk of a husband set her up."

Jack nodded, chewed his lip. "Yeah, you know it, and I know it, but does the cartel know it?"

The agents stayed quiet. Jack had a point.

Joe said, "Okay. It's crystal clear that none of the three of us want the cartel to get their hands on Porter." He was stating the obvious, but it needed to be said in order for them to work together on this.

Max nodded in agreement, and for the first time, Jack's posture relaxed.

"Well, then, it's set," Jack said. "We're all on the same page. You two want off this assignment, right? And I want this over as well. And we all want Porter safe. So, how about we work together on this— unofficially? If the cartel has a guy on her, we'll catch him together. Bring this all to a speedy end."

Max said, "I'm in. Yes, I want off this job, but mostly, I don't want anything to happen to her. None of this was her fault to begin with. She just married the wrong guy."

Briefly, Jack had a faraway expression, then he looked at both of them. "Thanks, guys."

Joe patted Jack on the shoulder. "She doesn't deserve any of this. We get it, man."

Jack nodded, patted the hood of the car, and walked to his bike. As he rode away, Joe turned to Max.

"What was all of that creeping-in-the-woods chatter?"

Max shrugged his shoulders and responded sarcastically, "What?"

"I thought you said he was in New York when you thought you saw someone in the woods."

"I was just cross checking."

Joe remained silent but gave Max a vexed glance.

~ 31 ~

As I chopped vegetables to add to a pasta salad, the house phone rang in a shrill, old-fashioned way, brutally extinguishing the serene silence.

"Hello."

"May I speak with a Ms. Porter Leighton?" a sharp, male voice sputtered from the other end of the line.

"Yes, I'm Porter. May I ask who is calling?"

The voice responded almost before I'd finished my question. "Yes, um, yes, hello. My name is Cedric Barton, calling on behalf of Mr. Frederic Barton. I work for the First Turnberry Bank. I have a letter here that instructs me to contact you upon possession of the Mitchell home in order for you to come to the bank and pick up the contents of a safety deposit box. I am to contact you within the first thirty days of your arrival, and well, uh, it's almost past that. It's just that I couldn't find your contact information. Anyway, well...it doesn't matter. You are Ms. Leighton, right?"

"Yes. I am." I tried to comprehend everything this stranger from the bank was saying. His tone was high-strung, to say the least.

"Can you come to the bank today? Ms. Leighton, are you there?" His voice gnawed at my eardrum.

"Yes, yes, I'm here. Can you give me the address, please?" I asked, assuming I'd be led to the big stone bank in town.

"It's 43 Main Street, the biggest building on the block. You cannot miss it." He spoke the words as if I should already have known. "So, I will see you today, correct? Oh, and please bring two forms of identification." His taut voice was followed by a click, momentary silence, and finally, a droning dial tone.

I finished my lunch and proceeded to drive the one mile to Main Street.

The bank sat right in the center of town—and I really didn't need the address after all. The bank must have been as old as the city itself. Once inside, I couldn't help but notice the height of the ceilings and the resemblance to the clock area in Grand Central in NYC.

I didn't know where to go, so I asked a teller where I could find Cedric Barton.

From behind me I heard, "I'm Cedric Barton." I turned. The jittery little man with oily hair, glasses, and a too-tight, brown suit spoke again, "Miss Leighton?"

I nodded, and he instructed me to follow him.

We entered a small and dated office with looming walls of mahogany paneling. Behind a large, fancy desk sat a man who looked to be at least eighty-five years old.

He spoke but didn't get out of his seat. "You must be Ms. Leighton."

"Yes." I walked forward to shake his hand, but he waved me back toward one of the leather chairs in front of his desk.

"Sit. Please."

I sat, thinking, *Have I entered a time warp?* The furniture looked European—well cared for, but antique. Large portraits of past bankers adorned the walls and were each lit by a brass sconce. I strained my eyes to see if any of the portrait plaques had the name Mitchell. *Two of the three did.* I stared at the one of Graham.

"ID, Cedric." The man behind the desk motioned to Cedric for him to check my two forms of ID.

Cedric took my driver's license and my standard-issue military spouse ID to photocopy for the bank's records. Cedric read aloud, "Porter Leighton Stone."

"I'm sorry, but that was my married name—Stone. My husband is, was...uh, he's gone." The look on the men's faces prompted me to continue. "I no longer use that name." I started to dig into my purse for my new social security card with my given name—Leighton. The old banker behind the desk waved his hand yet again, but this time in a "don't worry about it" sort of gesture, with a touch of annoyance.

"Ms. Leighton, Cedric will assist you with getting your items."

Cedric led me out of the office and into a small room with a table and two chairs. He then gained access to my box and an accompanying inventory list from the security box clerk. Then they both left me to review the contents in private.

Inside the box, there sat stacks of paper and a blue velvet pouch. The papers looked old and seemed to contain a lot of legal language. Those could wait. I opened the pouch. Inside were three items: a small, rectangular, silver pillbox with gorgeous sparkling stones set into a dragonfly pattern; a stunning sapphire ring with too many little diamonds to count; and an old non-descript skeleton key.

The ring fit my ring finger as if it were made just for me. The pillbox contained a single slip of very old and yellowed paper with some numbers and dashes written on it: L12- - - -R25- - -L15- -R0. *A combination? The safe under the stairs, maybe?*

~ ~ ~

As soon as I arrived home, I made a beeline to the front hallway and into the secret closet. Crouching in front of the safe, I spun the dial on the lock quickly a few times before aligning it to zero. Carefully, I tried the combination, again and again for over thirty minutes. No luck.

There is also the vault.

But if memory served me correctly, I hadn't seen a combination lock on the vault. The handle had looked like a ship's wheel. Besides, I didn't want to go back down there just yet—especially not alone.

~ 32 ~

For several days, I had been wearing the ring from the safety deposit box. Now I stared at the gorgeous blue sapphire, watching it sparkle as my hand rested on the steering wheel. By the time I pulled into the lot at Hatch, the clock read 2 p.m.

Mr. and Mrs. Tillman waved to me from opposite sides of the restaurant. I waved back, a little embarrassed, but also happy to be treated like a regular so soon. However, I was keenly aware that I had made a lasting impression, only because I had dined with Cecil more than a couple times over the past several weeks.

"Hi, there, Porter." Mr. Tillman chimed out from behind the pick-up counter. He moved around the diner at lightning speed.

"Hi, Mr. Tillman. Thanks for saving me a seat at the counter." I winked.

"You always have a seat at our counter, Porter. Hey, by the way, I've been meaning to ask you...how is the house coming along? How's the neighborhood treating you? Have you met some friends?"

"Still working on it, Mr. Tillman. I've met one neighbor, Rose Blanchard, and of course, you know Cecil. In fact, Cecil and I are walking the dogs together some mornings. But I do need more of a break from being in the house so much. This afternoon, I'm heading to the library for a while."

"Oh, good. It sounds like you are settling in nicely. Yep. Cecil is one of our favorite customers—an old-timer like me. Ah, Rose. She is an interesting one at that."

"Now, Mr. Tillman...you know you'll have to explain what you mean." I grinned as I spoke, knowing he had goaded me on purpose.

"Maybe some time when there isn't a rush, I'll bring you up to date on Turnberry gossip."

"I'll hold you to it." I finished my sandwich and iced tea and headed out the door to the library.

The weather had taken a sudden change for the worse. Black clouds blanketed the sky, and the air hung heavy with the faint scent of approaching rain. I hurried down the sidewalk, crossing the empty street at the corner. Only one more block to go. It appeared as if almost everyone had left downtown in anticipation of the impending storm.

Just as my feet landed on the front steps of the library, huge raindrops began to fall. As the large, Gothic, wooden door closed behind me, I heard a familiar voice say, "Talk about perfect timing."

"You're not kidding." I brushed a few drops of water from my clothing and walked over to the help desk, instantly recognizing Patsy. "Hi there. I don't know if you remember...we met at the pastry shop?"

Patsy's hands flew in the air before she clasped them together, her eyes gleaming. "Oh yes! Porter, right? Of course I remember. You're the only new person to move to this town in quite a while." She giggled. "How are things? Are you settled in? What brings you to the library?"

Even amidst the interrogation, I felt an affinity for Patsy. She seemed bubbly and fun, and marvelously theatrical. I could already envision a friendship forming.

I smiled and cleared my throat. "Well...where to start? I moved into the old Mitchell house, and I'd really like to know more about the family history. It's a little unusual, I know, but the family left pretty much everything in the home, and I feel a little bit like a guest amongst their ghosts." I laughed.

"The Mitchell house, oh?" Patsy looked serious, apparently missing my attempt at humor. "Well, ummm..."

Worried I had said something wrong, I quickly added, "I don't want to pry just out of curiosity. I feel like knowing more about the family will make it more like home to me. That's all."

Patsy leaned closer. "No. It's just, well..." Her words trailed off for a moment. Then she seemed to shift gears a bit, forcing a more chipper tone. "It's just that you've definitely picked the most interesting family history that Turnberry has to offer." She tapped her chin. "Hmmm, you know, I recall telling you there wasn't much to this town, but I guess really that's not completely the case. If you go over to the microfiche and look up 1925, you may begin to scratch the surface. But you won't find the real story in the papers."

"Oh really?"

She nodded enthusiastically. "Hey, you know what? If you want to meet up later, I can at least tell you what I know. I get off at 8 p.m. most evenings. I'm free tonight."

How could I say no to that offer? "How about a late dinner, then?"

She grinned. "Absolutely! I don't have anyone waiting for me at home. Do you like Italian?"

"Yes, I love Italian food. Thank you so much for offering to share information."

"My pleasure, and I happen to know the perfect place. It is called Marcello's, a couple blocks away. They serve the best carbonara."

"Marcello's it is," I said with a smile. "See you tonight."

As I navigated my way through the rows of books toward the microfiche area, I noticed a group of young children and their mothers all huddled around a lady dressed like a princess. She sat front and center reading them a story. For a moment, my heart sunk. Five years ago, I would have predicted that I would be one those mommies sitting there. I quickly swallowed the lump in my throat and continued on my way. The children's voices faded into the distance as I entered the dimly lit microfiche room.

Over an hour later, I finally came across an article titled, "Turnberry Philanthropist Dies." The article explained Sophie Mitchell's death and mentioned an unknown illness. Apparently, Sophie had died in her sleep after a grand charity dinner that served to raise $25,000 on April 27, 1925, for the Turnberry Historical Society. However, the story didn't end there. Apparently, after the gala, an artifact on display had been robbed of its jewels, a crown that had belonged to the Turnberry family. The two events begged for a connection in the way the article had been written. Between what Cecil had told me earlier and this new information, my thoughts were spinning.

Suddenly, I heard a loud crack and then booming thunder. Then, all went black, and the background filled with the children's shrill cries.

"Great, a blackout. Just what I need after an hour of searching for one measly article," I muttered.

A male voice called through the darkness, "Library is closing. A main power source to the building was struck. Anyone need assistance?"

I shouted back to this faceless being, "I'll manage my way to the door. Just help the others." I could definitely get out of a library in the dark, considering all the places I had been during the search for Will—a lot of them places no one should ever go.

"Okay, Miss, I will be back in a few minutes to check on you," and off he went.

Finally, I edged my way back to the circulation desk at the entrance. There stood Patsy, directing everyone. "Hi, there, Porter. I was wondering if we would ever find you back there."

"Thanks for the vote of confidence," I joked.

"See you at Marcello's at 8:30, then?" she said, smiling as always.

"I'll be there." Then I added, "If they have power."

Patsy's eyes widened. "Oh, good point. Let me give them a ring to find out." She picked up the phone and spoke with someone at the restaurant. After a quick conversation, she disconnected and gave me a thumbs-up. "We're all set. Power's still on at Marcello's."

I couldn't wait to spend more time with this lively woman—and maybe learn more about the Mitchell family as well.

~ 33 ~

After a warm shower and a quick change into a dark sweater, jeans, and boots, I arrived at Marcello's a little before 8:30 p.m. The small little restaurant tucked into a row of buildings on Main Street wore a most understated single-door entrance. Hesitating, I wondered if I had come to the wrong place until an unexpectedly dapper doorman appeared and welcomed me inside. The romantic Tuscan atmosphere served as the perfect backdrop to the delicious aromas wafting throughout. From where I stood in the hostess area, I could see the glass-encased wine selection room. *Patsy knows how to pick a place, that's for sure.*

The crisply dressed staff circulated around the restaurant with precision.

"Porter, Porter, there you are." Patsy ran over.

"Hello there! Wow, this place is lovely."

Patsy nodded quickly. She seemed anxious. "Porter, I have to tell you something...about the Mitchells. I wanted to tell you earlier, but I was at work and we just met. Well, it's not like we know each other now, really. Oh, goodness, I'm not making much sense, I know. Let's get a booth in the back. Come on." She pulled me through the restaurant.

"Shouldn't we wait for—"

"Don't need to be formally seated. It's my uncle's restaurant," she said as we walked to a small, private booth. Immediately, two glasses of water and a basket of steaming bread were placed in front of us. The waiter carefully poured a plate of olive oil for dipping.

"Do you like red or white?" Patsy asked me.

"I'd love a red."

"Me too." She ordered a bottle. "We may need more than one glass," she said with a giggle.

As I looked around, I was grasped by the memory of a the little Italian restaurant in London off Mews Street where Jack and I had spent many evenings rehashing our findings in the search for my husband, and just for a second, the separation between the past and present dissolved. Part of me felt the warmth of my memory, and the other part felt the icy sting of missing Jack.

Patsy leaned across the booth as if we were lifelong friends and spoke in a hushed voice. "Don't get upset, and please don't worry, but I have to tell you something. I just have to tell you. Okay. Here it is." She took a long pause. "For a couple of years now, there have been rumors that the Mitchell house is haunted. And you're there all by yourself! Aren't you?" Her eyes were bugging out.

I held back a smile, laughter. "Patsy, I'm all right, really. Surely it's just a rumor. Besides, ghosts don't scare me at all." I winked, then added, "People, on the other hand..."

Wringing her hands, she ignored my joke and continued. "But...people have seen lights go on and off at all hours. There have been shadows across the windows. Porter, it isn't safe."

I thought to myself that the shadows and lights were most likely from someone, a human, not the dead—maybe the same someone who may have been snooping around in the basement and back yard.

I must have sat too long in my silence.

"Porter, you look...well, just...are you okay? I'm sorry to have told you, but I would want someone to tell me."

Shaking off the serious moment, I rallied and spoke reassuringly. "Patsy, I am fine, and I will be careful. Thank you for letting me know. Besides, I have two dogs with me that have probably already scared off any ghosts."

Luckily, the waiter came along and took our orders, and the tension faded.

She spoke in a calmer tone. "Porter, I do have some other information about the Mitchells, but like I said, it happened a long time ago; I'm not sure it's even true. Okay, here it is. The story." She cleared her throat but barely took a breath as she dove right in.

"So, there was a big gala on the night Mrs. Mitchell died; her name was Sophie. Anyway, she was said to have been ill for a while, but on that night, she had been the belle of the ball, hadn't seemed sick at all. Sophie had presented a new artifact to the Historical Society, a jeweled crown that had been owned by her family." She cleared her throat again. "After the ball, her husband had driven her home, but not before she allegedly had witnessed him and his mistress in a bit of a row in the parking lot. Here's the thing. The story doesn't end there. As it so happens, someone reported having seen Mr. Mitchell promptly return on foot to the empty building where the soirée had been—where the jewels were stolen. And sometime around then, Sophie died." Patsy paused, then added, "Or was murdered in her bedroom—in your house."

I could only nod and waited for more as our dinners were placed in front of us and we dug in.

"This Bolognese is divine."

"Everything here is." Patsy beamed. "You know, Porter...rumors about murder, the heist, Mr. Mitchell," she waved her hands in the air, "they've circulated for years. It almost sounds made up. That's why you should check the library and do some research, of course."

I was taken aback by this additional information, and I knew my expression showed it. "No, not all of it sounds made up. I'm just shocked, that's all...because I did, in fact, find an article on microfiche about the gala and Mrs. Mitchell's unknown illness and death. It mentioned the jewel theft being on the same night, too." *And Cecil told me Rose's mother had been Mr. Mitchell's mistress.*

"Oh. Wow." Patsy looked down. "I had hoped it wasn't actually true."

"Don't get me wrong. I'm not convinced it is *all* true. That's a lot to happen in one night, for sure. I am surprised that no one was arrested if there was a murder. At least, I didn't see that in the article. I'll have to go back and read more when the power is back on." I smirked a bit at Patsy. Then we both sat in silence.

I realized that we weren't going to solve this decades-long mystery tonight. I decided to lighten the mood a bit. "So, where do the young people hang out in this town?"

Patsy laughed. "Here. You are looking at the only young people in this town, my friend—yep...you, me, and the wait staff."

I overdramatized a bit with my response and dragged out the words, "You cannot be serious."

We laughed.

"Pretty close. To be fair, most of the people our age are people I've known since preschool, so I never think of the men as eligible. It seems weird, in a big family kind of way. But you, on the other hand, are new to Turnberry. Maybe one of these grownup versions of boys I knew when they were snot-nosed little hellions will interest you." Patsy winked. "Unless you have a boyfriend."

I smiled and took a sip of the Black Rooster-certified Chianti sitting in front of me.

After we wrapped up dinner and said our goodbyes, I saw someone out of the corner of my eye. *It can't be.* I looked squarely in the man's direction, but he already had his back turned. Still...the same hair, height, build—*Jack?* My heart raced. I started to rationalize: *it's just your heart controlling your mind.* Yes, I missed him, and no, I didn't want to. My hands started to shake.

"Dammit." I got in my car. "Dammit, dammit." I sat on my hands, trying to force my anxiety away. Ten minutes, fifteen passed. Finally, the shaking stopped. I turned on the ignition and started driving, all the while fighting thoughts of Jack, but painfully losing the battle.

My skin tightened with the memory of that humid night in Georgia. Jack and I had been on our way back from a trip to Washington, DC, and decided instead to fly to St. Simons Island to talk to a retired major who had worked with my husband. We had stayed over at a historic circa 1920s resort gloriously named The Cloister, pompous and formal, and we had adored it all—the pretentious, illustrious South at its finest. Heading back to our suite that night, we had held hands, walking slowly until we approached the middle of a little bridge. There, we had stopped in unison and turned toward the dimly lit pond filled with tadpoles and koi. The sound echoing throughout the humid darkness had reverberated—unreal, otherworldly, raw, and relentless...

"Jack," my voice breathless, "what is that noise?"

"Frogs." He said only that one word as we stood entranced by the sound.

My skin glowed from the humidity; his hair curled ever so slightly at the ends as the ancient, primal calling of the frogs beat on in the darkness. My breath caught in my throat as his heart-stopping gaze moved closer, his hands gently touching my face. The moment before our lips connected, I felt a spark, as if we were creating our own charge in the night air. My whole body felt his kiss, deep and passionate. I never wanted to leave that moment. The dampness of his skin pressed against mine, the weight of the thick heat, the backdrop of steady noise from the pond—all of it captured my heart, touched the core of my being. I wanted to crawl inside his soul, take refuge in his strength, his love. But, as things do, the moment ended. With the guilt of feeling that I was betraying my missing husband, I pulled back. I pulled away. He understood, as he always did, and gallantly gave me the space I thought I needed.

Looking back now, I was wrong. I should have followed the desire of my heart and dove into that moment and the perfection that was Jack.

The tears flowed as I pulled into my driveway.

~ 34 ~

"Porter has been gone all evening." Rose spoke aloud to her cat. "I could be over there right now. I have to find it before she does." If only Porter had an established routine, then Rose could plan her search visits.

"I guess she doesn't have to work like the rest of us did at her age." She cringed as she thought about her own life as a bookkeeper. Ending up in this house later in life just wasn't enough. She should have lived a life of privilege from birth. And she felt owed for that injustice. Her mother had told her many times over that she had the same birthright as any of the Mitchell children.

Rose's mind raced, even though she needed to go to bed. Just as she moved away from the window, she heard an engine sound. Not a car, more like a motorcycle. Her curiosity strong, she looked one last time out of the window. She thought she saw the silhouette of a man darting from the garage to the back yard of Porter's house, but she still heard the motorcycle idling.

Rose continued to peer into the dimly lit yard. Yes. There near the guest cottage sat someone on a motorcycle. What was going on over there? "Maybe thieves, or maybe jilted boyfriends," Rose whispered, believing the latter more likely.

She knew she should care more for Porter's safety, and maybe even call the police, but instead, she decided to simply watch for a bit longer. Besides, what if it turned out to be just a result of having a young, single woman living across the street? The man in the yard seemed to have disappeared, and the one on the motorcycle pulled away. Just as his taillights faded into the night, Porter pulled into the driveway.

Rose thought about calling Porter, but then she rationalized herself out of it. "Porter is not my responsibility. Besides, she's in my way. Maybe she'll get spooked and move out. *Hmph!*"

Then the dark figure from the yard appeared once again from behind the house. The man stared at Porter as she struggled with unlocking the side door. Rose gasped; her heart raced. She steadied herself as she leaned in closer to the glass to see better. If he wanted to hurt her, now would be his chance. Rose held her breath, waiting for him to attack Porter. *If he grabs her, then I'll call the police.*

Suddenly, Porter froze. Rose gripped the curtain tighter with one hand as she watched, chewing on a nail of the other. Porter slowly looked over her shoulder toward the edge of the yard. At the same time, the dark figure moved back silently into the shadows. Finally, Porter disappeared inside the house, flipping on lights as she went.

Rose released the curtain as she let out a breath she'd been holding. "It's time for bed. She's safe inside."

~ 35 ~

Jack sped down the winding road away from Porter's house and toward the river house. Tonight, he had accidentally seen Porter in Marcello's having dinner with another young woman, and he had quickly left the restaurant to avoid the close call of what could have been a very public reunion.

He didn't want to approach her there, and he certainly didn't want to sit in the dark from the shadows of her yard waiting for her to come home. It all felt wrong, even just keeping a close eye on her these past weeks as she transitioned to this new place. Jack wrestled with how to define his being in Turnberry, his driving by Porter's house, his avoiding her seeing him, his fronting a second month's rent just that morning. He found himself in a tough spot, as if he stood directly on the fine line of love and obsession. Jack knew the difference, though, and deep down, he knew that any watching he did had been for surveillance purposes to make sure she was safe in this new place.

If Porter could have seen Jack's face that night in Marcello's, she would have seen the longing in his eyes, the unconditional love he could not hide.

Jack thought about approaching her, had even moved toward her in the restaurant. As he drove, he imagined going to her, holding her close, but somehow, she seemed so out of reach.

At Marcello's, Jack couldn't take his eyes off of Porter, the way the candlelight had caught the golden stands of hair that framed her face, the glint of green that he could see even from a distance in her eyes.

Jack arrived back at the river house. He parked the bike and stood in the quiet night air, barely breathing. The last thing he wanted was to watch her from a distance. In fact, he wanted exactly the opposite; he wanted to be her safe place.

~ 36 ~

Early on Wednesday morning, Rose slid muffins and peanut butter dog cookies into the oven. She wanted to be at Porter's door first thing, bearing gifts for all. She would charm those dogs and Porter, too.

Rose still hadn't decided if she would mention the dark figure she'd seen last night. She had a lot to lose if Porter set up a security system. Suddenly, it dawned on Rose that she didn't actually know if Porter was okay. The dark figure hadn't approached Porter as far as Rose had seen, but anything could have happened during the rest of the night. Rose looked out the window at Porter's house. No sign of movement, but lazy mornings had proven to be normal for Porter.

~~~

The doorbell rang over and over in my dream; then I awoke—but the doorbell chimed on and on.

"Who could be here this early? Who rings a doorbell incessantly like this?" I really needed to sleep in this morning after being out late with Patsy and then browsing the internet for more information about the Mitchells.

Ugh. Maybe I'll just let it go unanswered. The doorbell rang yet again. "Okay. Okay." Grabbing my robe while still groggy, I struggled to tie it and traipsed downstairs.

I looked at my clock. Still three hours before my scheduled walk with Cecil.

Through the peephole I saw that familiar gray head of hair. "Rose," I said under my breath with a big sigh. What could she want this early?

I opened the door. "Hi, Rose."

"Oh my, darling, did I wake you?" The woman looked particularly wide-eyed, wired really.

"Ah, well...yes. I was out late," I said as politely as I could muster.

"I'm sorry. I brought over some treats for you and the dogs. You know, Porter, I'm very good with animals and happy to watch the dogs for you any time you need someone to check in on them while you're out and about." She held out the basket of goodies, and Porter reluctantly took them.

"Thanks, Rose, but my two are real handfuls. Thank you for the breakfast." I started to shut the door, but she persisted.

"Just let me know, any time."

Perplexed, I wondered why she would even have thought to offer to watch my dogs. *What's in it for her? Is she really so lonely? Is watching my every move from her window not enough entertainment?*

"Okay, Thanks, Rose. I appreciate it."

This seemed to satisfy Rose, and she turned to leave.

No way am I going to ask her to watch the dogs. That's nuts.

~ 37 ~

"Morning, Porter," Cecil called out in his cheery voice. He patted Gatsby and Ripley.

"Good afternoon," I said in a mocking tone and knelt down to ruffle Blue's silvery fur.

"Uh-oh...do I detect sarcasm, Porter?"

Cecil casually pointed in the direction we would walk—his hand showed signs of years of writing and typing, his fingers standing a little crooked with the remnants of calluses he'd earned from putting millions of words on paper. I stared at him for a moment and thought about what an interesting life he'd had as a journalist and eventually the editor-in-chief at the local paper. He must hold such valuable memories of the history of this place. If only the human mind could be preserved like books and papers and photographs.

"In fact, you do detect sarcasm. Miss Rose Blanchard woke me at 7 a.m. this morning after I had a leisurely dinner with our local librarian, followed by a late-night internet search on the Mitchells."

We walked a few steps just to establish our stride. Before I could delve into the jewel theft on the night Sophie died, Cecil stopped abruptly and pointed in the direction of my guest cottage.

"What's going on there?"

I looked, and there on the far side sat the black SUV.

"Old friends." I spoke with jest. Cecil gave me a questioning glance. So, I elaborated. "It's a long story. The gist of it is that I'm kind of under government surveillance." I spat out the sentence quickly so that I couldn't change my mind. I had enough secrets. Besides, it just felt right to be honest with him. He'd had a lifetime of experience discovering secrets—he would have known if I lied. It wasn't worth the tension that would most definitely build between us.

"Porter, why would you be under government surveillance?" Cecil looked genuinely concerned.

I hadn't thought about my follow-through, so answering Cecil took a minute. "Honestly, I don't know why I still am. I can tell you why it all started, but it may take up our whole walk and then some."

Cecil looked at me in the way a parent looks at a child who says they didn't eat the chocolate but has a telling ring around his mouth. "I have the time, Porter."

I nodded. I needed to tell him. The truth, I needed to tell someone. "The thing is, some things from my past followed me here."

I spent a few minutes on the highlights of the crash, my husband's disappearance and possible death, and the illegal drug smuggling. Then I told him about how I had been implicated. I glazed over the cartel piece, trying my best to minimize the danger I could still be in, because even I didn't fully understand that part.

I knew, though, that the cartel wanted either Will or the money that Will may still have owed. However, since none of us knew if Will had survived or not, my black ops team had surmised that, ultimately, the cartel needed to watch me in order to try to find the money. The alternate theory, which I had wanted to believe more, had been that the cartel watched me to try to get a clue as to where Will may have been hiding. There had been other theories, too, but none made as much sense as those two. The ops team had assured me the cartel seemed to want me alive and well. It would be in their best interest for finding either Will or the money, or both. Jack still worried, though. He knew the cartel's patience ran thin and harming me could be used to smoke Will out of hiding or to appease the boss when the money didn't surface in time. I often joked that the government surveillance team served as free protection. Neither the ops team nor Jack had appreciated the humor in that perspective. I had to cope in some way with the stress, though. I wasn't naïve to the idea that the cartel could still be waiting and watching.

"Okay, Porter. I hear you. I can respect your privacy with your past. But…I don't know…it just seems strange that even though you've stopped searching, they're still watching," Cecil said with a serious tone. "Porter, maybe you need to get a security system."

"I have an alarm system, two actually." I laughed and pointed to the two border collies. "And maybe three—Rose doesn't seem to miss much out of her window."

"Porter, I'm serious. And speaking of Rose, why did she wake you up so early this morning?"

"She asked if she could help me with my dogs when I'm not there. Is she a bit senile?"

"I don't know. Maybe she's lonely and bored and trying to fill up her time."

He shrugged.

I shrugged.

We continued walking in silence for a bit.

"Back to the alarm, Porter. I'm serious." Cecil again stared intensely at me. I could see the light glimmer in his blue eyes, which kind of resembled small ponds.

"Yes. Cecil, I can tell. I hear you and will look into it. On a different note, do you have any experience with picking locks?" I gave him a sly look with a tilted grin.

"Oh good Lord, Porter. Where is this conversation going now? I'm an old man, you know."

"Ha! Starting to regret our friendship so soon?"

He shook his head with a wry smile that reminded me of how my dad looked whenever I would tell him I was about to do something risky. "Well, I do remember offering to help you bust open your vault. So, maybe I walked right into this one."

"It's not for the vault, Cecil."

Cecil looked inquisitively at me.

"I'll explain once you agree." I winked.

"Okay. Okay," he said in a playfully defeated voice. "I have a confession, too, actually. My dad was a locksmith, but that was a long time ago. I still have his tools, but I'm sure they won't help you with a modern-day lock. Why? Did you lock yourself out of your car or something?" He chuckled.

"I can't believe that you have 'locksmithing' in your lineage." I paused. "Well, fate certainly is on my side with this one. No, not a car, but maybe we could meet Friday morning at my house for coffee and some indoor lock-picking. Bring your dad's tools. I feel sure they'll be perfect."

"So, what's this lock, then?" Cecil prodded.

"Um...let's keep it a surprise."

"Is that all you're going to tell me? Like I said, I am an old man. I could pass away before then."

"Cecil!" I exclaimed. "I *will* see you Friday." I waved goodbye and sprinted off with the dogs toward home.

"Show off!" he yelled. "I'll be over about 9:15."

I waved again. "Thanks, Cecil!"

~~~

Max looked up from his newspaper. "Hey, who's that old guy with Porter?"

"I don't know," Joe said.

Max, just a few years older than Porter and never married, stared at the two. "Why would a young beautiful woman like that..."

"Do I hear some jealousy?"

Max put the paper down. "No. Don't be stupid."

Joe smirked. "Calm down. They're walking dogs."

The two sat in silence and watched. Max added, "I wonder what Jack would think about this."

Joe shook his head while staring at his partner. "Uh, nothing, Max. He'd think nothing. Good grief."

~ 38 ~

I decided to get some fresh air, and so I walked to Main Street to eat dinner. On my way out, I noticed the black SUV had left. Good. It appeared to me that the surveillance seemed to be getting spotty—more like a couple days here and there instead of 24/7. *Maybe they really are backing it down.*

Dinner at Marcello's was once again delicious, as was the impromptu mini wine-tasting Patsy's cousin had bestowed upon me, which made me very happy that I had walked and not driven. As I started toward home, I decided to make a small detour and popped in the market to speak with Stan and Peg. As jovial as ever, they gave me one of the new raspberry champagne-flavored cupcakes to test.

"Make sure to let us know how you like it," Peg called out to me as I waved and left.

"Will do. And, Peg, I need to bring you the photographs of the paintings from my basement soon."

"Ooh, yes. I'm looking forward to seeing what you found."

"Don't get your hopes up, but maybe you'll see something in one of them that I didn't. Thanks again." I gestured a toast with my cupcake as I turned to leave.

The night air felt crisp and fresh as I approached my house. In what had become a habit, I glanced up at Rose's window. For once, her house looked completely dark. Maybe she had gone out for the evening. Strange, though, because so far I had not seen her leave at all. She had groceries delivered every Tuesday and Friday, and a healthcare provider stopped by once a week. Come to think of it, her flower garden seemed to be the farthest she dared to venture.

I guess she went to bed early. Very early, really. Should I check on her?

You don't want to open that can of worms.

Does that make me a bad person?

It makes you a smart person.

I headed straight for my own home, trying to stop arguing with myself. I let the dogs out and stared over at Rose's house the whole time. Finally, I gave in to my conscience. After putting the dogs back in the kitchen, I walked over to Rose's house, rang her doorbell, and waited in the dark on her front porch.

I mumbled to myself, "Does she even own a car?"

I walked toward the side yard, peering around her house toward the garage. Suddenly, I heard a rustling in in the trees lining the edge of her property—probably a deer. Or, with my luck, a recently escaped zoo tiger or bear...or even better, Sasquatch. I held back a snicker. *Definitely something big, though.* I hightailed it back to the porch.

I knocked loudly a couple of times on her door and still no answer.

~~~

From Porter's attic window, Rose discreetly moved the drape, looking out to assess the situation. She had flipped off the light when she had heard Porter come home—the dogs' excited little barks had been her cue. Rose watched as the petite figure crossed the street toward her own dark house.

Rose thought how she'd love to be home right now. She'd been over here for far too long, having slipped in after Porter left around 5:45 p.m. Her watch now read 7:23 p.m.

Rose wondered why Porter had walked over to her house. She had never come over before. Then, Rose saw someone else. "Who is that on the side of my house? Is that a man?" She blinked and squinted. "Where did he go?" Her heart rate picked up as she wondered if it was the same man she had seen skulking around Porter's house.

This would not do. No, not at all. She needed to call the police, but she had to get back home first...and without getting caught snooping around Porter's attic.

Then, the man came out of the cloak of the tree line again, moving slowly along the edge of her yard. Rose gasped and instantly her hand went to her mouth.

Now he's watching Porter!

Porter must have heard something because Rose saw her scurry back to the front porch. The whole thing was becoming scary for Rose. What to do, what to do...

Then the man looked up toward the attic window.

"Oh!" Rose exclaimed, letting the curtains fall and backing away from the window. *Did he see me?*

Full panic set in. It was well past time to leave. Rose made a run for it.

She prayed the dogs would be closed up in the kitchen, which would allow her to easily exit through the French doors that led to the far side of the house, away from the garage. The French doors opened to a very private dining courtyard, so Porter or the man wouldn't see her, and she could wait to cross the yard until Porter went inside. Rose's biggest problem would be getting safely past the mystery man.

"It's now or never," she said aloud. "Darn." Annoyed, Rose had to turn on the attic stairwell light because it had gotten too dark to see without it.

At her age, she couldn't move too quickly. The old attic steps creaked, as did the door at the bottom. It seemed like hours as she descended the stairs. Finally, Rose made her way slowly down the second floor hallway, past Porter's bedroom, and down the staircase. Just then, she heard whining from one of the dogs in the kitchen. Rose breathed a sigh of relief as she made a beeline to the French doors and finally stepped outside onto the cool stone patio. "Phew."

Carefully, she peered out toward the front yard to see if she could see Porter, but the darkness did her no favors. She couldn't see a thing. Then she heard a commotion with the dogs inside and the faint sound of a woman's voice. Porter was home.

"The coast is clear." Rose hurried across the damp grass toward the street in the dark, worrying about the man lurking in the shadows. She ascended the front porch steps, unlocked the door, and then hurriedly locked herself inside the safety of her own home. After settling in, which included a much-needed stop at the powder room, she made a sandwich and grabbed a glass of water. With that, she went upstairs.

Just for a moment, she looked out her window, taking one last glance at Porter's house, and her heart dropped.

She'd forgotten to turn off the attic light.

Nothing she could do about it now, though. Just as she was about to look away, movement caught her eye. Again, she peered out. The male figure was walking briskly away from Porter's garage.

Then he turned and looked up, staring directly at Rose. Rattled, she shied away from the window.

As she settled into bed and took a bite of her sandwich, she thought about how the two of them, two strangers, were watching Porter—and both of them apparently had secrets to hide. If she exposed him, would he expose her?

So, it's an unspoken agreement, then.

Suddenly, she wasn't so worried anymore.

~ 39 ~

Back at my own house, convinced that I had done all I could do to check on my neighbor, I decided to call it a night.

I had checked Rose's front, side, and back windows for light. I had knocked on both her front and side doors. I had called through a couple of the closed windows as loudly as I could. In fact, nothing had seemed out of place, except for me.

With the dogs in tow, I walked toward my bedroom, ready for a good, long night's sleep. From the corner of my eye, I noticed a faint ray of light illuminating the hallway floor. The soft yellow glow crept out from the bottom of the attic door. *Strange, I haven't been in the attic for weeks, probably not since I first moved in, and I know the light hasn't been on this whole time. So, why would the light be on now?*

My heart pounded as I remembered my conversation with Patsy about the house being haunted. But I didn't believe in haunted houses, so there was only one possible explanation: someone living had turned on the light. The government spies, the cartel, a run of the mill burglar...who? And just maybe it was the same unwelcome someone that explored my basement not so long ago. My hands started to shake a little. *Please don't let it be the cartel.* I didn't want to die in a fiery blaze from opening a trip-wired door or be tortured for weeks in my basement's secret room.

My mind began racing and cataloging the past hour of events.

Had I left the house unlocked when I went exploring at Rose's house? Yes, I had. What if someone had slipped in then? I had heard something or someone in the wood line at Rose's. *Darn it. Why didn't I lock the door?* Maybe someone had offed Rose, and they were going to kill me next. Oh my God, I was losing it. "Jack," I said as if calling out his name would make him suddenly appear. I needed him here.

Porter, stop.

"Stop." I spoke sternly to myself. I needed to curb the panic that brewed deep inside. Try as I might, I could not contain the wave of fear that rushed over me. My mind raced as it became all too real that someone may be in the main part of my house, not just the basement. Someone moving around in my space, manipulating my environment. My heart pounded. I felt dizzy. *Breathe.*

Clutching my chest, I backed up slowly in the direction of my open bedroom door, praying no one was in there. I peeped in. All clear. I reached into my nightstand drawer and grabbed my knife. The floorboards creaked, and my heart pounded as I ran downstairs to the kitchen to get the dogs. *Why don't I have attack dogs?* I focused on Jack and how he would have told me to breathe and move forward—just keep moving forward. I wanted to scream at my husband for putting me in this situation. For everything he had done, for being the reason that I walked away from Jack. But I was the fool that landed myself here, my life, in this moment, proof of all of my mistakes.

Outside, the dogs and I ran down the driveway. "No, no, no," I whispered as I realized that I had left my keys and cell phone inside. As I looked around, I noticed that Rose's upstairs window was now glowing with the light of a television.

I mumbled sarcastically, even amidst my panic. "At least that means she's probably not lying murdered on the rug over there."

That statement would have provoked an eye roll from Jack.

I didn't want to, but I had to go over there. *Really, what are my options at this point?*

As I walked, I rationalized my fear. Regarding the basement, the light could have just been on from the start and then blown out while I had been down there. I had a million more excuses for the basement. But as for the attic, the light had not been on; I knew that for sure. And the basement had several other entry points. Besides, I had locked the dead bolt from the house to the basement. A person didn't actually need to enter through my part of the house to be in the basement. A weak defense, I knew. *Let's face it; I really didn't believe anyone had been in the basement until now.*

"The attic is a different story, though." I reviewed the facts, the first being that the attic required access through the main house and right past my bedroom. I just could not fathom going back in there without searching the house tonight. And I didn't want to search alone. *Jack, I wish you were here.* I needed a plan, but in this moment, I needed a safe haven more. So, I once again stood in the darkness, waiting at Rose's front door.

~ 40 ~

Rose heard a knock at the door, then the bell rang. Startled, she sat upright as she considered that it could be the stranger she had seen outside earlier. She carefully peeked out the window and, to her immediate relief, saw Porter standing on her front steps. She shuffled to the door and said, "Just a moment." As Rose began to unlock the door, her relief faded as she wondered if her uninvited visit to Porter's attic earlier had anything to do with Porter's visit now.

"Rose, Rose. It's Porter. I have my dogs."

Porter sounded anxious.

"Okay, dear. Just give me a minute to unlock the door." Rose fumbled with the old dead bolt.

Finally, the door opened to a defeated young woman with sad eyes, standing with the only two faithful companions she seemed to have—those hairy, obnoxious dogs.

"I'm so sorry to bother you, Rose. But could we come in? I didn't know where else to go."

"Certainly. Come in, please. What's the matter?" Rose tried to add an element of concern to her voice to mask that she knew a lot more about what happened at Porter's house tonight than Porter probably knew herself.

"It's a long story Rose, but I think someone may be or may have been in my house tonight." Porter placed her hand on the doorframe as if she were feeling unsteady on her feet. She also looked pale, maybe even scared.

Rose wondered if Porter would faint right there and then, so she quickly helped her and the dogs into the foyer. She immediately showed Porter into the living room and offered her a seat. "I'll make some tea," she said, patting her neighbor on the shoulder briefly. She mostly wanted an excuse to leave the room to calm her own nerves. After seeing how visibly upset Porter looked, Rose had begun to feel a little shaky herself—and a lot worried.

Within a few minutes, Rose came back with a tray of tea and sat listening intently to Porter's version of events.

"Rose, could I use your phone? I left my cell at home by mistake."

"Sure. Can I call someone for you?" Rose asked, wringing her hands.

"The police," Porter said without hesitation.

"Darling, are you sure? It was just a little light, wasn't it?" Rose laughed nervously as she spoke.

"No, it's not just a little light," she nearly yelled, and Rose startled at that. Porter puffed out a long breath and said, "Sorry. I'm just..."

Rose leaned back in her chair, staring at the intensity of the woman's green eyes, her fine features plagued with unease. Finally, Rose looked away, unsure what to say.

"Listen, Rose. It's just that I don't want to be worried someone is still hiding in my house somewhere. I'd like to sleep tonight." Her words were calmer this time, which Rose was thankful for. She didn't need anyone becoming unstrung right in front of her. She had enough to worry about.

"I understand," Rose said. "But think about it—you have the dogs. Wouldn't they know if someone was in the house? I'm not trying to minimize this at all, but are you entirely sure that you didn't accidentally bump the light switch?"

"That's the thing. I haven't been in the attic since right after I moved in. So, I am absolutely sure I didn't leave it on. I would have noticed by now. The light coming from under the doorway would have been hard to miss for well over a month."

Rose pursed her lips and nodded, silently cursing herself for her mistake. "Porter, it's late. How about you stay here for the night? I'm sure everything will be better in the morning." When Porter didn't answer right away, she added, "We can walk over together and lock up, in case you forgot to do that."

Porter shook her head emphatically. "No. No, I definitely don't want to do that. Can I please just use your phone so I can call the police? I guess I'll just use their non-emergency number at this point, if you have that."

Rose lifted an eyebrow, but after a few moments of studying her neighbor, she relented and went to get the cordless telephone. She scribbled the number for the local police on a sticky note, and handed both the phone and the paper to Porter. "Are you sure you want to involve the police?"

Porter didn't respond, though her fingers hovered over the keypad as if she were reconsidering it. Or maybe she was thinking about calling someone else, though Rose would have no idea who that might be.

Finally, she dialed.

Rose watched as Porter looked first confused and then annoyed.

"Everything okay?" Rose questioned softly.

Porter covered the receiver. "No. This is the cable company's phone number."

Rose waved off her words as she said, "No, no, no. It's the same office as the police. Just say you want to talk to the police."

Porter looked back at Rose with complete disbelief. Then she spoke into the phone asking to talk to someone at the police station— in a slow, drawn-out way that signaled her doubt in what Rose had just said. When she hung up, she said, "The police are on their way. I think."

"Wonderful," Rose said, though she didn't feel it. What if they found some telltale sign that she had been there? She'd be hard up to provide an explanation. She shook the thought from her mind, and they made uncomfortable small talk as they waited for the cops.

~ 41 ~

The police searched my house, questioning me and what felt like my intelligence as well.

That's when I realized that I shouldn't have called, after all. *Rose was right, darn it.* Lying and omitting information didn't come naturally to me under the best of circumstances. In contrast, bringing up government surveillance and cartel threats when they had asked if I knew of anyone that may want to get into my house seemed like an even worse option. I should have called Jack instead. I had even started to dial his number, in fact, but changed my mind because Rose was sitting right there. Besides, I could handle this. I could. Right?

Unfortunately, the police thought I had accidentally left the light on, too, and that maybe living alone in such a big house spooked me. So convinced were they, in fact, that they didn't even consider checking for fingerprints. The police asked if I knew that the French doors in the dining room were unlocked. Again, they showed no huge concern about that, either, noting that both doors had been tightly closed, and there had been no sign of a forced entry. When asked if I had used the doors recently, I explained that a few days ago, I had, indeed, while checking out the area to see if it would be a good spot to plant some herbs. I grimaced internally when I remembered that little tidbit. *Had I forgotten to lock the doors?*

"Do you remember locking the doors at that time," one female officer asked me.

I shook my head. "I really don't remember."

She and her partner gave each other a quick glance, one of *those* kind of looks, like I was just a worrier, exaggerating things in my head.

Now, I just wanted them to leave. They had checked the whole house, and the dogs had been all over, too. Clearly, I had been mistaken and everything was fine. But it didn't feel fine. Still, what more could they do?

Before they left, they "schooled" me on checking the locks every evening, explaining that these old houses tend to have sticky doors that sometimes appear locked even when not. Reluctantly, but politely, I listened to their suggestions of getting a security system or a roommate or even a live-in housekeeper. *Is this town so pretentious that the cops would suggest live-in help to the residents for their safety?*

When the police finally left, I sat exhausted on the soft leather couch in the study, the dogs resting at my feet. Taking a sip of scotch and letting it warm me from the inside out, I surmised that this didn't feel like a government surveillance stunt. *So, maybe this is it—the cartel people have found me.* The black ops team I'd hired said it could happen at some point. That if the cartel thought I had access to the money or to Will—if he was still alive—then they may do a search of their own in my home. I tried to replay the agent's words. Something like, "The cartels follow no rules. They have no respect for American soil. I know it's unnerving, but you need to be aware of your surroundings at all times. If they do anything, it will be when you aren't expecting it. Most likely, they will try to upset you to get you to make a move toward what they think you have." The one fringe benefit to the government surveillance had always been the extra protection from the cartel.

I leaned back, putting my feet on the coffee table, my mind taking me back to the day Jack and I arrived at the black ops office. The lead agent, a tall, athletic type named Kurt, had met us at the door...

"Can I get you any coffee, water, scotch?" Kurt asked, not kidding. This guy had seen a lot and probably knew that sometimes words went down easier with a bit of whiskey to dull the pain.

"Just water, thank you." My voice cracked.

"All right. There's really no easy way to start, so in cases like this, I find it best to just lay it all out there. So, my apologies in advance, Porter, if this seems impersonal in any way. I simply want to give you as accurate information as possible."

"It's fine. I understand." My voice sounded small, unrecognizable. Jack's hand clutched mine.

Kurt began. "I have evidence—ranging from photos, to dates, recorded meetings, transport records, phone records, bank transfers, security footage, and much more—that corroborates your husband indeed aided in the transport of drugs between enemy camps, as well as into the United States, for monetary gain."

Kurt pushed the files toward me. All of it blurred together. My breath shallow, I felt faint. Hold it together, Porter. I repeated the sentence in my head several times.

Kurt continued. "We also found evidence showing that Will used your name on bank transfers, storage units, hotel stays, and other documents directly related to the transport and storage of the contraband."

I heard Kurt's words, but they weren't sinking in. They seemed unbelievable to me. How could I accept that my husband, whom I had known since college—almost a decade—was a liar, a drug runner, a traitor even? No. Will would not have put me in harm's way. "There's some kind of mistake." I whispered almost inaudibly. Jack's hand moved to my shoulder. Kurt passed me another water.

I felt tightness in my stomach and sought out Jack's gaze. "She was the bad guy. Not him." She had masterminded the drug smuggling.

"Porter, I couldn't give two shits about that bitch," Jack growled. "Yes, she may have been the catalyst, but Will made his own choices. Will put your name on all of those papers."

I believed in my heart, though, that my husband's female copilot was the one who had sabotaged my husband's integrity and our life. Maybe she had been the one to use my identity. I had told my husband early on that she seemed like a bad seed, with her arrogance and aggressive nature. He'd seemed to agree at the time, but the unit assigned the two of them to a mission, which spanned about twenty-two months. The mission required that they trust each other fully. And that was what I felt had weakened him—trusting her. In the end, her body wasn't officially found, either, according to the US government, and I hadn't lost one night's sleep about that.

I argued with Jack. "It wasn't his choice; he got caught up in someone else's evil. She ruined my life. She hijacked my life story."

"Porter, who cares what happened to that piece of garbage? Will betrayed you, he betrayed his unit, his country. He gave up his honor. He was a grown-ass man, an officer in the United States military, trained to deal with much worse. I'm telling you, it was his choice. You need to accept that. Hold him accountable. She is not worth your time. She's beneath you, all of us. He's the one that hurt you. He's the one who had access to your personal information—to your identity. He wasn't the person any of us thought he was. Period."

Infuriated that Jack could believe it all so easily, I screamed at him right there in front of Kurt. "Shut up. You shut up. I knew him. I loved him. He wouldn't do this. Not to me. Not to me..."

I remember the tears flowing then, and I knew Jack had weathered my words like punches. He let me say terrible things to him, but he never punished me for those words. He held on through the pain, his valor, compassion, and loyalty never wavering—characteristics found unfathomable to most human beings.

That fight, the one Jack and I had over and over, became the sticking point I could not get past. I believed Will had become caught up in the corruption somehow and he couldn't get out. Maybe in some really messed-up way, he hadn't been trying to destroy our life together, but actually was trying to protect it—somehow. Jack believed Will had chosen greed over everything else. Over me.

Strangely, I slept remarkably well, considering the whole attic-light saga. The glass of scotch had probably helped. Around 8:30 a.m., I heard a knock at my side door in the laundry room just off the kitchen. As I headed toward the door, I could see Patsy standing outside through the adjacent paned-glass window. She smiled and waved.

I opened the door. "Hi, Patsy. What brings you over so early?"

"Well, my brother lives a street over and saw the police at your house last night. And from what I saw by your guesthouse just now, they posted a couple cops on watch—thankfully."

"Oh, that." I looked down and stepped aside for her to enter.

"Yeah, oh that." Patsy used a friendly mocking tone.

"Come in. I have coffee and donuts."

Over the next fifteen minutes or so, I explained the happenings of the previous night to Patsy, her eyes wide the whole time and her jaw opening and closing now and then. However, I didn't clarify that the black SUV parked by the guesthouse belonged to the government and not the local police. It felt like too much to put out there in the moment. After we first met, I had mentioned to Patsy that my husband had passed away in the line of duty, but I had given no details. Out of kindness, Patsy had not pried for more, and I had never brought it up again. I intended to leave it that way at least for today.

"Thank God you're okay, Porter. The police checked everything, right?"

"Yes. They said that if there was an intruder, the person had most likely entered and exited through the dining room French doors. And, Patsy, they emphasized *if*. I don't think they believed someone had been here. Not that they thought I made it up, just that they thought I left the light on and forgot to lock the doors. Basically, that I am an idiot."

"Maybe a ghost?" Patsy looked around.

I gave her a "really?" kind of look.

"I know. I know. But this is serious, Porter. So, what did the police say you should do?" Patsy asked, showing genuine concern.

"Well, since they couldn't find a forced entry, they suggested a security system, roommate, or live-in housekeeper."

Patsy tilted her head and pursed her lips. "A live-in?"

I smirked.

"What about changing the locks? You did change them when you moved in, right?"

"I meant to. The property manager had offered, but I never followed up with him. I meant to deal with it after I moved in. And, well, I never got around to it."

"No, I get it. I think." Patsy looked around again. "Did you stay here alone last night?"

"Yes. But my neighbor, Rose Blanchard, offered for me to stay at her house."

"Well, why didn't you?"

"Patsy, her place is creepier than my house with an intruder." I paused and added. "Or a ghost."

We snickered over that one.

"It's like a time warp over there, floral Victorian couches, knickknacks galore, and that musty smell like in the pages of old library books."

"I know that smell all too well." Patsy rolled her eyes.

"And there's this eerie energy, kind of like the house is actually breathing."

That sent Patsy over the edge. She belly-laughed. "Well, regardless, you probably should not have slept at your house last night. I have a spare bedroom, too, you know."

"Thanks Patsy, but I didn't want to bother you that late, and not with the two dogs. Besides, the police checked everything out, blah blah blah. Anyway, I'm fine." I waved my hand in the air dismissively.

"Porter, I haven't known you long, but it's long enough to know that you are dauntingly stubborn, and to be clear, that is not an insult. I happen to adore stubborn people. Just promise that you will call me if anything else happens."

I couldn't help but chuckle a bit at her honesty. She did know me pretty well, it seemed. I loved friends that would tell me like it was. I hugged her. "Thanks, I promise."

~ 43 ~

Max tossed the file to Joe as the two sat in silence parked outside Porter's guesthouse.

"So, you think someone was actually in the house?" Max looked over toward Porter's front steps as he spoke.

Joe stared straight ahead. "I don't know. But someone upstairs does because we are back on surveillance pretty close to full-time again."

Neither spoke for a few minutes. Then Max said, "I'm guessing it was one of two individuals, either the old lady or lover boy."

Joe nodded. "I'm guessing the old lady. Jack's not that dumb. The problem is that the bosses are concerned it could be cartel."

"I don't think so. We would have seen signs." Max looked at Porter's house as he spoke.

"Maybe. I agree, things are different than in the '80s when the cartel would kidnap or gun someone down just about anywhere, including here on American soil. However, there are still runners and hired hands."

"But what would they even want with Porter at this point? They know she's a dead end, essentially. And they know we're tailing her," Max said.

"We *were* tailing her. We weren't actually on assignment when this 'break-in'— he did finger quotes —occurred."

"So, what are you saying? This was cartel?" Max eyeballed Joe with some intensity.

Joe held up his hands in a defensive posture. "Hold your horses, cowboy. No, I'm not saying that. I actually think it was no one or someone unrelated to the whole missing-husband thing. But the fact is, we weren't here and that leaves a pretty large window for speculation."

Max stayed quiet for a long moment and then asked, "So, what's the deal with the nosy neighbor? What could she want in Porter's house, if it was her?"

Joe looked out the window towards Rose's house. "I don't know, but maybe it's time we try to find out."

"So, you *do* care." Max grinned.

"Yep. I care that we are now back on watch, and it could be because of that old bat."

~~~

I knew the SUV had come back early this morning and parked next to my guesthouse. *It's my fault they are here again.* I had called the police and no doubt stirred up the hornets' nest. To be honest, though, the Feds being out there took a load of worry off my shoulders. No one would want to break in while they were on watch. *At least I hope not.*

It had crossed my mind that perhaps those two government idiots were the ones snooping in my house. But I highly doubted it; it wasn't their current playbook, I believed. Plus, I was pretty sure they'd been pulled off the assignment—meaning, following me. Until now, of course.

No, it wasn't them. But someone with maybe not the best intentions had come in, possibly twice now. I just wished I knew if the SUV had been out there during the basement incident. I knew for sure it hadn't been for the attic. Maybe I should be keeping a journal of sorts, or at least be marking my calendar with the dates I see the SUV. *That's just one more thing to keep me tied to the past, though.*

A little after eight in the evening, I decided to relax by pouring a glass of red and flipping through one of the old books that had come with the house. As I skimmed through the pages of Volume IV of *Thackeray's Works*, I couldn't stop thinking about how I still had not escaped the torment of Will's choices. I felt myself sinking into the depths of defeat.

Could I not get one moment of peace in my brain?

I argued with myself: *Think about it. Don't think about it.* Then more firmly: *Do not go there, Porter!*

But I did. I began to think of all the unanswered questions that still weighed me down. And the only person that could really answer them, my husband, had been declared dead.

The pain started to surface. *Had my whole marriage been a lie?*

The more time that passed, the worse things had seemed between us. Maybe Will had wanted to have a life with me, had wanted to be a good person, but maybe the other part, the broken side of him, had been stronger. Did I still love him? How could I, really? If everything we uncovered was true, then the Will I thought I had known had never really existed.

My thoughts shifted to Jack and more questions, but these only I could answer.

Why had I pushed him away? Why couldn't I see that he was the better man all along? Why didn't I let myself love him? Will was gone, right? I could love Jack without the guilt of betrayal.

Jack had stood by me the whole time, supporting me. In fact, he turned his life upside down to help me.

Jack accepted the truth, all of the disgusting things about my husband, his friend, from very early on in our search, yet he had still supported me and handled my emotions with kid gloves, letting me digest it all slowly. Only well into the third year of the search had he started to push me to accept some hard things.

And I had needed to be pushed. I knew that now, looking back.

The only problem was I walked away. *I'm sorry, Jack.*

Attempting to still the echoes of my wounded heart, I spoke aloud. "Porter, someone was in this house last night. Reminisce later."

The more I reviewed everything in my head about the basement and the attic, I knew someone—not something, like an electrical issue—had entered my home. *An actual human being, not a ghost, Patsy.* I smirked.

And to be quite honest with myself, I cared much more about the *why* than the *who*. If I had learned anything through my ordeal with searching for my husband after his plane went down, it was that people were a lot like chess pieces—the actual people never held the same level of importance as the depths of the power and motivation behind their actions. Even the least regal pieces could hide some of the biggest demons.

People used to amaze and disappoint me without notice. I believed what they showed me about their lives reflected truth. But the wiser and, yes, more jaded version of me listened to her gut a little more over time, and maybe that was a good thing. Even if it hurt sometimes.

Like with my husband. His true character had been tested, and it could not rise above the toxicity of greed. He'd lost his sense of honor as a result.

But Jack...Jack never lost his honor. When fate tested his character, his truth and strength shined through like the sun through the rain clouds. He did not falter.

How could I have hurt him? I imagined Jack's pure blue eyes—but not the way his eyes looked on the day that I had walked away, the day I broke his heart...and mine, too. Not those eyes with the veil of pain, the questioning, but the ones that lit up when I walked in a room. Those eyes that could look straight into my soul and know me, care for me, support me unwaveringly. I wanted to look into those eyes at this moment. I wanted to laugh and see that sparkle again.

And here I go, reliving memories of Jack again.

I remembered the first time we met. I was married at the time, but our eyes had locked for just a moment, and I had seen a flash or spark— something—in his eyes. I had felt a stirring in my soul. But I had denied it, pushed it down and away because I loved Will. Eventually, Jack became as much a friend of mine as he was Will's. We learned quickly how to manage the undercurrent we clearly felt for each other. I relabeled it as a deep affection—like for a sibling. Easier that way. *But it wasn't ever really that easy, was it, Porter?*

The telling moments played through my head like a movie. The time he had pulled me close in the street to keep me from walking in front of traffic, and he'd kept his arm around me until we reached the car. My husband ahead of us, focused on something—anything but me, as usual. I did my best to ignore it at the time, but looking back, I know what I felt.

I held back tears and a chuckle all at once as I remembered the night at the military ball, when my husband was nowhere to be found for most of the night and had left me on my own. I had never liked how Will ignored me, but I hadn't felt it my place to demand his attention. I had wanted to respect Will's independence. Jack, however, had noticed me standing alone. He was surrounded by a group of single, interested women, all dressed in their most glamorous frocks, but Jack looked only at me. Our eyes locked, and I didn't see anyone in the room but him as he held out his hand to me. I approached, and the sea parted, and he hugged me close. I heard gasps and protests from his admirers. But Jack hadn't cared. I had known then, too, what I felt, but we both had been too loyal to my husband to be inappropriate.

I didn't know why I bought into my own excuses for Will and why I ever put up with being ignored, especially when the man who could see no one else in the room but me was right there. Hindsight truly did shine clarity on a situation. I couldn't have admitted any of this back then. Did Will ever really love me? Distance made me question that a lot.

When I thought of the man I was married to for all of those years, I only remembered how lonely he made me feel. Was I conveniently rewriting history? Had it all been that bad? I thought about Will and his temperament.

Really, Will had not been a nice guy. However, as convenient as it would be, I couldn't blame only Will. I always made excuses for how he treated me, throughout our entire marriage and even after he was gone. I had settled for someone that didn't put me first because I didn't value my own worth. Because of my own choices, the brutal truth was that Will wasn't the villain. It was my fault, all of it. I had chosen to marry him, and I thought I loved him then. But looking back, I hadn't known what love looked like.

I thought of Jack and knew he didn't deserve any of this madness with me. I wished for his sake that he'd never met me...or Will. Jack deserved happiness, love without boundaries. I had to leave to set him free of the poison Will and I had created together—one of the thousand reasons I had to walk away that day.

~ 44 ~

At 9:15 Friday morning, the doorbell rang.

"Cecil. You're right on time." I couldn't help but smile at my friend who stood holding a large florist box of white roses.

I opened the door wide and stepped aside. Cecil entered, "Punctuality is my strong point. And, I wish I could say these were from me, but..."

I interrupted. "I'll stop you there, Cecil." I winked. "Hey, when opportunity knocks, take the credit for the front door delivery service, at least."

Cecil responded slyly, "Okay. Okay. I won't pry. So, how is everything else, Porter?"

"Well, funny you should ask." We walked to the kitchen and sat at the table. As I shared the sordid details of the attic saga, his face remained serious, interrupted only by eyebrow raises.

"And before you say anything, I am looking into getting a security system. I called just before you arrived to set up a consultation for next week."

Cecil nodded his head slowly, "Good, good." Finally, his gaze met mine across the table. "Porter, do you have any idea who it could have been?"

Should I tell him everything now? Everything I hadn't said during our last conversation about my past? About Jack and the Colombian drug runners?

"Okay, Cecil. You know a lot, but not all." I leaned back and began the long story.

Cecil listened and when I had stopped talking, he said simply, "I'm so sorry, Porter."

"It's okay." I felt a lump in my throat.

"No. What Will did to you was not okay. But I think you already know that. And Jack sounds like a good guy just trying to do the right thing in an impossible situation. Pardon my candor, but I've been around the block a few times, and one hundred percent of the time, I've learned it's best to call it like you see it from the get-go." Cecil looked at me with compassion.

"I know. Trust me. And, Cecil, you're not wrong." I looked down at the table. I didn't want to cry, not now. So I switched the conversation back to the attic. "I don't know enough yet to be sure who it was in my house—cartel, feds—I just don't know. What I'm sure of is that I didn't leave the light on up there."

Cecil agreed, but added, "There is one thing that bothers me, though. The activity is not in the main part of the house where your personal belongings and information are—as far as you know, anyway. The only things that are in the attic and basement have to do with the history of this house, not you. Maybe I'm just looking for peace of mind, if that's even possible in a situation like this, but I don't think the cartel or government would be interested in anything other than your belongings."

Cecil's perspective—honed, I was sure, by many years as a newspaperman—caught me off guard. "You have a point. I never thought of it that way."

We both sat, thinking.

"And, Porter, for what it's worth, I don't think for a second that you left the light on, and I'm glad you called the police. If anything, it sends a message that you're taking this seriously and, more importantly, that you're aware someone was there." His voice resonated with caring, understanding, no judgment.

"Thank you, Cecil," I smiled at him warmly. "But do you have any idea what could be in this house and who would be looking for it?"

"Porter, I wish I did, but no. Let me think on it a bit, though. I'll go through some of my old notes and articles. Maybe something will jog my memory. And I'll give my daughter a call. Maybe she remembers something."

"I really appreciate that." After another pause, I said, "Now, are you ready to try your hand at lock picking?"

Cecil seemed as relieved as I was to change the topic. "As ready as I'll ever be. Point me in the direction of this vintage lock that has you so intrigued," he said with a wry grin.

"Follow me." We headed into the front hallway.

Cecil looked inquisitively as I pressed both hands onto the wall beneath the stairs. The panel popped open. The novelty didn't elude Cecil as he gave a slow clap.

I turned on the light, waved my arm theatrically in the direction of the safe, and said, "Here she is."

"Wow. That's a real museum piece. I'm almost a little afraid to tinker with it. The safe itself is valuable. You know that, right, Porter? The safe is a collector's item. Are you sure you don't want to hire a real locksmith?"

I shook my head. "I want to keep this as private as possible. Honestly, I'm not concerned about the value of the safe. If dynamite wouldn't bring my house down around us, then I'd say yes to trying that, even."

We both laughed.

"Okay, I hear you, loud and clear," he said.

I watched him with his father's locksmith kit still in its timeless oiled leather case, like something straight out of a movie. His eyes sparkled as he carefully and quite astutely put on a special pair of glasses with a magnifying appendage. He rolled up his sleeves revealing a long scar on one arm.

Anyone with a scar like that is a survivor of something.

Cecil caught me staring, and in a slow voice, he said, "Now, don't look at me like that, Porter." Cecil's tone softened as he glanced down at his forearm. "That's just a little shrapnel souvenir from Nam. It's been there longer that you've been alive. Yes. I've lived a couple lives at least. I served my country in one of them. Now, that's all I want to say about that." He gave me a quick wink, then went about his business.

I felt a small child who has just been scolded.

I understood not wanting to talk about the past. Often, experiencing the tragedy itself proved only the beginning and, as it turned out, maybe the easiest part of the journey. The real work came with somehow letting go enough to live with the memory and ever-present pain of the past.

I pushed it all aside. Cecil meant no harm. "Oh, I almost forgot," I said and leaned over Cecil to grab the yellow scrap of paper I had left on top of the safe. "Here, I have this. I found it in some of the Mitchell's belongings. I thought it could be the combination, but now I don't know. I have tried it a few times. Maybe I did it wrong."

"Let's see." Cecil took the slip of paper containing the list of numbers and dashes: L12- - - -R25- - -L15- -R0. "Before I start the combination, show me what you did."

I knelt and spun the lock several times to the right landing on zero. Then, I made a left turn to the 12, a right to the 25, a left to 15, and ended with a right turn back to the 0. I tried the handle. Just as the other times, the safe did not open.

Cecil grinned and proceeded to try the combination.

He first counted aloud as he turned four times to the left and landed delicately on the 12. He made three right turns landing on the 25, two left turns and stopped on 15, and a final right turn to 0. He gently pulled on the door, and the safe opened. "And...here you have it, Open Sesame." He grinned.

"How...how did you do that?" I couldn't believe he'd done it in one try.

"You see, this safe has a Mosler lock. The number of times that you turn between each number matters as much as the numbers themselves. See the dashes between the numbers? Each of those dashes represents the number of turns that you should make to the preceding number. With a Mosler, you do not start at zero. You clear the lock by turning it to the left the amount of times indicated by the first set of dashes after the first number. Each number stop is done according to the dashes that follow it, with the ending number of the combination being zero. That's why these are very secure locking systems, especially for the 1920s era."

"I have no idea what you just said." I laughed. "But thank you. Thank you so much."

Cecil stood up.

"Let's see what's in here." I said, pulling open the door.

First, I lifted up the stack of papers and quickly fanned through them: legal documents, mechanical sketches, letters—who knew? — But all were older than I was—and probably Cecil, too—and not very interesting in the moment. There were a couple boxes of old coins and a pretty marble-handled letter opener. Then my eyes caught the glint of metal on the top shelf—I reached in and pulled out a Smith & Wesson revolver with a six-chamber barrel. A box of ammunition sat on the shelf next to it.

"A .45, and it's loaded." I said in a soft voice.

"Careful, soldier." Cecil paused, then added, "You know Porter, guns in Virginia, traditionally, are not a red flag. Most children from my generation grew up sleeping, eating, playing, and, in fact, living with loaded guns in the house. Any well-respected Southern home would have had a small arsenal, especially during the era of this gun. I'd have to research a bit, but I'd bet this gun once adorned the hip of a WWII solider."

I listened, taking it all in.

Then Cecil read the words etched into the barrel out loud, "MADE IN U.S.A. Most definitely military issue."

History preserved and revealing itself right in front of our eyes. Even the air in the safe seemed to have a different consistency— staleness, like the contents hadn't been moved since the day it had been locked for the last time. Out of respect for the stories these items carried, I delicately placed the revolver back to the spot where it had resided for decades.

He looked at his watch and sighed. "Porter, I think I'll leave you to it. Mastering the lock will have to be enough for me for one day. I have to get going. My daughter sets my doctor's appointments, and I'll get an earful later if I don't show up."

"Everything okay?" Concern veiled my words.

"Yes. Just old age and an overprotective daughter." Cecil chuckled.

"Okay. But if I find anything life-changing in here, you'll be the first to know."

"Sounds good to me." Cecil smiled.

~~~

Max looked at Joe. "I'm hungry. It's almost one o'clock. That old guy left a while ago, and the old lady across the street is probably watching anyway. We can leave it up to her. How about we go get lunch at that diner?"

Joe gave Max a sideways glance. "Hatch?"

"Yeah, that one." Max's stomach growled, and he grabbed at his belly and chuckled. "The sooner the better."

Joe was thinking it over when Porter walked out the front door, her dogs at her heels. The two men watched as she headed in the direction of downtown.

Joe started the engine. "Yeah, why not? We have to eat, right? And there hasn't been anyone unusual hanging around. I don't think an hour at lunch will hurt. Besides, she's headed out for a walk with the dogs. She'll be gone at least that long herself."

Max readily agreed.

Over lunch, the two discussed Joe's daughter's new job—she'd gotten the offer right after graduation. Max shared how he and a few buddies were planning a fishing trip in Alaska for next spring.

After the small talk, Max said, "Joe, do you think Porter is really in danger?"

"I don't know. The cartel is fickle. Hopefully, they've moved on from Will and all the fallout he caused." Joe took a sip of his iced tea.

Max shoveled in some more food, chewed, swallowed, stopped to breathe, and then said, "She seems like a nice person. How do you think she got caught up with a guy like Will?"

"Look it's not our job to judge that. We just need to keep watch. Make sure she's safe." Joe could tell Max wasn't satisfied with that answer. "Listen, when you've been in this business as long as I have, you realize you can't judge a book by the cover—or by the pages, for that matter. She probably didn't know what she was getting into."

"It's just...oh, never mind. I don't know." Max crumpled his napkin in frustration.

Joe knew Porter and Max were about the same age. "Look, Max, I have eyes, too. She's a looker. And seems sophisticated and smart. If I was your age, I'd be wondering, too."

Max, a little embarrassed, simply nodded and went back to his food.

~ 45 ~

After returning from a walk with the dogs to deliver the photos of the paintings to Peg at the gallery, I decided to go check out the contents of the safe again. I had gotten off track once Cecil left, and the day had taken on a life of its own. As I knelt in front of the safe, my hand gripped the cool brass handle that still shone a bit, even after the passing of several decades. The door opened slowly, exposing the same array of objects. Now that I was alone, this felt dodgy, like going through someone else's private belongings—probably because that's exactly what it was.

Then something caught my attention at the back of the top shelf: a small, black, velvet pouch. We hadn't noticed it earlier. Carefully, I removed the pouch from the safe and loosened the strings to look inside. "Jewels." I shook my head in disbelief as I dipped my finger into the bag as if giving an indulgent stir into a dirty martini.

Suddenly, the hairs on the back of my neck prickled. I felt a presence, like someone stood behind me. I froze. *I don't believe in ghosts. Is someone in the hallway?*

I picked up the loaded gun, knowing full well the danger of using one that had sat unmaintained for years, decades. Startled by a creak in the hallway, I silently moved toward the door and looked out into the foyer area. I saw the front door open just a tad, swaying slightly. *The wind?*

"Hello?" I called out.

I couldn't be sure, but I thought I heard quick footsteps outside.

I felt my breathing get heavy and quick.

Is the person from the attic, the basement, back?

Holding the .45, I walked to the front door, looking back at the far end of the hallway to the closed kitchen door. I heard the dogs rustling on the other side.

As I walked toward the door, I heard a motorcycle—the engine revved. Without thinking, I ran outside to the driveway. I caught a glimpse of the black motorcycle speeding away. "What the hell?" I yelled. Not afraid anymore, but angry.

~~~

Jack rounded the bend to Porter's house and caught a glimpse of a guy in black darting down the front steps, across the driveway, and into the wooded area near the guesthouse. At the same time, Porter rushed onto her porch, holding onto something with both hands. A gun? Fury ignited in Jack as he spun the bike around and sped off after the guy. He knew that if he could get to the other end of the wooded area first, then he could wait for him. The guy would need to emerge at some point, and Jack would be ready. Max and Joe were nowhere to be found, but then again, his watch read just past lunchtime, and Joe didn't look like one to miss a meal. "Those idiots."

Jack waited at least ten minutes. No one exited from the wooded area. Frustrated, Jack raced back to Porter's house. The guy must have doubled back.

Jack pulled up aggressively next to the guesthouse at the same time as Max and Joe.

He wasted no time dismounting the bike. "You're doing a bang-up job, fellas." Jack's hand pounded the roof of the car just over Joe's head as he stormed past on his way to the edge of the guesthouse to survey the yard near the house.

"Hey. Easy there, fella." Joe called out.

Max chimed in with a loud, "Yeah. And thanks, hotshot, for the performance review, except I don't remember asking your opinion."

Jack froze, spitting out the words. "Listen, you two knuckleheads. While you were having your leisurely lunch, sipping sweet teas, someone was snooping around. He ran into the woods right over there."

Joe sheepishly looked down at the two Styrofoam cups with bent straws sitting in the center console.

"Well, why didn't you stop him?" Max asked, leaning over Joe so he could eyeball Jack through the open car window.

Jack dismissed Max's comment and turned back to Joe. "I rode my bike to the other end of the clearing to wait for him. He must have doubled back."

Max pushed Joe on the shoulder. "See, I told you I saw someone a while back."

Jack asked, annoyed, "When?"

"A few weeks back. He ran into the wood line over there." Max pointed behind Porter's garage.

Jack thought for a moment. "This guy is smart. He knew you two weren't here. He waited for an opening. In fact, he was at her front door."

"What? Why do you think that?" Joe questioned.

"Porter was on her porch with a gun, I think, as he was running away. I don't know. It all happened in a split second."

"That's bold," Max said somberly.

Joe and Jack made eye contact.

The cartel.

Jack felt his heart pounding. What if the guy went back to the house? What if he was in there with Porter, right now? "One of you idiots needs to go check on her. Now."

"What?" Max looked wide-eyed. "That's not allowed. We are not supposed to interact."

Joe added, "He's right. We're here to watch her, as in 'investigate,' not act as personal security guards."

"How do you two sleep at night?" Jack fumed as he marched a few steps in the direction of the house. He didn't want to confront Porter this way, but he had to make sure she was okay. *She's had her space— enough is enough.*

Just before leaving the last bit of cover provided by the guesthouse, Jack stopped abruptly and stepped backward a couple feet. He had seen Porter emerging with the dogs through the side door. Luckily, she hadn't had the chance to look in his direction.

"Lose your nerve?" Max goaded.

Jack turned and glared at Max, putting a "shush" finger to his mouth.

He walked over, leaned into the car, "She's fine. For now."

The agents showed visible relief.

"I need to be able to count on you two. I have to try to find this guy. And I need you to keep a close watch until I do." Jack's eyes had almost a look of defeat as he spoke.

Jack had no authority to make such a request. But Joe decided to let it go. He understood Jack's predicament. The guy couldn't be in two places at once, hunting the fugitive and watching his girlfriend.

Max added, "But we aren't here during the night, so...."

Joe turned to Max with a "you're really bringing that up now?" type of look.

Jack took in a deep breath, let it out. "That's a problem, then, guys."

~ 46 ~

Rose rubbed her eyes as she looked out her top floor hall window that faced Porter's house. She watched as a man dressed in all black ran down the front steps of Porter's house. Could it be the same man whose silhouette she thought she had seen a couple other times? She couldn't be sure, but this was indeed concerning. Suddenly, the figure disappeared into the tree line. Then she saw the other guy rev up his motorcycle and speed away down the street. And, there, in the midst of the chaos, Porter ran out the front door holding... a gun? No. Porter wouldn't have a gun, would she?

Rose was almost paralyzed by the scene. "Should I call the police?" Maybe that man hurt her. The corners of Rose's mouth tightened. She didn't like that Porter had moved in, but she didn't want anyone there at all—it wasn't personal to Porter. And she certainly didn't want to see Porter hurt. "But she looks okay," Rose muttered, trying to convince herself. Besides, more police activity could put an even bigger wrench in Rose's plans to continue searching the house.

Just as Rose started to move from the window, she saw the SUV and then the motorcycle pull up again. Porter emerged onto the side yard with the two dogs briefly. The men in the car and the guy on the bike spoke for a few minutes, and then the motorcycle left in a hurry.

"Oh, forget it." Rose closed the drapes and walked away.

~~~

Jack breathed hard as he raced along the curvy roads that lead to the river cottage he had rented. He revved the engine, driving way too fast; suddenly, he pulled off onto a side road and shut off the engine. Angry with himself for letting her come here alone, letting her leave in the first place, his hand slammed down on the seat of the bike.

"Dammit." Jack knew if it the cartel really had found Porter and decided to do something, things could get bad, fast. He thought for a moment and wondered if his recent trip to Colombia had instigated this. "I should have wrung that little hombre's neck right then and there in that cantina."

He had to do something. It was time he revealed himself to her—somehow. Let her know what he knew. Yes, Jack wanted to protect Porter, but he also missed everything about her—getting lost in her smile, looking into her green eyes, just breathing in the scent of her. He worried that his emotions would cloud his judgment as to what to do, but there they were just the same.

He pushed his feelings for her aside and weighed his options in terms of *protecting* her. He had to make a move soon. If the guy worked for the cartel, there wouldn't be room for error on Jack's part. He thought about the best way to handle this. He needed to talk to her in a way that would make her listen. Going back to his original plan, he still felt a letter would be best. That way, she could not interrupt. She'd be forced to hear him out. Until then, he would amp up his own surveillance, crossing his fingers she didn't catch him. That wouldn't go over too well.

~ 47 ~

Frustrated, I plopped down in the leather chair in the study that faced the fireplace on the far wall and replayed the basement, the attic, the motorcycle, and the open front door incidents. Had I really left the front door unlocked when Cecil left? Probably. I had been distracted.

One thing I had decided for sure: no police. And I'd have an alarm system soon. What more could I do at the moment? As crazy as it sounded even to me, I pushed the thoughts of the mystery motorcycle and possible intruder away. *Boy, I'm becoming a pro at living in the midst of denial.*

I refused to let my mood paralyze me, so I called Patsy. She had said to call anytime. After three rings, she answered.

"Hello." Her cheery voice made me think twice about telling her what I'd just experienced.

So, I did my best to feign lightheartedness. "Hi, Patsy. How are you?"

"Porter, I'm glad you called. I'm fine. The bigger question is, how are you? Everything still quiet? Any updates from the police?"

It's decided. No way I'm telling her what just happened. I responded as briefly as possible. "I'm great, and no, nothing more from the police. Everything is fine. But I am in need of a little social time. Do you have plans for tomorrow?" I said, my tone almost pleading.

"Actually, I do have plans, but you're in luck; there's room for one more." She paused for a moment, then added, "You're probably the only person on earth that would answer 'I'm fine' after what you went through with the police and all that."

"Yeah, yeah," I said in a *let's move on* tone. "I am intrigued about your offer to join you tomorrow. Do tell...what do you have planned?"

I asked in a playful voice.

"Well, I'm going to my first yoga class ever this Saturday. There's a yoga studio here in town that is all the rage. It's really exclusive and rarely ever has openings to join. Tomorrow is open enrollment for invitees and their plus-ones. I didn't have a plus-one until now—that is, if you're up for it. I've been on the waitlist for almost three months."

Am I up for it? I could barely contain my excitement. I turned my eyes to the ceiling and mouthed a thank-you before replying, "Yes. Patsy, you are a godsend! I haven't been to yoga in way too long—yes, yes, yes."

"Wonderful. Meet me at 10 a.m. at Hard Yoga just off Main, on Water Street. Parking is in the back."

"I'll be there with my yoga pants on." I found myself grinning. This was just what I needed right now. A reprieve from the crazy.

"Please wear a yoga top, too," Patsy said with a quick cackle.

Energized at the thought of getting back on the mat, I decided to take the dogs for a late afternoon walk. I locked every single door and left lights and a radio on inside.

~~~

The cool April air on my face felt brisk and raw. The dogs and I were well on our way to the river, which as only about a mile and a half from my house. My old self would have walked there a dozen times or more by now—we were overdue for a visit. I felt torn between the fear of all the strange happenings at my home and the stubbornness to keep this new life untouched by my past. The adrenaline surged in my veins as the residue of old and the sting of new anger started to take hold. I wanted to run—the irony of which did not escape me. I had been running from my past for so long, and now I wanted to run from my new beginning as well. I stared into the distance as if staring into my very own future—why did I think peace resided somewhere up ahead?

The dogs suddenly stopped to sniff something, not unusual for them. I took a moment to look around, and then I looked up to see the canopy of branches above my head shrouding the sky like lace. I felt overwhelmed, sad. I tugged the leashes and pushed on.

As I reached the street that led to the river, I paused for a moment and looked behind me. There it was again—that feeling of being watched. I saw a man dressed in dark clothing. He looked my way and then quickly vanished into a storefront. I couldn't make out his face, but something about his presence jolted my soul.

No, I reassured myself. *No one is following me.* Yet my feeble assertions relentlessly faded into my uneasiness. *Could it be the same person who'd opened my front door this afternoon?*

And just like that, the old feeling of doubt and darkness overcame me like billowing black storm clouds. Much like the giant clouds that were seemingly coming from nowhere and turning the whole sky above me a dark, ominous blue-black as well. *Of course.*

Then, as if poetic justice were shamelessly at work right in front of me, I knew that instead of gaining solace from the water, I instead would be tormented by it in an imminent downpour. *What a fun walk home this will be.* I caught only a quick glimpse of the river, which proved mesmerizing with its choppy gray water. The water looked exactly how I felt inside: uneasy, cold, and breathless.

With moisture brewing around me, I could smell the impending rain and felt an electric charge in the thick air. The people moving around in and out of stores became a blur, my awareness shifted to the task of getting home.

As I turned back, sheets of rain started to fall like walls of water...and then I thought I saw Jack. *How strange.* My mouth opened as I started to call his name, but then the other man, the one in dark clothes, darted around the corner holding up a newspaper to shield his face from the pelting raindrops. Suddenly, the man stopped, lowered the paper from his face, and briefly glanced at me before running down the street.

But the other man...Jack? I thought it was Jack, at least. He looked in my direction for a moment and then turned and ran after the man in black.

I stood frozen, questioning my own eyes. "Jack?" I wanted to chase after him, but my legs didn't move.

Why would Jack be here? And who was the other guy?

None of it made sense.

Confused as to what or whom I had or had not seen, I stood there, water pouring down my face, heart pounding, my hair and clothes becoming saturated. Then, as the cherry on top, the dogs started to shake the water from their fur.

Was it really him? I felt like I was losing my mind.

"Miss? Miss! Come out of the rain."

I turned toward the voice calling out to me through the raindrops.

The thin, dark-eyed man wearing a white apron motioned to me from a covered, outdoor dining area.

"But my dogs." I looked down at the furry messes.

"It's okay. Dogs are allowed in the patio dining area. Please, Miss. Please, come out of the rain." He looked at me with concern and reached out a hand to help with the dogs.

I nodded, appreciative of the rescue. "Yes. Okay. Yes. Thank you."

Immediately, he handed me a white cloth napkin to wipe off some of the water.

I tied the leashes to the railing next to the table. The waiter disappeared but quickly returned with a cappuccino and an array of decadent Italian cookies.

"Thank you, but I don't have my wallet with me. I was out walking the dogs."

"It's on me. I brought enough cookies for the dogs, too." He winked.

"Thank you. I can stop by and pay you tomorrow," I said gratefully.

"No need. It's my pleasure. Just promise to come back for a real meal sometime soon." He smiled.

"You have a deal. I look forward to it."

Finally, the rain slowed enough for me to walk home.

After walking briskly for a few minutes, I could see my house in the distance, lights beaming from the windows. It definitely didn't look like I had gone out—in fact, it looked as if I could be entertaining twenty-five people, except for the lack of cars parked out front. I also saw the side of Rose's house, and from the flashing blue light in the window, I assumed she was watching TV.

"Good." Maybe she wouldn't see me walking home, drenched, with two wet dogs. Not that it mattered anyway. *She sees almost everything else.*

Once inside, I started pulling off my damp clothes in preparation for a hot bath that held the promise of thawing out my fingertips and toes. I let the dogs have the run of the house. Selfishly, I needed the reassurance that no one had slipped in while I had been gone. If someone lurked about, the two border collies would find the unwelcome guest. I wished I'd relied solely on their senses of smell the night of the attic incident, but that was in the past now.

As the warm water heated up my body, I thought about seeing Jack—or had I?—and that other man on the street, the man who seemed to be staring at me. Or was he? I wondered if maybe my mind had just played an elaborate and cruel trick on me. It wouldn't be the first time.

My heart ached at the thought of Jack. Even though I tried not to, I thought about him every day, but I'd never slipped far enough that I actually imagined seeing his face. Not until today.

Am I going crazy?

Quickly, I began to worry about my ability to heal from the past. I needed a plan. Step one, I moved here. *Done.*

Next, I needed to formulate step two. Making new memories, a new life. I thought about my new friends, Cecil, Patsy, Peg, and Stan. I had acquaintances, too, and a nosy neighbor. Wasn't I already working on step two? Then why did I feel like something was still missing or as if this was all just temporary? My heart knew the answer, but my mind fought the truth.

The answer, of course, was Jack. Nothing seemed enough without him.

Wrapped in my fluffy robe, I opened a bottle of red wine with a gorgeous artsy label—a charcoal drawing of a crooked vine. I'd bought it weeks ago at the suggestion of Stan. Jack would have loved going there with me, picking wine, chatting with the owners. Still feeling chilled a little, I started the gas fireplace in the study, curled up on the cozy leather sofa, sipped the spicy wine, and flipped through an old book I had picked out of the beautiful row of leather-bound novels adorning the shelves in this room. This had started to become my new normal with only one thing missing.

Maybe I should call him.

~~~

Jack had chased the guy for several blocks. The slew of umbrellas had made it hard to see and to navigate the sidewalks.

Frustrated that the guy had gotten away again, Jack sat on the couch at the river cottage. He had called Joe to make sure they would keep watch tonight. Now he stared at the pen and paper still on the table from the other day when he'd tried but failed to write to Porter.

He wasn't sure if she had seen him. But it was just as likely as not. It was now or never. If she had seen him, he needed to explain. Soon.

Jack picked up the pen and began writing. The words came easier this time. He sealed the stationery envelope and put it in the center of the table.

Now he just needed to decide how to deliver the letter. It shouldn't be in person, because that would defeat the whole purpose of forcing her to listen and not talk.

Jack sipped his whiskey and looked out the large window at the dark river.

"Just come back to me, Porter. Just come back."

~ 48 ~

I woke to the sound of the doorbell. "Not again." I didn't have to be anywhere until 10 a.m. not to mention it was a Saturday. I glanced at the clock on my bedside table: 7:30 a.m. *You have to be kidding me.*

The doorbell rang repeatedly. "I give up."

The dogs followed me and sat near the bottom step as I looked through the peephole. Then I saw it—the familiar gray head. "Rose," I muttered under my breath and looked at the dogs, who wore the saddest expressions. I couldn't help but giggle at that. "Not Rose fans, either, huh?"

I opened the door slowly and peered out, still squinting my eyes in an effort to look sleepy and annoyed...because I was.

"Good morning. Oh, did I wake you? Well, you young people sleep so late. Anyway, I wanted to bring the cookies over early in case you're heading out today. Oatmeal raisin." Rose's voice sounded far too chipper.

But...darn. I do like oatmeal raisin. "Yes. I do like to sleep in sometimes, especially on weekends. *Hint, hint.* Thank you for the cookies." I took the plate and started to close the door.

"So, are you going anywhere today?" Rose leaned in to subtly stop me from shutting the door.

"What? Oh, umm, yes. I'm going to yoga. Thanks again, Rose." I held up the plate of goodies. "For these."

"Do you need any help with the dogs?"

"No, thanks. I won't be gone that long." *Not this again.*

"Are you sure? What time is your class? Maybe you want to go to a lunch or grab a coffee or shop around with the other girls after. I will be home all day, so I can come over and let the dogs out, and that way you won't have to rush back." Rose seemed eager, and that was just so weird to me.

Confused at her motivation, I responded the best I could without being rude. "Thanks, Rose, but maybe next time." I forced another thank-you and slowly shut the door. *What is wrong with that woman?* I took the cookies straight to the kitchen, plopped the plate on the counter, and decided to take the dogs out back. I needed to restart my morning.

Coffee.

I practically inhaled the first cup. With my second cup in hand, I went upstairs to get ready for yoga. I put on my favorite black yoga pants and a purple spaghetti-strap top that made my arms look far more toned than they really were. I grabbed my cardigan and flip-flops and caught a quick glimpse at my unpainted toes. With a shrug, I decided not to worry about that at the moment. Other than the missing pedicure, I had successfully gotten ready with a half an hour left to kill. *Focus on the wins, Porter.* I snickered at myself as I headed to my car.

~~~

When I arrived, Patsy stood waiting for me just outside the front door. As we entered, I couldn't help but take in the beautiful interior of the place. The studio sported ultra-smooth reclaimed wood floors and mystical murals on the walls. The classroom had an entire wall painted to look like a deep, dark woods backlit by a fiery sunset—something out of a grownup fairy tale.

Patsy and I quickly picked spots near the back to place our mats side by side. The dimly lit room flickered with the glow of tiny twinkle lights and salt lamps. A line of colorful crystal chakra singing bowls sat near the front of the classroom by the instructor's platform.

I whispered to Patsy, "This place is legit."

"I know. I'm not sure if I should be excited or scared." She did a little sweep of her hands over her plump frame. Her left eyebrow lifted and a sarcastic grimace appeared on her face. I tried not to, but I laughed a little.

Just then, the instructor floated in like a pixie. Her blond hair short and her body toned to perfection, she commanded the room from the moment she appeared. After a brief studio introduction and membership-package description, class began. It was challenging and exactly what I needed.

After the Savasana that followed the hour and twenty minutes of working hard through challenging poses that the instructor considered "beginner," but that I knew at any other studio would be considered "intermediate," Patsy and I rolled up our mats and headed to the dressing area.

"Patsy, I loved it," I blurted out while we gathered our shoes and sweaters.

Patsy only said, "I'm going to be sore."

I giggled. "You'll be fine. Thank you so much for bringing me. I'm going to sign up."

"I am too. Let's go find the list. I need this. As they say: no pain, no gain."

As we entered the lobby area, we noticed a line forming at the front desk. One after another, we took turns filling out the registration paperwork.

"I'm famished." Patsy said.

"I could eat, too." My pre-yoga breakfast had already worn off, and besides, going home didn't seem too appealing. I liked this distraction from my life of spies.

"Let's walk around to Main and find a nice café with an *outdoor* patio." As she said this, Patsy made a face implying we may not smell fresh enough to sit inside.

I laughed a little. "Actually, I know the perfect place. I owe them a visit, and there is an outdoor patio where we can sit."

Patsy nodded, giving me an impressed look. "Oh, really? Where are you thinking?"

"Well, yesterday when I was walking the dogs, the little bistro down the street—Fromage, I think—offered me and my dogs shelter and sustenance during the downpour. I didn't have my wallet, but they didn't care. I promised I would come back for a proper meal and repay them."

Patsy appeared to be searching a street map in her head. Her eyes lit up. "Oh, yes, Bread and Fromage is a fantastic little place. Let's go."

We arrived at the bistro, and the same gentleman who rescued me yesterday greeted us. "Hello again. Welcome."

"Hi. Thanks again for yesterday. The cookies were absolutely delicious."

"My pleasure. It's so nice that you could come back so soon."

"Trust me, now that I know about this little gem, I'll be here quite often." I felt more myself today, so I didn't mind the friendly conversation.

"We look forward to it, Miss...?" He paused as if he wanted me to answer with my name.

Awkwardly, I answered, "Miss Leighton, Porter Leighton."

"Well, Miss Leighton, would you and your guest prefer inside or outside dining?" He winked at Patsy because, as with almost everyone in this town, he'd known her his whole life.

"Real cute, Tony," Patsy said sarcastically.

"We'd love a seat on the patio." I looked knowingly at Patsy. He nodded and gestured for us to follow him.

"I think you have a new admirer," Patsy whispered, smirking.

I waved off the comment and smiled a little, thinking about Jack. We took our seats outside and placed a quick order. Our iced teas were brought out immediately.

"So, Porter," Patsy said, leaning toward me over the table, "everything quiet in the attic still?"

"Thankfully, yes. No more attic incidents. Actually, I haven't even unlocked the door since then, but I probably should go up there soon. There are a lot of clothes and boxes that probably need to be thrown out or donated."

"Girlfriend, you know you don't have to go up there alone. I'm happy to come over and go with you. We could make it fun. Maybe order in, I know a great pizza shop that will deliver, and I could bring a bottle of wine."

"What a fantastic idea. Yes. Let's do it." I didn't even try to contain my excitement.

"How about Saturday night? I'm only working at the library until noon. So, maybe I could come by around 6:30?"

"Perfect. It's a date." I smiled and sipped my iced tea. Actually, I felt a little relieved that I wouldn't have to go up in the attic alone.

And with that, we changed subjects as our meals arrived, and we dug in, famished. Patsy told me all about her brother and his new baby. Patsy seemed like a terrific aunt. I loved how she beamed when she spoke of her family. I didn't have any family left. In fact, my family tree could potentially stop growing with me. It brought me joy to know that Patsy's family still had lots of branches.

I walked with Patsy to stop in at the library. While she chatted with another employee, I walked into the small historian area. Large glass cases adorned the room, some containing relics from Turnberry's past, some fashion from the different eras, and some news articles that documented pivotal points in the town's history.

One case in particular held a large crown. As I examined the piece, I realized that the stones were missing—all of them. The placard in the case read: *Lady Turnberry jeweled crown 1842. The crown had been brought over from England on a ship and belonged to the Turnberry family. Unfortunately, the jewels were stolen on April 27, 1925, while on display at a charity gala hosted by the Mitchell family, owners of the First Turnberry Bank, where the crown had been kept secure for decades prior.* My heart raced a bit. This was THE crown. Then, I thought of the bag of loose jewels I had found in my house in the safe.

No. They couldn't be the missing jewels.

I waved to Patsy and headed to the microfiche room, and in less than thirty minutes, I had printed a stack of articles about the heist. On the scene, the police had found a bag of replacement stones, fakes. Apparently, the thieves had gotten spooked halfway through and had left the job unfinished.

~~~

As soon as I arrived home, I took out the black, velvet pouch. I began laying the jewels onto the large picture of the crown I had printed. So far, the jewels were matching up—exactly.

What do I do?

I knew I had to tell Patsy, but I thought maybe I should tell Cecil first—in person. I had to see his face.

~ 49 ~

I could barely get out the door fast enough to meet Cecil for our usual Wednesday morning walk. I could not hold onto my discovery much longer; it had already been days—I might burst.

"Hi, Cecil," I said as I ran down the driveway to join him.

He chuckled. "Someone has a pep in her step."

"Yes. Well, you may too after I tell you this. Remember when I said you'd be the first to know if I found anything earth-shattering in the safe?"

With a raised eyebrow, Cecil said, "Yep."

"Well, I think I may have solved the case of the missing crown jewels." I could feel my mouth stretching from the large smile I wore. I bounced on my toes, feeling electric with my discovery.

Quiet for a moment, Cecil seemed to be thinking. Then, his eyes shone bright. "The crown at the library in the Historian Room?"

"Yes. In the safe. I found a bag of jewels. When I compared them to the library crown, they seemed to be an exact match."

"Good grief, Porter. That mystery has spanned decades."

"So, here's the thing. I want to give the jewels back. Do I call the police?" I made a *please say no* face as I spoke because after the attic light saga, that qualified as the last thing I wanted to do.

Cecil thought about that for a moment, "Okay. Okay," he said, nodding. "I think that's the obvious right thing, but..."

"But...?"

He shrugged. "Well, it's an old crime, and this is just an old cynic talking, but shouldn't you make sure you don't have the fakes first? As I recall..."

I interjected. "That's right. I did read about the fakes. But wouldn't the police have those or a record of them, or something?"

Cecil continued. "That's a good assumption. However, times were different. Small town, everyone was someone's cousin or brother, and so on."

"How's that different, now?" I teased.

"I can't argue that." He chuckled. "Anyway, the point is the Mitchells were the most powerful family in Turnberry at the time. Who knows what kind of pull Mr. Mitchell had over the police? This crime is, for all accounts, ancient—closer to a legend than fact. Maybe confirm some things first. Then, if necessary, tell the police."

"I was thinking maybe I should talk to Patsy," I said. "As for determining their value, I'm not sure."

"Good idea. Patsy's been at the library a long time and should know who to contact as far as the historical collection is concerned. Maybe there's information about the crime that didn't make it into the newspapers in the archives. As for the authentication, here's what I suggest: Take one or two stones to H&H Jewelers just off Main, on Carolina Street. Ask for Alan. Tell him Cecil sent you. Just have him check to see if they are real or paste. If a couple of them are real, I'm betting they all are."

"Okay. Then it's decided. I'll keep you posted." I felt good about the decision. "Oh, one more thing."

He gave me the raised eyebrow again but said nothing.

I eagerly continued. "Well, I actually have a proposition for you. It involves more lock-picking, though. Are you interested?"

"Now, now, Porter, did you lock yourself out of the safe? Remember the combination pattern I showed you?"

"No. It's much better than that." I enjoyed teasing him like this.

"Oh, good grief. Okay, lay it on me." Cecil did a mocking, crossed-arm stance.

"Brace yourself...." I paused for dramatic effect.

He gave me a sideways glance that oozed sarcasm.

"Okay, so do you remember the article in the paper a month or so ago about the Prohibition vault?" I asked. Of course, I knew he would remember.

"Why, yes, I do." Cecil looked at me. "Okay, young lady. Let's have it. What's up?"

"Do you want to pick the lock?" I giggled.

Cecil burst out in a good-natured laugh. "How could I pass up an opportunity like that? But there is something I want to tell you first. I probably should have said something the day you mentioned the article."

"What is it?" I asked. I wondered if it would be good or bad news.

"Porter, many moons ago, when I worked at the paper as an inexperienced reporter, I actually took the photograph of your vault. Now, I didn't see inside. No one opened it while I was there, so it being a Prohibition vault couldn't really be confirmed, but it made for a great story—twice." He winked.

Speechless, my jaw dropped. "You were the photographer? I wasn't expecting that."

"I probably should have made that clear the other day." Cecil looked down as he spoke.

"Well, regardless of all of that, we're on the same page now. And I do have a real favor to ask of you. By the way, if it pans out to be a prohibition vault, just maybe I'll share some of those outlawed libations with you." I fiendishly brushed my hands together to lighten the mood.

Cecil's demeanor rallied. "You're on."

"So, Mr. Lock Expert, when do you think you can fit me into the schedule?"

He answered readily. "Well, let me see. You know my services are in such high demand. Hmmm..." He pretended to be deep in thought, as if checking a mental calendar. Then the corners of his mouth curved up into a sly grin. "How about tomorrow afternoon?"

This is going to be fun.

~ 50 ~

Jack hung up the phone. He'd made a few calls to Porter's former investigative team, as well as to a few intelligence officers that still worked in Colombia, regarding the man dressed in dark clothing whom he'd seen twice now—near Porter's house and on Main Street. From what he had gathered from Joe and Max, they may have seen him one time as well. Anyway, the best bet remained clear; this guy had been sent by the cartel. Jack just needed to find out what he wanted and why.

He needed to catch the guy. Soon, before the man could harm Porter. Jack's contacts in Colombia and DC said they'd put out feelers, but he knew the best way to get answers would be straight from the proverbial horse's mouth.

Unfortunately, that meant Jack would have to start watching, too, not just checking up on Porter, and that felt creepy. But if she got hurt or worse, he couldn't live with it, so appearing a little creepy definitely outweighed the alternative.

However, to do this right, Jack needed to go home to Sleepy Hollow to get some tactical supplies. That meant Porter's safety would fall solely on Joe and Max for a day or two.

Jack picked up the phone again.

"Joe, here." The voice on the other end completely lacked enthusiasm.

"You got a minute?" Jack asked.

"Yep. Who's this?"

"It's your new pal."

After an awkward pause, Joe replied. "Okay. This is new territory. Be careful. It's a government line, you know."

"I worked for the government, too—for a long time. Remember?" Jack said flatly.

Joe said, "I'll call you back." Before he could hang up, Jack heard Max ask who was on the line. "It's Jack. Drive to the motel. I want to use the phone there instead of the cell." Then he disconnected.

Jack muttered, "Tweedle-dumb and tweedle-dumber." He waited impatiently. Finally, his phone rang.

He picked up, but before he could say anything, Joe spoke. "Well, since you've gone to the trouble of calling, let's hear it."

"Here's the deal. I believe the cartel guy is watching Porter. From what I can surmise, between the three of us, we've seen him a few times. I need to make a trip back to New York to get some things and stop off in DC to meet with someone. I need you guys to stay sharp. Keep a closer eye than usual. It's critical," Jack said firmly.

"Okay, okay, hold your horses, lover boy. What do you mean 'between the three of us'?" Joe asked.

"You and Max saw that guy. You thought it was me. It wasn't."

"Right, right. But Max only *thought* he saw someone. But I hear you. I get what you're saying."

Jack let loose a small sigh of relief. "Good. The point is, I think she's in real danger, and I need your help. Besides, if we catch this guy, you two slackers can take all the credit. Maybe get a raise or a promotion."

The line stayed quiet for a moment. Then Joe said, "Okay, funny guy. You have yourself a deal. How long will you be gone?"

"Two days, tops. I leave tomorrow morning."

Joe grunted but agreed, and with that, Jack hung up the phone.

~~~

Joe got back in the car where Max eyed him, waiting for an explanation.

"Drive, drive." Joe motioned impatiently. "It's going to be a long two days." He then explained the plan.

Max took the news well. Neither of them wanted Porter to be harmed. "I'm up for it. I'd love to catch one of those scumbags. Let's do this," Max said.

Joe shook his head. "You young people."

Max grinned.

~ **51** ~

"Darn" was the only comment I could muster as all four of my winter coats fell off the hangers and onto the floor of the guest-room closet. The closet in my bedroom lacked space, and moving the bulky coats seemed like a good idea with summer on its way.

That's what I get for trying to move all of them in one trip.

While leaning down to pick up the pile of jackets and hangers, I noticed a glimmer out of the corner of my eye, something gold behind the leg of the dresser. Reaching under the heavy mahogany dresser, I gently grabbed the delicate gold chain, but it wouldn't budge, and I didn't want to break it.

I attempted to move the dresser. I leaned into it, using my body weight to push. No luck. Then I tried to pull the dresser.

"Not happening," I finally said aloud. *This thing weighs more than a refrigerator.*

As a last resort, I bumped my hip hard into the side of the dresser hoping to jar the leg just enough to release the chain.

It worked. "Got it."

As I held the necklace in my hand, I could see that the pendant was old. Vintage, classic, gorgeous. Perfectly centered in the middle of the oval pendant sat a monogramed M. I ran my finger over the letter and felt the swirling grooves.

Undoubtedly, it had belonged to a Mitchell—no big mystery there. Without thinking, I unclasped the necklace and put it around my neck. As I stood in the mirror adoring the new find, I imagined how special it probably had been to someone long ago. Maybe even a gift.

I knew sentiment well. When I was nine years old, my father had given me a beautiful heart pendant necklace. I wore it every day...until one day I was feeding breadcrumbs to fish off a dock, and as I leaned over the railing, something caught the necklace and ripped it from my neck. I heard only a small sound as it hit the surface of the water. My heart had actually ached as I watched it slowly disappear into the deep, dark abyss. I never told anyone what had happened. I had felt too sad and a little ashamed for being careless. I wondered if the person who lost this had felt the same way.

Getting back to the task at hand, I finished organizing the coats in the closet and then headed out with the dogs. I planned to walk to Main Street to pick up a few odds and ends and to stop by H&H Jewelers. I grabbed two of the stones, tossed them in a little plastic zipper bag, and stuffed them in my jacket pocket.

As we walked down the driveway, I noticed Rose clipping the spent flowers off her azalea bushes with deliberate precision.

Suddenly, one of the dogs made a sharp little bark. I gave the dogs a stern look, not wanting to draw attention to ourselves. Too late. Rose turned her head toward the sound, and when she saw us, she waved.

"Hi, Rose," I called out and then looked at the furry traitors and quietly said, "Thanks a lot."

Rose stood up slowly, her hand on the tree trunk next to her for support. She dusted off and walked over to where we stood on the sidewalk.

"Hi, there, Porter. Good afternoon. Taking the dogs to burn off some energy, I see."

I nodded and forced a smile. "That's the plan."

Rose raised a hand, still donning a gardening glove, to block the sun as she looked up at me, seemingly staring at my neck.

Instinctively, I reached up and touched the pendant.

"Is that new?" Rose asked.

"This necklace?" *What does she care?*

"Yes. Is that your initial on there?"

"Actually, I found it in the house. It's an M. I'm assuming it belonged to one of the Mitchells."

Rose stood silent, still staring.

Then it dawned on me. "Rose, do you recognize this necklace?" From her face, the answer seemed pretty obvious to me. She definitely had seen it before.

"Yes. Well, maybe. The Mitchell children all had them, each generation received their own monogramed pieces."

"Very traditional." I responded cautiously, remembering my conversation with Cecil about Rose maybe being one of the Mitchell children.

Rose seemed to be lost in thought, a faraway look in her eyes. "Yes. I remember it now. I thought that pendant had been lost."

"I think it kind of was. I found it behind a dresser in the guest room."

Rose pursed her lips and continued to eyeball the necklace.

Ready for the awkward moment to end, I said, "Rose, I need to get on my way. I have to run errands on Main. It was nice seeing you." And with that, I walked away. I briefly thought about her comment, *"I thought that pendant had been lost."* As if it was hers maybe? Well, she hadn't said it was hers, so I wasn't going to dwell on it. Rose was an odd bird, and I had other things to do today than worry about her fixation on the necklace.

~~~

Her enthusiasm for gardening extinguished, Rose left her garden pruners right in the flower bed and stomped inside. She couldn't believe Porter would just put the necklace on like that, not even stopping to think who might be the rightful owner.

She mumbled, "She's barely there three months. Who does she think she is? It doesn't belong to her. It belongs to me."

She grabbed the faded hatbox from the back of her closet and began to riffle through the old school pictures she had stored inside. Finally, she found the picture she wanted. Her finger, crooked now from arthritis, traced the pendant Mr. Mitchell's daughter wore in the photograph.

Rose remembered how jealous she'd felt every time she looked at it. All the generations of Mitchell children had worn monogramed gold jewelry as if they were royalty, little lords and ladies of Turnberry. Rose seethed at the memories and felt her own neck where a pendant should have been. Mr. Mitchell's daughter had passed away in her young twenties from complications from the flu. Rose knew the young woman had not been buried with her pendant because Rose had seen it in her room after the funeral.

"I should have taken it then. Why not? Who would have known?" Rose chided herself.

She remembered how things had been so chaotic during that time. Later, after the grief had settled and the family had found a new normal, Rose often spent time over there with her mother, helping out with household duties.

She thought about all the places she had searched in the house back then...and even in recent years. The latest being the attic, where a lot of clothes and personal belongings were stored in wardrobes. But not that piece of jewelry.

"Behind the dresser, of all places," Rose huffed. "That necklace belongs to me. It's my birthright."

~~~

Joe tossed his bag in the trunk and then sat in the driver's seat, waiting for Max to emerge from the motel office. When he finally did, the young man tossed his bag in the trunk with Joe's, slammed it shut, then looked around the lot, ruffling his hair with his hand. Joe knew Max was worried. So was he.

"Did you get in touch with him yet?" Max asked Joe as he clicked his seat belt.

"No." Joe stared straight ahead.

"I just don't feel right about this. We told him we'd keep watch."

"I don't either, but we don't have a choice. The Bureau pulled us. We can't stay."

Both men just sat there. Joe's hands rested on the wheel, but he didn't start the car.

Joe's phone rang. "Joe here."

Max looked hopeful, mouthing, *"Is it him?"*

Joe shook his head. Max's head dropped.

"Okay. Yes. We're leaving now." Joe put the phone down and started the car.

The two drove off in silence.

A few days had passed, and the black SUV that had seemed to be a permanent fixture once again had disappeared. As much as I didn't like being watched, it had been a bit of comfort lately, especially since the security installation had been delayed—old house issues. *No, I won't let any of this dampen my spirits.*

Cecil arrived promptly as always, and we made our way into the basement to try our hand at picking the second lock. The damp, cool air made me grateful that I had on a cardigan. Cecil, dressed in his typical flannel and khakis, carried his father's leather locksmith case along with another canvas bag hanging from his shoulder.

"Cecil. Let me carry something," I offered.

"I've got it," he casually replied and kept moving.

Once at the bottom of the stairs, Cecil looked around and whistled. "It's as if time has stood still down here. Now, if memory serves me correctly, that room over there is the coal storage, and there's the help's bathroom, and there behind that wall of garden tools is the vault."

"Yes, but what do you mean by coal storage?" My brain got stuck on that new piece of information.

How had I missed that?

I looked to where Cecil pointed, and sure enough, I saw a small door. Opening it, the old hinges squeaked loudly.

I looked around the small, soot-covered brick room, which had one greenish-glass window near the ceiling. I pointed at it and looked at Cecil curiously.

He explained. "The heat for this house used to be coal powered. See that window? It opened to the outside for coal deliveries. And that iron door that looks sort of like an oven on the wall— that's where the coal fed into the furnace to heat the house. Lots of nineteenth-century homes were heated this way."

"But wouldn't someone have had to shovel this coal several times a day?" Then I got it.

Cecil nodded, as if he'd seen the light bulb go off in my head. "Yes."

I interjected. "The help." I felt my eyes go wide in disbelief.

"Precisely, my dear Watson."

"Wow, this house must have such stories in its walls." I felt the magnitude of the history all around me.

"No doubt. No doubt..." His voice trailed off.

I clapped my hands together softly once. "Okay, back to the task at hand."

We opened the secret panel.

My mind flashed back to the night I had seen the unexplained light. I hadn't mentioned the footsteps or the tunnel for that matter, when I originally told Cecil, and I didn't really want to now. However, at some point, I'd probably need to address the elephant in the room.

I moved to step inside. "It's pitch dark in here."

"Porter, wait. Let me turn on the flashlight."

"Oh right, that would be better." I laughed nervously.

Cecil shone the light into the room. I entered, pulling the string for the ceiling light. Instantly, the room illuminated. Guiltily, I noticed the tunnel door still obstructed by the boxes that I had pushed against it.

Cecil stared at the vault, visibly enamored. "I forgot how big it was."

"I know. Seems like overkill," I said, half joking.

Minutes went by as we examined the challenge that loomed in front of us. The tall, battleship-gray door had a large brass lock front and center.

"That's a serious lock," I said.

Cecil popped on his glasses and leaned in close to read aloud the inscription etched into the brass. "CHATWOOD'S—PATENT LONDON."

I moved closer, too, and read the other smaller words, "Manchester, Leeds, and Works Bolton."

Around the brass lock system, we investigated a series of etched numbers 17, 18, and 19 along with depictions of two handles—one that suggested it twisted, and another that appeared as if it would pull.

I looked at Cecil. "The door looks like it belongs in the basement of a 1920s bank."

"Well, Porter, let's hope we don't go down like the 1929 stock market crash. This is quite a complex lock."

"Come on, Cecil. We can do this." I pumped a fist in the air. "Bonnie and Clyde time...with a better ending, of course."

"Okay. Let me get my bearings. You do know that my father was the locksmith, not me."

I grinned slyly, cutting my eyes at him.

Cecil moved his glasses up and down on his nose several times. "Porter, did you see this?"

"See what?" I leaned in.

"The lock is made for a key."

"Okay. What should we do? Is that easier?" I was hopeful.

"I don't know. I can try some of these tools." He put one of the tools in the keyhole.

"Wait." I had an idea.

He paused.

"I'll be right back." I darted upstairs and went straight to the study. I opened the drawer where I had stashed the skeleton key from the safety deposit box.

Breathless, I returned to the basement. Cecil stood looking at me questioningly.

"Here, try this." I reached out my hand, exposing the old key.

Cecil carefully inserted the key and began twisting the handle: one, two, three loud mechanical clicks. Then he grabbed the other handle and pulled, grunting a bit at the weight of the door.

Stunned, I watched as the vault opened.

Pitch dark inside and eerily chilly, the vault resembled a tomb. Cecil reached out his hand. Instinctively, I placed the flashlight in his open palm.

The glass bottles sparkled like stars as he swept the beam of light across the space. Lots and lots of glass bottles—hundreds of bottles all stacked perfectly on rustic, wooden, crisscross racks.

"Who would have thought..." Cecil seemed mesmerized, as was I. "I know I have been down here before, but I never saw behind the door..." His voice trailed off into the glorious glimmering silence.

"Cecil, what are all these bottles?"

As we walked into the vault, Cecil stopped and put his arm out straight in front of me to block me from walking further. "Wait, Porter. Grab a couple of those boxes and block the door open. We don't want to get trapped in here. No one will ever find us."

"Good idea." I couldn't believe I hadn't thought of that myself.

Once again, I pushed boxes around the room. "Okay, secure."

Cecil examined the shelves of bottles with a focus akin to an archeologist who had just unearthed long-lost treasures in an Egyptian pyramid. "Porter, these bottles are definitely Prohibition era. And they are labeled with names of people. I think this may have been a bank of sorts for liquor."

I carefully lifted a dusty, cool bottle off the rack. The glass felt heavy and different from modern-day bottles. I passed it over to Cecil and said, "This looks like a prescription label."

He nodded. "That makes sense."

"It does?"

"Yes. During Prohibition, drugstores were able to sell liquor through a legal loophole, as long as it was prescribed by a doctor for medicinal purposes." Cecil picked up another bottle.

"Then why hide it here?" I asked, still not understanding fully the extent of what Cecil was saying.

"Well, I don't know for sure, but I have a feeling that quantity was also tightly controlled. Just speculation here, but you see, if someone had one bottle for a cough or arthritis, let's say, it wasn't a problem. However, if someone had fifteen bottles in his home for arthritis, it could raise suspicion. But if your bank could store your backlog in a secret vault, then purchasing in bulk probably was cheaper and safer. Delivery of a case was less risky in the long run than having a couple bottles at a time transported. Also, it guaranteed a supply was readily available when needed."

I stood mouth agape for a moment, taking it all in the best I could. "This is unbelievable. I expected a few leftover bottles of spoiled moonshine. I did not expect this Smithsonian-worthy display of prohibition liquor. Honestly, this is amazing."

Cecil continued to survey the shelves as he spoke. "Porter, I'm with you. I could not have imagined this. Even decades ago, when I took that photo of the front of the vault, I didn't think something like this was behind the door. I truly believed that maybe there were a dozen or so bottles of old rancid liquor left in a box in the corner."

We stood in disbelief for a few moments longer.

I felt a smile appear. "I have an idea."

Cecil chuckled. "Oh boy."

"Well, shall we?" I motioned toward the bottles. "Let's have a toast to successfully picking two locks under one roof." I giggled.

He grinned. "I don't see why not. Except we really didn't pick either."

"I won't tell if you don't. And, being that you are the hero of the day, please choose a bottle or two to open."

He shook his head but played along. "I would be honored." He returned his gaze to the shelves and began surveying the options.

I glimpsed a twinkle in his eye, and that made me happy.

"I'll be right back. We need glasses." I headed off to the kitchen.

"Don't worry. I'll be right here exploring the bottles," Cecil's voice trailed after me.

I ran upstairs at a record pace to gather supplies for our illegal liquor tasting. I grabbed a canvas shopping bag and began filling it. I threw in a dark-chocolate bar flavored with chilies and one with salted caramel, and of course, cocktail napkins, a dishtowel, and the silver corkscrew monogramed with an M for "Mitchell." Lastly, I grabbed two antique brandy glasses. "Perfect." In a brief flash, I scurried back downstairs.

"Did you bring the kitchen sink, too?" he teased.

I laughed, a little breathless. "Well, if we're going to do this, we should do it right. I see you found the light switch in the vault."

I pushed a box inside the vault to use as a makeshift table.

"Impressive," Cecil said from behind me.

"Well, thank you." I finished my setting up and turned to him with a raised eyebrow and wry smile. "Now that I've done my part, did you do yours and sanction a bottle for us to try?"

He rubbed his hands together eagerly. "I sure did."

"I get the feeling you know a little bit about the one you have chosen for us."

"I have to admit that I do." Cecil feigned an air of smugness. "Now, this prized specimen is a delicate moonshine that has been aged in an oak whiskey barrel."

"How do you know that? The label says all of that?"

Cecil nodded and returned to his normal manner. "Yes, it does, and there is more. This bottle was made especially for Gerald Barton for digestive issues."

I gave Cecil a blank stare. He smirked. The label was old, yellowed with time. Even from several feet away, I saw the beautiful handwritten script, which closely resembled an official certificate of sorts, with red numbers and filigree edging. "I hope after all of these years, it doesn't have the opposite effect and give us digestive issues."

Cecil smirked. "You see, Gerald Barton was the mayor of this town in the late 1920s. He's infamous for his dealings with the 'drugstores' of the time."

I understood immediately. "Of course! The 'drugstores' like in *The Great Gatsby*."

"Exactly. And for several reasons, including the stature of the intended recipient of this magnificent bottle, I'm going to take a stab that this is probably one of the best bottles down here." Cecil pursed his lips and nodded slightly.

I said, "Well, I can't argue that. Let's get to it, shall we?"

With that, Cecil and I sat down on the floor next the box. The only thing that would have made the scene even more theatrical would have been a sterling silver candelabrum and a ghostly shadow or two. Cecil opened it easily with the corkscrew and held the bottle up to the light, illuminating the slightly amber liquid that had been preserved in time for over seventy years. Almost ceremonial in his actions, he poured two glasses. The cut-glass snifters sparkled like diamonds in the orange glow of the vault. Without hesitation, we raised our glasses in unison. "Cheers." The crystal made the most beautiful ping—a sound seemingly straight from the past, timeless. And in that moment, I truly felt like a piece of my shattered soul fused back into place.

After a few sips for me and a second glass for Cecil, I noticed him staring intently behind me into the room outside of the vault.

"Porter." He paused. "I know this liquor is strong, but I don't think I've had enough to hallucinate. Is that a tiny door over there on the wall?" He pointed, and I turned to look at the door I had been avoiding discussing. "No, there was a large bookshelf over there last time I was here years ago. I'm sure of it."

"Oh, that," I said sarcastically. Turning back to him, I attempted to escape the awkwardness of the omission with jest. "I must have forgotten to mention that hobbits once lived under this house."

"Very funny."

"Why, thank you." I breathed a sigh of relief and took a dramatic bow while seated cross-legged in front of our cardboard box table. "Actually, Cecil, I had no idea that a tunnel was down here until I found this hidden room." I laughed at the absurdity of the sentence that had just come out of my mouth. Cecil chuckled, too. Gathering my composure, I said, "And now that we know this is definitely a prohibition vault, I'm starting to put the puzzle together as to why this room was hidden. And that small door must have been the delivery entrance for the illegal liquor. However, there's still one big question..."

Cecil waited for me to continue.

"Where does the other end of that tunnel let out?" My words sparked a silence between us.

Then Cecil took another sip and responded. "Porter, I agree. I feel sure that must have been a tunnel for the booze." He put his glass down and stood, battling his stiff legs with a grunt. He walked over, pushed the boxes out the way, and opened the door. The screeching hinges brought chills down my spine.

"Porter, grab that flashlight for me, will you?" In investigator mode, Cecil didn't seem to feel the same apprehension that I had originally about peering into that tunnel.

As instructed, I walked over with the flashlight. Cecil shone the light into the dark tunnel, and, instantly, we heard a skittering sound. My body shivered. "What was that?"

"Mice or bats." Cecil said matter-of-factly. The idea of critters in the tunnel did not deter him in the least. "I'm going to walk in a few feet. Stay here in case it caves in on me."

Hearing his chuckle, I knew he was joking, kind of.

"It's a long tunnel. I still cannot see the end. It bends left. Hold on. I'm coming back out."

I reached for his arm to help stabilize him as he ducked under the doorframe.

"It's a tight fit in there. I feel for the person who had to transport liquor hunched over like this. It looks like the same brick as the coal room. I don't think this tunnel was an afterthought." He placed a hand on his lower back and groaned.

Relieved that he was out, I said, "Okay. Well, there is no urgent reason to explore in there tonight. Let's close it back up. I don't want any of those critters moving into the house." I decided not to share my real reason for wanting that tunnel closed—I didn't want whomever may or may not have turned on the light in this room to come back any time soon.

Cecil ruffled his hair to remove any remnants of dust. "Well, Porter, you never disappoint. I don't even need to watch TV anymore. I can just come over here for a suspense-filled evening courtesy of the Mitchells."

I pursed my lips and nodded. This move had not been what I had expected in many ways. "Tell me about it."

"Well, I hate to end this party, but I need to get home. Shall we wrap it up for now?" He grabbed the locksmith's bag.

"A parting gift," I said as I handed a bottle from one of the shelves to him.

"I couldn't."

"I insist." I smiled.

"Well, maybe I could."

I walked Cecil out to the part of the main driveway that curved in front of the garage. Twilight was in full bloom. We were saying our goodbyes when a motorcycle engine revved behind us. Startled, we turned and saw a matte-black motorcycle, its rider dressed in a leather jacket and jeans, speed away.

Oddly, something felt familiar about the rider. I just didn't know what exactly.

Cecil offered an acceptable explanation. "He must have been turning around."

All I could manage was a "Yep."

"Porter, you okay? You look like you've seen a ghost."

I pushed back an uneasiness that had been stirred by the sight of the rider. "Yes. No. I mean, I'm fine. Just tired, I guess." I managed a small smile. "Maybe too much prohibition liquor."

"Okay then. Get some rest. Thank you for the adventure...and for the parting gift." He held up the bottle as he walked toward his truck.

"Have a good evening. See you Wednesday for our walk."

And, just like that, alone again, I stood anxiously wondering if the motorcycle rider could have been that same someone who kept prowling around my house.

Then the loud, intrusive engine of a motorcycle once again filled the silence. The mysterious rider pulled into my driveway for a second time, stopping abruptly as if shocked by my presence.

Should I run inside?

The headlight illuminated a light blanket of mist as the rider dismounted the bike and approached me.

My heart raced. My body froze. *Run, Porter, run!*

But the man hesitated as well. He stopped, not coming any closer. Was he going to shoot me or something? I could see his eyes through the slit in his helmet. Our gazes locked, just for a moment.

And suddenly I couldn't breathe. "Jack?" I stepped forward as if being pulled in that direction by some unknown force.

He moved back a step, mumbled, "Sorry, wrong house," and in the blink of an eye, he turned, mounted the bike, and sped away. Dumbfounded, I stood there, mouth agape at the emotional absurdity of the moment. After at least five minutes, I gathered myself and walked back inside.

"It could not have been Jack." *Porter, you are lonely and tipsy.* "No more prohibition whiskey for me." I dropped my head in defeat and admitted that I missed him entirely too much, and my heart ached so that I had to clutch my fist at my chest. My other hand brushed my cheek to wipe away my tears. I had done it again—imagined Jack. *What is wrong with me?*

~~~

Jack jetted into the driveway of the river house, which, quite frankly, had become all too familiar, parking haphazardly. Once inside, he flung the helmet onto the couch, flustered, mad, at his wit's end.

"Why did I leave like that? You idiot." He paced around the room. Stood still and then paced some more.

Jack had heard Porter say his name, and it had nearly torn him to pieces. Her voice had sounded different, sad or maybe lonely. Maybe hopeful? But he'd freaked out, acted like some sort of weirdo. That was all she needed in her life—another jerk.

Grunting as he sat on the couch, he let his head fall into his hands. He leaned back, heart aching with frustration. "Slick move." Jack's voice resonated the anger he felt at himself. What had he been thinking?

He had gotten back from DC that morning and let his emotions and fear make his decisions for him. True, he had been eager to catch the informant that he now knew for sure had been assigned to watch Porter for the cartel. With the wheels still turning in his mind, Jack surmised that if the cartel's intent had been revenge, they would have done that already. No. They were watching, maybe even searching for something they thought Porter had, and it appeared that the US government was allowing it to happen. Jack fumed inside. He knew he didn't yet have all of the pieces, but he intended to dig those out, and catching that informant was top of his list. Jack knew better than to go straight up Porter's driveway on his bike like he'd just done. That wasn't the smart way to confront her with all of this. However, if he had been observing his own behavior from the outside, he would have thought he *wanted* to get caught. If he were honest with himself, he kind of did. The whole process of protecting Porter on the sly proved exhausting. Yes, part of him wanted to give her the space she desired, but the other part really wanted to protect her by just being there, holding her, and reassuring her with his words.

Jack thought about how he had just compounded everything by being elusive and by probably making Porter afraid. That had not been his intent. He needed to send the letter he had written to Porter soon. Or he needed to man up, get over there, and talk to her face-to-face.

He picked up the phone and dialed Joe's number. It rang several times. No answer.

"Damn it. Where are those morons? I told them to keep a close watch."

Beyond frustrated, Jack propped his boot-clad feet on the edge of the coffee table—but just for a moment. Abruptly, he stood up and grabbed his helmet.

"Someone has to watch out for her." Jack started the bike and rode back to Porter's street. This time, he parked down the street and walked up to the spot by the guesthouse where Joe and Max should have been. Jack took a seat on the porch of the guest cottage and settled in for the long night of keeping an eye out for the Colombian scumbag.

~ 53 ~

Saturday arrived, and I could hardly contain my excitement for the evening ahead. Patsy would be coming over in a few hours for a retro-inspired girls' night, something I had never done—ever. It would be a night of sipping expensive wine, ordering in pizzas, and trying on glamorous, vintage dresses in the attic. Oh, and probably some gossiping, too. Just a little. I chuckled at the immaturity of it all. I'd never been one of the giggly, bubbly types. *But if it brings me a few hours of escape from thinking about the strange happenings of late, then count me in.*

Dusk started to fall just as I finished readying everything for Patsy's arrival. I had set out two perfect bottles of small batch reds and ordered the pizza to be delivered at 7 p.m. I also had taken the liberty of stopping by the market earlier and buying two very decadent pints of locally made gelato, which Stan recommended, of course. And to top it off, unnecessarily, I had chilled champagne—my defense being that fine boutiques always offered a glass of bubbly during fittings. *If we get through all of these bottles, Patsy may need to stay in the guest room.*

Just before seven, I heard a knock at the door, and I practically danced over to open it. A frazzled but smiling Patsy stood in front of me, her arms overflowing with gift bags and yet another bottle of wine. Red, of course.

"I come bearing gifts," she said breathlessly.

"I can see that. Let me help you." I started taking items from her as we moved inside.

Patsy followed me toward the study, but then awkwardly paused, peering around the foyer.

I laughed aloud, remembering that Patsy thought the house to be haunted. "I promise. I asked all the ghosts to take the night off."

Patsy tilted her head and waved a hand at me dismissively. "Pfft. I ain't scared of no ghosts." Then, she walked over to the vase of white roses on the entry table, leaned in and inhaled with her eyes closed. "Oh my. These are absolutely gorgeous...and so fragrant, too."

"Thank you." I decided not to mention that white roses had shown up every single Friday since I had moved into this house. Jack hadn't stopped our little flower tradition. And I didn't think I wanted him to.

With the first bottle opened and the wine poured into glasses, the chatter commenced. I savored every sentence Patsy shared about her day. My regrets about leaving Jack barely on my mind, I felt a little bit like the old me. I listened intently as Patsy talked about her co-worker at the library and how he couldn't shelve the books correctly. She smiled and leaned back as she kicked off her shoes. With Patsy, it was easy—I could give the occasional head nod or laugh without having to actually speak about myself. Not much later, the pizza arrived, and we took our time devouring it before transitioning to the attic.

On our way out of the study, I grabbed the second bottle. "Shall we?" I gestured toward the staircase in the foyer.

"Ooooh. Yes. But I need to use the powder room first, if you don't mind."

"Of course. That way," I said and pointed in the direction of the downstairs guest bathroom. I waited by the flowers, enjoying their sweet fragrance. When Patsy emerged from the hallway, she wore a strange look on her face.

"What is it?" I asked.

"Well, the reality of my reflection in your ever-so-lovely powder room struck me with a bit of panic."

"What do you mean?" I said, truly confused.

"This is a little embarrassing, but as I hate to point out, we are two very different dress sizes, and well...what if none of the dresses fit me?"

I actually had not thought about that possibility, but I wasn't going to let that ruin our night. I had to say something to make her more comfortable. "What if none of the dresses fit either of us? Besides, what are the chances that they will fit both of us? So, whichever of us gets lucky, we'll just have to promise to go dress shopping with the other soon. How bad could that be—a second shopping trip?"

Patsy grinned. "Great idea. In fact, I hope they fit you, since this is your house and all. And besides, there is a cute shop downtown that you have to buzz to go in, and I just haven't wanted to go alone. So, you'll be on the hook if the dresses in the attic don't fit me."

Phew. Crisis averted.

On our way up the first flight of steps, Patsy said, "This house...well, it's just magnificent. Every detail is just perfect—the chandeliers, the woodwork. It's, well...it's such a beautiful homage to craftsmen of a different era. Really a lost art."

"Thank you. I wish I could take credit, but all I did was move in." I looked around as the words slipped over my tongue. True, I didn't design this house, but I felt like parts of it were made specifically for me.

Once in the attic, Patsy joked that she felt out of breath after two flights of stairs and plopped down on the blue velvet couch with her wineglass in hand. She reached out for the second bottle of wine to pour a refill and said in a theatrically snooty tone, "You may start."

I laughed aloud and headed into the wardrobe room. *It's stuffy up here.* I opened the small French-style windows to let in the cool night air. That's when I heard it, the faint sound of a motorcycle, briefly. I chose to ignore it—purposefully denying that I even heard anything at all.

To begin this ridiculous fashion escapade, I put on a sparkling, pale-blue ball gown, cut in a flapper style with a high neckline. I came out doing my best version of the Roaring '20s, which left much to be desired. Patsy almost spit out her wine before bursting into laughter.

Her eyes sparkled. "What we need is music."

My eyes landed on the old tabletop radio in the corner.

Patsy followed my gaze. "My gosh! That thing is as big as a microwave. Does it work?"

I shrugged. "It's worth a try." I flipped on the switch and turned the dial. Yep. It worked, but sounded awful. "How about we imagine music?"

Patsy looked at me with a raised eyebrow. "Umm. Yes. Please turn that off."

We giggled, and I happily clicked the radio off.

"Okay, then, I'll just top off this glass while you try on another dress. By the way, that one doesn't look bad," Patsy said genuinely.

I tried on two more dresses, a tea-length silver one covered in large jewel-shaped beads, and a long, straight, black-beaded dress with silver and gold threads running throughout.

"You can do better. Keep trying, Porter," Patsy teased with a swish of her hand. I could see that she had gotten very comfortable on the little couch, with my fashion failures as her entertainment.

"Okay, one more, and then I'm taking a break." And I wasn't kidding.

After a zipper struggle, I emerged in a flowing emerald-green gown made of layers of sheer fabric with wispy edges that caught in the breeze from the open window.

Patsy just stared, silently.

Is she speechless or horrified? A little embarrassed, I asked, "Is it that bad?"

"No. No. It's that good. You are stunning in that dress. Porter, I didn't know your eyes were that green. The dress makes them absolutely electric! Honestly, it looks as if the dress had been made for you and only you. The fabric fits your delicate frame so elegantly. Yes. That's the one."

I felt a flush in my cheeks, uncomfortable with the compliments. "Thank you." And then, I laughed. "The one, and I have nowhere to go."

We both belly laughed like two goofballs. Then Patsy's expression turned serious. "Girl, we have to think of someplace you can wear that dress."

She's serious.

I belted out a quick follow-up laugh, "Ha!" and turned to go take off the dress, hoping to divert this train wreck of thought.

"Porter, I'm not kidding. You have to debut in that dress. Take your position in Turnberry society. You've been here long enough. It's time. Let's throw a gala."

"Whoa, Patsy, I'm not sure I'm up for all of that." I knew the shock of her suggestion showed on my face.

"You just need a push. That's all." Her tone sparked with relentless determination.

She's really not going to let this go.

I tried again to extinguish her proposal. "Patsy, we can't just throw a gala for the sake of this dress. We would need a cause. We've had too much wine. This is silly. Let's go downstairs."

Patsy didn't falter. "That's just a technicality. Porter, leave it to me. I'll find a reason." She had a faraway look in her eyes that honestly scared me a little.

"Okay, well, we obviously won't be able to decide anything tonight. Your turn?" I pointed at the other dresses.

"Uh, yeah. No. I think not."

"You sure? That was our plan."

She stood. "Well, plans change. I'm thrilled with what we've done already. Besides, I want to take you up on that shopping trip." She batted her eyelashes.

"Okay, fine. Let me change back into my jeans and blouse, and we can head downstairs for dessert."

"Dessert? What's for dessert? Oh, who cares? Sure. You don't have to ask me twice." Patsy raised her hands in mock defeat.

~~~

Patsy left close to midnight—we needed to wait for her last glass of wine to wear off. I stood in the driveway, waving as she left. Walking to the house, I felt a tingle on the back of my neck, like someone stood behind me, watching.

Slowly, I turned toward the garage, peering into the darkness. I didn't think the SUV had been around in days, but maybe they'd come back. But, so far, those guys had never been purposefully creepy.

What was that?

Something moved near the garage, maybe. *I don't know.*

I started walking back to the house again when I heard a faint sound. A grating of pebbles? It was hard to tell. I stopped. Turned.

"Hello?" I called out into the misty night air.

I waited. Nothing. A few crickets chirped. *Okay, stop it.* I recognized the old feeling of panic and knew exactly where it would lead. So right then and there, I made the decision to refuse to spook myself any further. I gathered my wits about me and went inside. The dogs had been asleep upstairs for over an hour, having lost interest in my and Patsy's antics. *It's time I joined them.*

~ 54 ~

Rose yawned as she cautiously watched out her window. She couldn't sleep anyway, and she had noticed that Porter's lights were still on. Not typical for her at this late hour. Seemed like she might be having some sort of girls' night.

"Porter has become quite the hostess recently," she muttered to her cat sitting on the chair next to the window. She felt annoyed that she had not been invited over at all. She would have understood if Porter's guests had all been young, but Cecil had visited several times, and he was old enough to be Porter's father.

"I just need to find a way to click with her." Rose ruffled her cat's fur, and the feline purred appreciatively.

Maybe another basket of muffins would do the trick. Rose needed access to Porter's house, and that had been harder since the tunnel entrance had been blocked.

She was pretty sure that Cecil and Porter had been in the basement together recently, and she knew for certain that Patsy from the library had been in the attic with Porter for hours tonight.

Frankly, the snooping in the attic made Rose more anxious than the basement because that's where most of the family's personal items had been stored. Porter had already found the pendant, but as far as Rose had seen, she had not found the blue sapphire ring. She felt certain that Porter would have been wearing it, showing it off as if it belonged to her.

Rose watched as Patsy drove off and Porter stood for a moment and then went inside. She started to close the curtain, but there, lurking next to the garage she caught a glimpse of the "shorter stalker," as she sarcastically had come to refer to him. The short guy usually liked to hang out at the wood line. The "taller stalker" who rode the motorcycle didn't usually stay long. The "SUV stalkers" never went more than ten feet away from their car and didn't seem to try to stay out of sight.

Yes, that short, pudgy stalker...he kept to the shadows. Honestly, Rose felt like waving to the others; it had become such commonplace for them to see each other watching. But not with this guy—the macabre one. Instead, Rose let the curtain go, and without a second thought about Porter's safety, she went to bed.

She didn't see the other man, the taller stalker, approaching Porter's guesthouse. And the short guy didn't see him either.

~~~

Jack sat on the porch steps of the guesthouse, getting more irritated by the minute. He'd hoped to get a crack at the drug runner's spy. It would suit his mood perfectly. "Where are Joe and Max? I can't believe they aren't here," he grumbled under his breath. "And now they're not answering my calls?" He pounded his fist into his thigh, then he got up and started walking.

As he rounded the garage on the far side, he heard something. Jack froze and waited. He could hear his own breath, but he could hear footsteps as well. Just then, Jack spotted the guy, short and a little heavy.

Jack called out, "Hey, you. Get over here."

Startled, the guy turned quickly to face Jack. His body language looked as if he would run.

"Don't even think about it." Jack pointed his 9mm straight at the guy.

The guy immediately raised his hands in the air. "Okay, Okay, don't shoot." His Spanish accent thick—Anger raced through Jack's veins. He had caught the cartel's guy.

"Walk slowly towards me." He motioned with the end of the gun.

The two of them met behind the garage, out of street and house views.

"Who hired you?" Jack got right to the point.

"I don't know...no se."

The guy was lying, and Jack knew it. "You better remember real quick. I'm not playing this game with you. Do you hear me?" Jack's words dripped with impatience and anger. "I know you're tied to the Colombians, the cartel, so just come clean."

The guy looked visibly shaken and nodded his head up and down several times.

"Yes. Sí, señor. I'm just supposed to watch her. That's all. Promise, señor."

Jack fumed. "Well, you're fired." He spun the man around and pushed the gun into his back, hard, right between his shoulder blades. The guy flinched but kept his hands raised. Jack leaned in close, his breath on the man's ear as he spoke. "Tell your boss I said if he sends you back here, only one of us will be walking away—and it won't be you."

Jack knew he needed to let the guy go, mostly because he didn't have any other viable options, but also because he wanted the message to get back to the cartel. Plus, shooting this guy would stir up all kinds of trouble with the police here...and the Colombians. Joe and Max were nowhere to be found, and Jack would surely go to prison without their protection.

Jack shoved the guy and told him to leave. In a split second, the informant ran straight into the woods, never looking back.

Jack leaned against the garage and sighed. "This has gone on long enough." He waited a while longer, and once the sun started to rise, he felt secure enough that the informant wouldn't be back, at least not that day. He walked back down the street to his bike and took off.

~~~

Just before lunch, Joe's cell phone rang as he sat at his desk inside FBI headquarters in Washington, DC. His stomach growled and he seriously considered not answering until he read the inbound number. He picked up. "Joe here."

"You had better be laid up in a hospital somewhere," Jack spat out.

"Okay, calm down." Joe's voice was even. "Listen, our assignment got put on a temporary hold. Nothing I could do."

"You could have called me."

"I tried."

Jack snarled, "I thought we had a deal."

"We got pulled. It's out of my hands. You know that." Joe shot back. He shouldn't even be talking with Jack, considering the circumstances of the investigation at this point. Things had gone flat, especially in regard to Porter. Surveillance had become harder and harder to justify when she hadn't even left Turnberry once since she had arrived months ago. In fact, the assignment would have ended sooner if Jack hadn't made that little visit to Colombia.

"Joe, don't play dumb. You know there's someone watching her. You saw him, too."

"Hey, I never actually saw anyone. That was you, remember?"

"Don't be cute, Joe. Max saw him, then."

"Maybe. Max *thought* he saw someone, but he wasn't sure. Besides, he could have just seen you."

"Joe, you know it wasn't me. I was out of town." Jack paused, and Joe heard him breathing heavily. *The guy's gonna give himself a heart attack.*

Jack continued more calmly, even though Joe could tell he was seething. "You didn't report any of what I told you, did you? Well, here's something else you can neglect to report. I caught the guy last night at her house. I tried to put the fear of God in him, but I had to let him go. No backup!" He barked the last two words.

Joe stayed quiet for a second before replying with, "Do you really think that was a good idea?"

"Of course it wasn't!" Jack scoffed. "But tell me, what choice did I have? The deal was to do this together. I just tried to buy some time by spooking him and getting a message back to the goon that put him there."

"Listen, Jack. Why don't you just patch things up with her? That way, if someone does bother her, you'll be there to take care of it." Joe saw that as the most reasonable explanation, and he'd often wondered why Jack hadn't done it by now.

"Yeah, well, you don't know as much as you think you do. Thanks for nothing, Joe."

The line went dead. Joe stared at the receiver for a moment and shook his head.

Max was staring at him from across the desk. "Was that who I think it was? He's not happy, huh?"

"Nope." Joe sighed, his thoughts far away.

~ 55 ~

Eagerly, I walked briskly to get to the library to meet Patsy—we had decided to meet every Thursday for lunch downtown. Between my weekly walks with Cecil, lunches with Patsy, yoga, and regular visits to Stan's market and Peg's art gallery, my schedule had filled up nicely.

As I swung open the large wooden door, I smiled at feeling a part of this town already—just a few months in—almost summer. *Jack would love it here, too.* I spotted Patsy at the circulation desk and waved. She gestured that she'd be done in a minute, so I marched straight away to the Historian Room to find the Lady Turnberry case. And as I examined the crown, I pushed away a twinge of guilt that the missing jewels lay hidden in my house. I needed to tell Patsy. I should have mentioned it at my house the other night, but as strange as it seemed now, I really had not thought of it at the time.

I'll tell her at lunch.

~~~

Patsy and I settled in at a small corner table on the patio at Bread and Fromage. Our regular waiter took our orders. Momentarily, I became lost in my thoughts.

I must have stayed quiet too long.

"You seem distracted. Is everything okay, Porter?" Patsy looked truly concerned.

"Yes. Sorry. Yes." I took a sip of my iced tea, feeling a little anxious about what I needed get off my chest and tell Patsy. "It's just that I need to tell you something, and...well, I feel awkward because I kind of forgot about it until today. The truth is, I should have told you a while ago."

Patsy's look went from concern to terror. *My dramatic friend.*

"Oh, gosh. Don't worry. Actually, it is a good thing." *I think.*

Patsy sighed with a hand to her heart. "Thank goodness. I thought you were going to tell me you were dying or moving or something."

"No. No. Oh, forget it. Patsy, I have the crown jewels."

Patsy shrieked. "You stole the crown jewels? You're an international thief?"

I dropped my head and shook it in disbelief. *Could this conversation be going any worse?*

"No. no. I mean I found the jewels to Lady Turnberry's crown in my house. The library crown, not THE crown as in the Tower of London."

Light dawned in Patsy's eyes. "Oh, wait. The crown in the Historian Room?"

"Yes. There's a safe in my house. Cecil and I got it open, and I found jewels inside. When I saw the crown, I put two and two together, and I think the jewels are exact matches." I couldn't get the words out fast enough.

Patsy looked dumbfounded. "Porter, do you know what this means?"

"I think so." I took another sip of my tea.

"This is so exciting. Well, I mean, are you going to tell anyone else?" She looked as if she could springboard right out of her chair.

"Yes. Of course. That's my point, actually. I want to give the jewels back so they can be put into the crown. But I don't know who or even where to start. The police?"

Patsy nodded. We sat in silence. Then she snapped her fingers and said, "Porter, I have an idea. Before you say no, just hear me out."

She explained her idea of hosting a 1920s-themed gala, primarily to raise money for the library Historian Room, which had already been in the works. "And now we can announce the reintroduction of the jewels to the crown. It's serendipitous." At the end of her spiel, she added, "And you can wear that green dress."

I thought about her idea, and other than making me and the green dress the center of attention, I liked it.

"Okay, Patsy, I like everything except the part about me being the guest of honor."

"But it has to be you. You found the jewels. You're donating them," Patsy pleaded.

"I can do it anonymously. I'd prefer that."

"Porter, it's for the library, and the new girl in town will draw a crowd. Please say yes. I'll be there every step of the way."

"I don't know." I could feel dread building at the thought of all of the attention.

"Okay, you don't have to say yes today, just don't say no." Patsy looked at me with puppy-dog eyes and pouty lips.

Porter snickered. *How can I say no to that face?*

~ 56 ~

Rose stared out her window as Porter and the dogs left for a walk around four o'clock. Impatiently, she waited for the trio to become small dots in the distance. Rose made a mental note of the day and time. She had finally started to notice a pattern with the walks and today she would take advantage of it. Clutching the old brass key to Porter's house, she hoped the locks hadn't been changed. So as not to be spotted, Rose walked around back to the service porch entry. Inserting the key, she heard a loud click and began to jiggle the door handle roughly.

~~~

Jack watched from beside the guesthouse as Porter left with the dogs, and just as he moved to mount his bike in hopes of heading over to the river house for an hour or so, he observed the older lady from across the street making a beeline for Porter's house. Silently, he followed her from a distance as she walked around the back of the main house. "What the hell?" He needed a closer look, so he rounded the corner, bringing into view the sight of the woman fiddling aggressively with the service door lock.

Without thinking, Jack called out, "Hey! What are you doing?"

The woman's shoulders jerked. She turned abruptly and then quickly shed the shock of being caught only to replace it with an apathetic tone. "Oh. It's you."

"Huh?" Jack was confused.

For a moment, the woman simply glared at him, then scowled and said, "It's none of your business. You of all people shouldn't be questioning me. You, mister, are a stalker."

Jack found himself taken aback by her harsh words, but from her perspective and pretty much anyone else's, he couldn't blame her for thinking so. That was exactly what he would appear to be. Feeling defensive and somewhat humiliated, Jack looked away for a moment. He mouthed the word *stalker*. Then he turned back and retorted, "That's preposterous. You don't know why I'm here. You're one to talk." Then, grasping to strike back, he sniped, "You're a burglar."

The tiny woman furrowed her brow and lashed back. "Hardly...and for your information, young man, I know enough."

Caught up in the moment, Jack added, "You don't know me or my relationship with Porter, for that matter. What we've been through together, how we are connected." He stopped his rant as he quickly realized the ridiculousness of the situation.

The look on her face said it all—confusion. He could only assume she was wondering why a perfect stranger would be telling her all of this. And rightfully so. Still, the feeble lady fired back with, "Well, if you're so close with Porter, then why are you always lurking, spying? That doesn't sound like a healthy relationship."

"Listen. The point is I'm no stalker, lady." Jack could feel the heat of embarrassment in his face and neck. This woman had gotten to him.

The lady stomped her foot and fumed, "And I most certainly am not a burglar."

"No? Well, then why are you breaking and entering?" Jack spoke with a cavalier tone.

They stonewalled each other with silence for several moments before the woman relaxed her shoulders and said, "Listen here, young man. This was my father's house. Somehow it got sold out from under me. I have every right to go inside."

Jack's anger turned to something more like pity as he looked at the shaking old lady. "Okay, okay. Let's calm down."

The woman looked down and mumbled, "Porter is the one who shouldn't be here." Then she looked at him again, this time with sheer anger glowing in her old eyes. "I'll tell her about you if you don't mind your own business."

Jack almost laughed at the irony of it all. But he kept his reaction to a small shrug. "Go ahead. But she doesn't know that you're the one going through her house when she's not home. I know it. You know it. Maybe she should know it, too. Hmmm?"

Jack saw her hands begin to shake, and her voice did, too. "How dare you threaten me! I'll call the police on you. They'll arrest you, they will. For what you're doing around here, watching her like you do."

Jack called her bluff. "The police won't find me or any evidence of me, but they will find your fingerprints all over this house, places where they don't belong. So, do you still want to call the cops?"

Then she made a loud huff and spun on her heels. "You'll regret threatening me." She shook her fist in the air and stomped away.

Jack stared at the feeble old lady as she made her way back to her house. Something about her seemed innately broken, pathetic. What did she want from inside Porter's house, anyway? Strange.

"Hey," he called out across the yard.

She didn't turn around. Jack ran to catch up with her. She stopped with a loud, long sigh. Jack spoke in a calmer, friendlier voice. "Listen, don't come over here anymore unless Porter invites you. I'm serious. Stay out of her house."

The lady stared blankly at Jack. He stared back. Then she walked away again, without a word.

Jack watched her go into her house and then, a moment later, her small silhouette appeared at the window, watching. He shook it off and walked back to the service entry of Porter's house. He looked at the door and saw the key still stuck in the lock. Instinctively, Jack relocked the door and tucked the key into his pocket.

~ 57 ~

The phone rang early Monday morning.

"Hi. Porter. It's Patsy."

"Good morning." I barely managed the greeting before Patsy chimed in again.

"I won't keep you. I just wanted to share the news—I just couldn't wait until our lunch Thursday to tell you."

"Yes. Do tell." I felt angst creeping in. I thought I knew what she would say.

"Well, Porter, I received the green light from my committee on the Lady Turnberry Fundraising Gala for the Historian Room at the library." Patsy made no attempt to contain her excitement.

My heart pounded against my chest. Exactly what I feared she would say. "That's great." *I think.*

"Yes, and we have a ton of planning to do between now and then. Just six weeks away."

"Patsy, six weeks? That seems too soon. Can we even get invitations printed and mailed and RSVP'd by then?" I tried not to be the voice of doom and gloom, even though it matched my mood.

"Porter, we can do it. Let's chat about the details at our next lunch." Patsy remained upbeat, completely ignoring my hesitation about it all.

We said our goodbyes just as my doorbell rang.

I opened the door. "Rose."

"Hi, Porter, Good morning. I just stopped by to..." Rose's words trailed off as she looked down at my right hand.

As a reflex to her stare, I lifted my hand and stared, too.

"Where did you get that ring?" Rose mumbled the question.

"Well, um, it's new, kind of. It's new to me, at least." I didn't know quite how to answer, considering how fixated she seemed. *Does she recognize this like she did the necklace? Weird.*

"It's just that I've seen that ring before. It belonged to Mrs. Mitchell." Rose seemed sad.

"Oh. I feel a little strange wearing it. I hope it didn't upset you," I said apologetically.

"Where did you find that—behind the same dresser?"

"No. Actually..." Then I stopped. Something about how Rose looked at me made me uneasy. She had a wild glare in her eyes. *Is she angry?* I needed this conversation to end. "Rose, I have to be somewhere. Was there something you needed?"

Now she looked confused.

"A reason you came over?" I prodded.

"Oh, no. Well, yes, but never mind." With that, she turned and shuffled back toward her house.

I thought about calling after her, but instead, I took the chance for escape and shut the door.

~~~

At home, Rose slammed her hand on the kitchen table. "She's robbing me blind over there."

First the necklace, and now the ring. Next, she'd be getting into the liquor stash—she probably already had found the key to the vault. Rose scrunched her nose, not that she cared about the spoiled old liquor—she just wanted Porter to stop snooping. "She's a regular Hercule Poirot, that one," Rose huffed as she sat defeated in the kitchen chair. Maybe that explained why she and Cecil had gone in the basement. That or the tunnel. Rose's shoulders slumped as the reality of losing the house, her rightful belongings, and any ties to her estranged family set in. What could she really do about any of this?

Out of habit, Rose got up and walked straight to the window that faced Porter's house. There on the far side next to the courtyard stood a man, one she had not seen before. Rose squinted to get a better look. From this distance, his skin looked olive-toned, and his hair very dark and wavy. The man smoked a cigarette as he eyeballed Porter's house. Frustrated at the whole situation, she let the curtain swing shut. She needed a break.

~ 58 ~

The phone at Jack's river house rang several times, stopped, and then rang again. Jack grew annoyed at the continued interruption, so he picked up without putting it to his ear fully intending to hang up without saying a word, but then he thought he heard someone saying his name through the receiver. That's odd he thought as he racked his brain as to whether he'd given out the number to anyone. Then he put the receiver to his ear.

"Jack. Jack. Are you there? It's Joe."

Curious, Jack readily replied, "Joe. Yep. It's me. What do you want?"

"Listen, I've been bothered ever since our last chat, so I put some feelers out about the informant. It looks like he went back to the cartel, told them about you, and now they've sent a replacement. I got an alert that the guy made it through customs yesterday and to Turnberry sometime late last night. And this guy has a reputation—not a good one."

"What?" Alarm bells sounded in Jack's head. "I wanted them to know, but I didn't want a new thug showing up."

"Yep. I hear you. Listen, I don't know exactly what they want from her, but I'm willing to bet they aren't going to stop just because you tell them to. And I'm also thinking you may have just upped the ante on what they're willing to, uh, do to her."

"Dammit." Jack's frustration permeated the air.

"Listen. We never had this conversation...and what I'm about to say, I never said. Do you understand?" Joe spoke in almost a whisper.

"Yeah, I get it. What?"

"One sure way to get us back on surveillance is to make it look like she's planning to go to Colombia. I don't know...maybe there's an airline ticket that gets purchased in her name or something."

"Yep. You never said that, and I'm on it. And Joe, thanks." The fear and gratitude in Jack's voice mixed together seamlessly. His breathing became shallow as the adrenaline surged.

"A guy has to be able to sleep at night, you know," Joe said.

"Thanks again, Joe. I mean it."

As soon as they disconnected, Jack dialed the airlines to book a flight to Colombia in Porter's name. He made the reservation for several weeks out to buy some time, since she obviously would not be showing up for the flight.

Next, he climbed on his motorcycle. His mind raced as he rode to Porter's house. By the time he arrived, it was just starting to get dark. This time, he parked down the street and walked through the side yard. He distinctly smelled cigarette smoke. Looking at the ground, Jack bent down and picked up a discarded butt, still warm.

Jack looked toward the old lady's house. "Yep. There she is, as usual, spying out the window." He dropped the cigarette and marched across the street.

After knocking several times, hard, on the front door, she finally yanked it open.

"And what do you want?" Her words hung thick with disdain between them.

"What I want is to know if you saw anyone hanging around Porter's house today."

"Why should I tell you?"

"Because if you don't and someone hurts her, then I'm going to tell the cops everything I know about you." Jack winced at his own words— they were weak and mean—but what choice did he have? He needed to know.

The tiny woman shook her head, stepped aside, and said. "Okay. Fine. Come in. Let's at least be civilized about all of this. By the way, my name is Rose. Your name is?"

"Jack. I'm Jack." A little breathless and a lot overwhelmed with worry, he stepped inside Rose's house.

"Well, Jack, would you like some tea?" Rose's face had softened, and she spoke in a friendly tone.

Caught a little off guard by Rose's sudden shift in demeanor, he politely declined the tea.

"Sit, then." Rose motioned to a very petite Victorian couch covered in a floral fabric. Jack sat awkwardly. It seemed impossible to sit normally on the undersized furniture.

Rose began. "So, today, I did see a man standing on the side of Porter's house. He just lingered there for an hour or more, smoking."

"Was he short and pudgy?" Jack asked.

"No. That's the first guy. This was definitely a different person. He seemed average in height and had browner skin—an olive complexion—and his hair was black, wavy." She wiggled her fingers around her hair and face, as if he needed the guidance.

"That's sounds like a different guy for sure. Did he do anything else? Did he have a car?" Jack fidgeted as he talked. He couldn't get comfortable.

Rose thought for a moment before responding. "No, he just stood there, smoking. I didn't see a car."

Jack nodded and stretched out his legs. He thought about the information he'd just received.

Rose cleared her throat and said, "Now, can you do something for me?"

He simply looked at her without answering.

"Can you get my jewelry back? Porter has my necklace and my ring—they were my father's."

Confused, Jack asked, "Why does she have your father's jewelry?"

"It was in the house. I told you, that was my father's house."

Jack tried to be patient. "Oh, right. Um. I don't really understand."

Rose began to explain everything, how she was the illegitimate love child of Mr. Mitchell and her mother, who was the housekeeper. How Mr. Mitchell gave all of his children monogramed jewelry and how the ring that had originally belonged to his mother was now on Porter's finger.

As strange as it all sounded, Jack kind of got it. "Okay. I'm sorry. That's a difficult situation."

Rose looked at him, blinked some sudden tears away, and said,

"So, will you get my things back?"

Jack's compassionate side was seeping in. "Tell you what. When this is all said and done, I'll talk to Porter for you. Then, the two of you can figure it out together. I'm sure she'll be very understanding. How's that sound?"

"But what if she says no?" Her voice sounded almost childlike, meek.

"I know Porter, and she always does the right thing," he assured her. Then the two of them exchanged phone numbers. "Rose, call me if you see that guy again, will you?"

Rose agreed. If it got her what she wanted, she had no problem helping this stranger.

~~~

Almost twenty-four hours later, Max sat finishing off the last bite of his candy bar as he and Joe waited in the SUV next to Porter's guesthouse. "Joe, I really never thought we'd be back here. And now it's hot and humid." Max plucked at the neck of his shirt several times in a futile attempt to cool himself.

Joe responded with only an "uh-huh."

The two had arrived that morning, a day after the airline-ticket alert had hit the Bureau.

"I knew I saw someone that day," Max added.

Joe stayed quiet and looked at the clock: 8 p.m.

Max crumbled the wrapper.

"Shhh." Joe leaned forward. "Look."

Max shifted his sights toward the far side of Porter's house. There in the shadows stood a man—olive skin tone, dark hair. "That's the new guy. He looks a lot more fit than the other one Jack described from before."

"Unfortunately, yes."

Joe picked up his cell phone and dialed Jack.

"Who are you calling?" Max asked.

Joe ignored Max's question and said only two words to the person on the other end of the phone. "He's here."

Max stared at Joe, waiting for an explanation.

"Who do you think? I called Jack," Joe said.

Max nodded. "Right."

Joe and Max waited and watched. After a few minutes, they could hear a distant motorcycle. Then silence. They watched some more. Then they saw Jack dart behind the garage, then the house. Next they saw the new intruder raise his hands as if at gunpoint.

Joe looked at Max and said, "None of this ever happened."

Max nodded but could not take his eyes off of Jack as he approached their car, practically dragging the guy alongside him.

Joe got out of the SUV, cuffed the dark-haired man, and pushed him into the backseat.

Jack got in next to him, still pointing his gun at his newly acquired prisoner.

They drove to the river house. And then the interrogation began.

Joe and Jack took turns questioning the guy.

"What do you want from her?" Jack's voice rose as he lost his temper.

The informant's thick accent caused his words to run together. "Dinero. She owes her husband's debt to my boss. If she doesn't pay, I'll take it—one way or another." He laughed mockingly.

Jack grabbed the guy and raised his fist. Joe put his arm on Jack's. Jack acquiesced and backed away.

The drug runner spat on the floor and said, "That's what I thought."

Joe pulled Max aside and instructed him to keep an eye on the guy, and then he led Jack outside to the back deck for a brief chat.

"Listen, Jack, I don't think they'd watch her just to get money." Joe didn't want to say the words, but someone had to.

Jack agreed. "There's definitely another reason. I just hope it's not what I think it could be."

Joe tilted his head. "I can think of a million reasons that aren't good. So, I'm going to need you to be more specific about yours."

Jack turned to look out at the river. "I'm worried they're waiting for Will to come find her. Or going to do something to her to make sure he does."

"What? I thought he was dead?" Joe leaned in, waiting for clarification.

"A lot of evidence suggested that, but I'm not so sure after my last visit to Colombia. The informant I met with had some of Will's possessions, and when I asked where he got them, he said from the pilot. Then, when I pressed him about whether Will was dead or not, he ran."

"Okay, that's not a lot to go on, but let's go try to find out what this guy knows. And stay calm, for chrissakes," Joe said, even though he himself looked anything but calm at the moment.

They heard a scuffle from inside, and a loud thud followed.

"What the hell?" Joe called out as both men scrambled to get inside.

Max was sprawled out on the floor, coming to from being knocked out.

The other man was gone.

"Dammit, Max!" Joe said, helping his partner to his feet.

"What the hell happened? Where's the informant?" Jack shouted. Without waiting for an answer, he ran out the open front door.

The agents quickly headed to the car. Max hung his head the whole way. When they were inside the vehicle, he said quietly, "He couldn't have gotten far."

Joe did not respond. He knew Max messed up, but there was nothing they could do about that now.

Back to Porter's house we go.

~~~

A couple of hours went by, and Joe and Max sat in their SUV near the guesthouse. Jack finally showed up on his motorcycle, pulling up next to Joe's open window. "Couldn't find him. That guy is a professional for sure—impossible to trail even handcuffed."

Max groaned.

"What, Max?" Joe looked as if he already knew what Max would say next.

"Well, that's the thing. The guy told me he had to go to the bathroom and either I had to help with that or remove his cuffs."

Jack just shook his head. Joe's jaw actually dropped. Max looked at them with a hangdog expression. "I'm sorry, okay?"

~~~

Rose hadn't slept well the night before, so she had spent most of the day napping off and on in her chair. She went to the window to look out for just a moment. She didn't see the new guy lurking around.

"I need some fresh air." She filled her watering can and went to tend to the ferns on her screened-in porch, located on the side of her house. That's when she saw just a sliver of the red taillight of the black SUV on the far side of Porter's guesthouse.

"Why are those guys back?" Then Rose saw Jack take off down the street on his motorcycle. Hastily, she plopped her gardening hat on her head and made her way to Porter's guesthouse being careful to stay out of sight. She could hear the voices of the men in the SUV, but could not make out their words. Frustrated, she tried to move closer.

Suddenly, Rose stumbled into full view of the SUV. Her heart pounded violently as she watched the younger man emerge from the vehicle.

He walked over. "You okay?"

"I'm fine." Rose leaned to retrieve her fallen hat. The man grabbed it first and gently handed it over. Rose thanked him and turned to leave. Then, she stopped and faced him again. "Are you helping Jack?" Her words hung in the air awkwardly.

"We're just doing our jobs, ma'am."

"So, you are helping Jack, then?"

"Um. Hey, Joe?"

Joe got out of the car. "What is it?"

"This lady is asking if we're helping Jack."

Joe brushed the front of his shirt and started to speak.

Rose cut him off, "Are you looking for that guy who hides in the woods?"

The two men looked at each other, eyes wide, and she knew she'd hit the nail on the head.

~ 59 ~

The weeks flew by, and the SUV surveillance came and went randomly, while Rose's watch remained constant and—if I let my imagination prevail—seemingly escalated. Luckily, I kept busier than usual as Patsy and I prepared for the gala. All appeared good and well with the preparations except that I still wrestled with apprehension about being at the center of it all. I needed a mental reprieve. I shook off the feeling, blaming my exhaustion on all the footwork and anticipation. However, the thought of going to an event without Jack proved harder to deny and made me feel downright blue. I wiped a few tears from my cheek.

It's time to call him. Way past time.

The doorbell chimed. I looked at the clock: a quarter past three in the afternoon. "I'll be right there." How could I have forgotten? Cecil and I planned to check out the prohibition tunnel today.

As I opened the door, Cecil said, "I have a surprise for you." Grinning, he waved a stack of papers my way. But upon seeing my expression, he stopped and asked, "Are you okay, Porter?"

"Yes. I'm fine. Just tired, I think. Come in, come in. Let's see this surprise." I tried to switch my mood.

"I can come back, if you need to rest." Cecil looked concerned.

I waved off his suggestion. "No way. Now, what do you have there?" I forced a smile.

"Let's just say that this is quite the comprehensive list of people who used to receive a certain medicinal elixir from the Turnberry Pharmacy during the prohibition. I thought it would be a nice accouterment to your little piece of history downstairs."

"Oh my," I almost squealed. "How did you get this? I cannot wait to compare the bottles to the names." *What a generous gift.* I felt my mood lighten for the first time in days, and it felt good.

"An old newspaper guy has his tactics." Cecil winked. "The medical justifications alone are quite entertaining. I'm sure you'll enjoy at least a few of them quite a bit."

"Thank you so much, Cecil. What a perfect surprise. Come on, let's go." I walked toward the basement door, and Cecil followed close behind.

Once in the basement, Cecil reached into his canvas bag and handed over a forehead light on a stretchy band. I burst into laughter.

"Don't curb your laughter just yet. There's more," he said playfully.

"I can't wait."

Then he revealed a walkie-talkie. I laughed so hard my cheeks hurt. "Actually, Cecil. I'm impressed. Even though we look like kids at a summer camp."

He splayed his arms in mock innocence. "What? You never know."

I couldn't stop laughing.

Grinning, he said, "Okay, okay, maybe we leave the walkie-talkies here, but I didn't want to be accused of not being prepared."

"No one can accuse you of that." I put on my headlamp and hooked the walkie-talkie to my waistband. "Ready when you are, sir."

He slid on his headlamp, and in unison, we both became quiet as we approached the hobbit-sized door.

"How do you want to do this?" I whispered.

Cecil looked at me. "Why are you whispering?"

"I have no idea," I whispered, then snickered. In a louder tone, I said, "Okay, enough fun and games. What's the plan?"

"Well, Porter, one of us should go in first and assess the safety. That way, if anything is unstable or something caves in, one of us is out here to call for help. I figure, if everything looks sound, then it's fine for both of us to follow the tunnel to its rightful end."

"I agree. Ready?"

Cecil and I pushed the boxes away from in front of the door.

I felt compelled to go first. He didn't argue, only saying, "It's your tunnel, your call."

I headed in, feeling the cool, damp air on my face. Feeling...*bold?*

The headlamp Cecil brought worked remarkably well and

illuminated the tunnel at least three feet in front of me. Fortunately, it looked to be in very sound condition; the walls, ceiling and even the floors were made of brick. I approached the sharp left turn of the tunnel and fumbled with the walkie-talkie. Static ensued as my actual voice intermixed with the choppy version coming through Cecil's walkie—a mess. I had said, "Heading around the bend." However, the sputtered mosaic of sounds didn't match the original message.

Cecil made a *hmph* sound and then said without the walkie-talkie, "Maybe we just call out to each other the old-fashioned way."

I couldn't help but smirk a little. "Okay, heading around the bend."

"I got that. Thanks," he said with a bit of sarcasm.

After the turn, the tunnel opened up, and I could stand much straighter. "Looks good to me."

"Okay. I'm heading in," Cecil said.

He caught up, but we couldn't look at each other because we'd be like two deer in each other's headlights. He gave me a strong pat on my shoulder. "Ready?"

"Yep." I started walking and thinking. Here we were walking in a wormhole of sorts, both figuratively and literally. I said, "It feels like we could pop out at just about anywhere."

Cecil added, "Hopefully, we pop out somewhere."

Feeling philosophical, I couldn't help but think that none of us really knows what the future holds, where each of us will end up at the end of our journey.

"Porter, you still with me?" Cecil's voice echoed a bit.

Pulled from my thoughts, I answered, "Yes. Just lost in my own head."

"Porter, how about a break for just a minute or two. Sip some water. Catch our breath."

I didn't really need a break, but I could tell Cecil did. We both tugged at our headlamps so that they hung down around our necks— no need to blind each other—and sat on the floor.

Cecil said, "Porter, there's something I've been wanting to ask you, but I don't want to pry."

"What is it? It's okay. You can ask me anything?" I took a sip of water.

"Well, I don't know how to say it other than to just say it. And today seems like the right day. You seem sad. And..."

"I'm okay, Cecil. I promise."

"I know. I know. But...it's just...well, Porter, I've lived a long time, seen a lot. I can see pain sometimes in your eyes, like a shadow. Today, though, it's more. Let me help if I can." He put a gentle hand on top of mine, the way my own father used to.

I tried to take a deep breath, but the lump in my throat continued to build.

I had told Cecil the facts, the logistics of things. I just hadn't highlighted the emotional impact that did, in fact, lurk just below the surface for me on most days. So, I sighed, and began to open up to my dear friend. "It's a long story. You already know most of it, just not what it did to me inside. I trusted my husband Will so much that I would have given my life for him. It shattered me to find out he had lied to me and set me up to take the blame."

Cecil nodded.

I continued. "There are many layers to what happened. A lot that still haunts me, and some that are still unresolved. So, you're right. I do hide pain, and yes, pretty much every day. But as time passes, I do find moments of happiness and peace. Sometimes I even count the number of breaths between the waves of pain. And, Cecil, the number of breaths is getting larger. That's my light at the end of the tunnel, pun intended."

"Ah, I understand. Trust me. I really do."

We both forced smiles before the weight of our conversation fell back upon us like a storm cloud.

I looked at Cecil and said, "However, it is my burden, no one else's. One that I, in some way...well, I'm sure I deserve."

"Whatever happened, I know you well enough to be certain that you did not deserve this struggle."

I shook my head emphatically. "No. I ran from the pain, from the whole thing. And the worst part, I left Jack, the man I love. Jack was so good to me. He truly cared about me. And I think he still does. So, ultimately, I betrayed someone, too." My voice cracked. "I'm a coward."

"No," he said firmly. "Not at all. You ran away because it was too much to bear. You didn't start the fire; you ran from the fury of the heat—that's natural, heroic even. You ran to survive. What you did is not shameful, you hear me? It's okay to break sometimes, but not to quit. And, Porter, you didn't quit. I know this because you are here in front of me now."

I told Cecil about the day the Army had handed me the flag that had covered an empty coffin and how I had told Jack I didn't think I could live with the pain. That it was all too much. And it was.

"And...Cecil, do you know what Jack did? He just kept saying, 'It's okay. Porter, I'm here. Hold on to me. Just hold on to me. I will fix you. I will fix everything. It's okay. Just let me. I will fix you.'

I took a breath. Cecil waited.

"Except that I was too selfish. I did not want him to fix me. I didn't want anything except to erase my past. But I just sat there; I let him think he fixed me. And then in the end, I left him, my truest friend. It isn't the Leighton way to be that weak—and that is who I really am, a Leighton. I should be stronger than this. I think I just lost myself somewhere in all of the pain. And I don't know if I'll ever find my strength again."

Cecil kept listening patiently.

"And even now, it all somehow seems like a movie. Sometimes, it seems like Will never even existed. Like I made him up."

"Porter. It's okay," Cecil said softly. Then he added, "Whoever hurt you has his own penance to settle. His own hell to face as a result. You...you listen to me, Porter. You stand tall, with your head high, you hear me? You. Are. A. Survivor."

I couldn't hold the tears back any longer; they trickled down my face.

He waited a moment then continued. "I'm going to let you in on a little secret. We survivors, we have each other. Whenever you feel alone, or you feel like you are disconnected from existence, just look around, and the other survivors...their eyes will jump out at you...our energies are different from everyone else. You can find strength in us when you are weak. You don't have to talk about it—our stories are all one. We all carry the same scars. You know the scars—the ones that can only come from the brutal pain of your soul splitting in two. Just keep moving forward. Keep being the beautiful soul you are meant to be. And I promise, one day, the pain will be only a memory; the person who hurt you, just a waning shadow.

Before I could respond, he added, "Focus on those breaths and your light. Your wings won't stay broken forever. They may remain blackened from the fire, but you will fly again. Wear those dark wings with honor. You survived."

Astonished, I blinked a few times at his words. Had I told him about the necklace I'd given Will? I couldn't remember. I must have.

Then he said the thing I needed to hear most. "And if you love Jack, tell him."

He reached into his pocket and handed me a beautiful linen handkerchief, pressed to perfection. I wiped my tears.

"My friend, you don't have to punish yourself. You deserve to be happy."

That's exactly what Jack always says. I could feel pieces of my soul coming back to life from the words. I mouthed a thank-you.

Cecil gave my hand a stern pat, then started to stand. "You'll get there. Trust me. Trust yourself."

His words replayed in my mind, striking me deep inside. *Trust myself.* Dammit all to hell. Damn Will, my despicable husband. Damn him. No, I didn't have to answer for his choices. And with that, I stood up—in more ways than one. "I'm ready. Let's go."

And I was ready. To be happy again. Truly happy. I knew what I had to do. But for now, we had tunnel business to take care of.

"Thatta girl." Cecil gave an encouraging pat on my back as we started to walk again.

Finally, the end of the tunnel came into view, and we could see a narrow, stone staircase about four feet away. Cecil said, "Moment of truth just ahead," then pointed.

He paused at the bottom of the stairs and looked up. "Well, I wouldn't believe this if I wasn't seeing it."

"What?" I quickly shuffled to his side.

"This staircase."

"Yes?" I prodded.

"Well, I've only seen one other staircase this ominous in my life."

"Cecil, the suspense is just too much...please divulge."

"Dublin Castle. This looks like the staircase coming straight out of the moat into the ruins of Dublin Castle. I swear, this is almost a spitting image, except for the wood supports."

I giggled at his comparison and took a better look. At the top of the staircase, I saw a flat panel made of dark, thick wood with iron hinges. "Well, it's still castle-like up there—look, a dungeon door." My words rang with sarcasm.

I climbed up the stone stairs and, once at the top, pressed on the panel over my head with both hands. "It's stuck."

"Is there room for both of us?" Cecil questioned. "Can I help?"

"Wait, something just clicked."

Suddenly, the door began to pull itself upward. I stumbled since I had been using the pressure on the door to balance myself. My hand reached for the wall, but it was damp, and I lost my grip. Then I felt a strong hand on my back. Cecil braced me so I could find my footing. "Thanks. You saved me from a not-so-fun fall. In fact, you've kind of been rescuing me all day."

"Any time." He remarked as the staircase filled with natural light. Then he explained, "That door is on a weighted pulley system."

As we climbed out of the tunnel, with surprisingly little difficulty, we came to find ourselves standing inside a small room with a stone fireplace.

"What...where are we?" I stood in awe. "I thought we'd pop up in the woods or a cave or something."

"Well, it looks like we are in someone's living room."

"What? Oh my God. Cecil, this isn't okay."

"Wait a minute. Look." He walked to the window and parted the sheer curtains. "That's your house. We're in your guest cottage, for heaven's sake!"

"What? Let me see." I peered out the window too. *Sure enough.*

"Porter, you haven't been in here yet?"

"Actually, no."

"Why not?" His brows furrowed in a perplexed fashion.

"You know, Cecil, that's a good question, and I really wish I could answer you, but I'm actually asking myself the very same thing."

We just stood, looking at each other, speechless, as we considered the discovery.

Cecil spoke first. "We're not the only ones who know about this tunnel."

I looked at him a little confused. "Why do you say that?"

"See that rug rolled up over there?" My eyes followed his gaze. "And see those dusty footprints?" He pointed.

I nodded. "I need to sit." I spotted two leather chairs, visibly the worse for wear. Then again, so were we. "Well," I said while clapping my hands together matter-of-factly, "since this my house, can I offer you a seat?"

Cecil replied, "I don't see why not." We plopped down into the chairs.

I brushed a little dust off my pant leg and then spoke. "I guess now is a good time to tell you this." I began recapping my story about the light in the basement, and this time, I divulged the part about the footsteps in the tunnel that I was sure I had heard. Cecil listened intently, and I imagined wheels turning in his mind.

After a few minutes, we left through the front door of the cottage. While crossing the driveway to the yard, Cecil gently put his hand on my back to guide me away from the angle toward Rose's house, where she stood staring at us from her garden.

"Yes. Let's avoid that. Does she look crankier than normal?" I asked.

He raised an eyebrow.

"I feel like she watches my house like it's a television program. Maybe it's my imagination."

Cecil closed his eyes and shook his head in slow motion. "Probably not."

"Okay. Then I'll try not to take it personally."

"And you shouldn't. She's just a strange bird."

"Yep. You have that right."

After Cecil left, I secured the tunnel door in the basement and then took a long, hot bath.

What an afternoon.

~ 60 ~

Jack knocked on Rose's back door, his mind heavy. Max and Joe had been back in DC for a few days for a reevaluation on Porter's surveillance—apparently things had been a little too quiet on the official reports. It didn't help that the recent cartel catch-and-release fiasco had to be kept off the record. But Joe had assured Jack that he wouldn't let the assignment get pulled again—he'd play up the plane ticket to Colombia that luckily still had a few weeks left riding on it. Plus, Joe asserted that it could be time well spent searching through some off-limits files that may shed some light on Will's loose ends with the drug runners. So, Jack had been doing the best he could, on his own, about keeping an eye on Porter, but he had needed help. That was why he'd decided to pull Rose in. She had surveillance down to a science.

They were developing a routine; he would stop by in the evenings here and there. She would update him on anything that she had seen on the street and at Porter's.

This evening, he held a bakery box in his hands as a thank-you for all she had done so far. Her eyes lit up when she saw the box of treats, and she quickly ushered him inside.

"What a lovely thing to do."

"It's nothing, really," Jack said, raking his fingers through his hair. He felt on edge, more so than usual.

"Everything okay, dear?" Rose asked gently.

"Yes, sorry. Long day." The countless hours of worry were starting to take their toll. He needed this to end. And he needed Max and Joe back, too. Rose had been great, but he knew the risk in relying on her. He could be putting her in danger. Not to mention the danger involved in him not being able to get to Porter in time even if Rose alerted him.

Rose began to update Jack on the week's happenings. She rambled on about this and that. Jack listened half-heartedly until Rose mentioned a tunnel, and that's when Jack interrupted. "A tunnel? What are you talking about?"

"Yes. There's a tunnel. It runs from the guesthouse into the basement of the main house. Porter knows about it. I saw her and Cecil coming out of the guesthouse." Rose stopped.

Jack's eyes widened. "Okay."

Rose looked at him in a *don't-you-get-it* way and said, "A prohibition tunnel."

"And how do you know Porter knows about it?"

"Because I saw them go in the house and then later come out of the guesthouse."

Jack tried to comprehend. He knew about Cecil, a friend that Porter had made in town. But he had no idea what Rose could possibly be trying to tell him. He waited for more.

"I'll be right back," she said. When she returned, she handed him a key. "It's for the guesthouse. See for yourself."

Jack took the key, but he had no intention of going into any part of Porter's house uninvited. Besides, he still had the other key that Rose had left in the lock that first day they had met.

Once Rose finished her update and they exchanged pleasantries, Jack said his goodbyes and headed to the river house. It would be a brief respite. He'd be back at Porter's in just a few hours. He still cursed the fact the cartel thug had escaped before they could get any real information out of him.

Back at the river house, Jack grabbed the FedEx envelope that had arrived on his porch, went inside, poured a glass of whiskey and tried to slow the gears in his head. But he couldn't. What to do, what to do—about everything. Suddenly, he sat up straighter, an idea forming in his mind.

Bottom line: he had to get the cartel off Porter's back. Period. The only way to do that would be to redirect them to Will and fast, if he really was still alive. And Jack believed, more than he ever had, that the bastard was indeed alive.

His suspicions about Will continued to grow as he read over the new information that Joe and Max had sent—apparently they had been busy over the past couple of days. "Those two may not be completely worthless after all." Jack couldn't believe his eyes. Apparently, not long after the crash, an American fitting Will's description and sporting several injuries, including a broken leg and a laceration to his arm, had chartered a plane out of Bogota to Costa Rica. Jack knew all too well that extradition from Costa Rica proved to be next to impossible, even with treaties in place. Besides, the government had deemed Will deceased, so in reality, if he had gone to Costa Rica, he could have gone under a completely new identity. Jack's gears were spinning—his heart pounded from the adrenaline.

Still, the big question remained. It burned in his brain. "If he is alive, why hasn't he contacted Porter somehow?" Jack needed to go to Costa Rica. Now. He couldn't think of a better way. He picked up the phone and dialed.

The voice on the other end picked up after only one ring. "Joe here."

"Bang-up job, and I mean it in a good way this time."

"You got the package, I assume."

"Yes. That's why I'm calling. Listen, I need to leave town. Soon. As in tomorrow." Jack spat the words out one after another.

Joe's response came after a pause. "But we aren't scheduled to be back until Thursday. Can it wait?"

"I don't think so. Can you get back sooner?" Jack felt anxious to get moving on this.

"Let me think." Joe made a *click, click, click* sound with his mouth before responding. "I can send Max ahead of me. I can get him there tomorrow afternoon."

Jack took an audible breath. "I guess he's better than nothing."

"Look. We aren't asking him to build a rocket here. He cares about her safety. He won't let her get hurt. He can do this."

"I hear you. Thanks Joe, really." Jack hung up and called his old pilot buddy to schedule a private flight to Costa Rica.

Between Max coming back and Rose on the lookout, Porter should be okay for a couple days. Besides, she and the librarian seemed almost attached at the hip lately. Jack grinned thinking how he loved that Porter had these new friends. He had not seen her this involved socially in a long time.

She's healing.

Jack packed a bag before showering and then rode back to Porter's.

~ 61 ~

After breakfast, I walked to Main Street to the little gift shop a couple of doors down from Stan's market and browsed. My hand caressed a smooth wooden box containing a set of whiskey stones and two beautiful crystal glasses.

I snickered as I thought of the time Jack tried to pour his forty-five-year-old whiskey into plastic cups for us. He had belly laughed when I refused and plundered his cabinets to find the closest thing possible to proper glasses.

"Perfect." I bought the box and had it inscribed with his initials, wrapped and shipped directly to his house in Sleepy Hollow from the store. I knew I needed to mail it right then and there, before I lost my nerve. Inside, I had placed a small heart shaped gift card that read simply, *"I miss you. Love, Porter."* I hoped it wasn't too late for us.

Next, I walked to the library to see Patsy. The gala planning had taken on a life of its own. Once word had gotten out, thanks to Patsy's social nature, people popped out of the woodwork all over town offering to help with everything from menu planning to entertainment. Patsy and I chatted for about twenty minutes, and during that conversation, she told me at least three times that I could sit back and relax. The guest of honor didn't need to do all of the work. I decided to listen, finally, and left her to it. I made my way to the wine shop and purchased a couple of bottles of small-batch reds and some more dark chocolate.

I felt better today than I had in a long time. *I hope this feeling lasts.*

As soon as I arrived home, Rose came flying out of her front door waving and calling my name. I tried not to roll my eyes. She sported an unusually pleasant look on her face. We chatted for a few minutes, before Rose went back inside. I was dumbstruck—that had to have been the most normal conversation I'd ever shared with her.

I pinched myself. This day seemed like a dream. A good one for a change.

On my way past the staircase, I recalled the stack of papers I had found in the safe. I grabbed them, a cup of Earl Grey tea, and settled in the study to read through them—why not? The first few pages appeared to be just legal documents concerning property and stocks. I flipped through a bit more. "What on earth?" A diagram? Then several more diagrams. "It can't be." The diagrams were of a crown. I had to call Cecil and Patsy.

~~~

Max and Joe once again sat in the clearing by the guesthouse, perspiring a bit in the mid-summer heat as they kept watch while Jack was away.

"I could have held down the fort, you know." Max's voice sounded small and slightly wounded.

"I have no doubt." Joe kept his response short to stave off any more damage to the bruised ego sitting next to him. Truth be told, Joe had fully planned for Max to come back early without him, but the assistant special agent in charge had misunderstood the request and authorized both agents' travel back to Turnberry. So, Joe just went with it.

Joe tapped his foot incessantly. Max rolled the window down further and shifted in his seat. Both felt the tension in the air—waiting and watching for the cartel thug to show up...or not.

"I need to stretch my legs." Joe opened the door and stepped out finding shade under the large trees lining the property. Max followed his lead.

Joe leaned on the trunk of the old oak, deep in thought.

Max said, "What's on your mind?"

"It just doesn't make sense."

"What?" Max popped a piece of gum into his mouth, enjoying the shade and slight breeze.

"Why the cartel would just watch her and for this long. If they wanted money, that should be a relatively easy get for a bunch of drug runners against a wealthy, single woman living alone. Jack thinks they're watching to see if Will shows up or to make him show up, and that makes a little more sense. But not completely. There's still something missing. I just know it." Joe spoke without making eye contact.

Max seemed to be thinking it over for a few beats. Then he said, "Maybe they're watching so that if and when they find Will, they have a bargaining chip—like protecting an asset."

Joe processed what Max had just said. The kid seemed to be making some sense.

Max continued. "So, let's put all the pieces on the table. Will ran drugs for the cartel. His plane crashed in FARQ territory. Was his plane full of drugs or money at the time? Let's assume it was money, since he was headed back into drug country. If he did escape, maybe he took the money and disappeared. Maybe he cost the cartel a lot of money, and maybe even their trafficking route. His crash definitely set off the red flags to the illegal activity and maybe even alerted the US government to it. So, let's say the cartel needs a way to make Will cooperate. If and when they do find him, and they have eyes on Porter, they can kidnap her to make him pay them back."

Joe shrugged, not totally convinced. "Seems like you watch too many movies, but I have to admit, you may have hit on something. But one question, why not kidnap her from the beginning?"

"Not sure, but maybe they aren't sure Will is alive either, or maybe they want him first before they mess with her. Maybe they want him to know that she's alive and well and at risk. If they took her years ago, she'd probably be dead by now."

That was concerning enough, but Joe felt in his gut there was still something more.

~ 62 ~

Jack sat in an open-air hotel lobby in a small Costa Rican beach town. Joe had sent him a map of the area before he left marked with all the places that the individual resembling Will had been seen. Jack studied it carefully. Donning his sunglasses and hat, he walked to the first location. Grabbed a coffee and pretended to thumb through a travel brochure. He barely had to try—his cover story, an American tourist.

After an hour, Jack decided to catch a cab to the next location, an outdoor market that sold an array of goods, from food to crafts. Jack looked around a bit, and then he saw a stand that had embossed wings on the sign. Jack recognized the wings immediately. They were just like the ones on the necklace Will carried and on the stationary that Porter had.

He walked over, and a little lady with sun-weathered skin and wiry dark hair asked him in broken English if he liked anything. He nodded and then reached in his pocket. He showed the lady a picture of Will. The lady nodded and said, "That's Mr. Jack."

His heart nearly exploded. He asked her where he could find "Mr. Jack."

Holding out his map for her to show him, the lady leaned in and then tapped a spot next to the ocean, "Aqui, señor."

Jack made a mental note of the location she had indicated and said, "Gracias." Then he eyed the array of jewelry and embossed stationary again.

"Something you like, señor?"

Jack pointed to one of the necklaces. "That one, yes, with the delicate gold wings." The lady handed it to him. He paid her, put the necklace in his pocket, and left.

As he approached the locals-only hangout, he noticed a few patrons sitting at tables around an outdoor dining area overlooking the ocean. He walked over to the open-air bar, and the bartender greeted him. "Can I help you?"

Yes. I'm supposed to meet Mr. Jack." He thought he'd give the name a try. The worst thing that could happen was the bartender thinking he was a little nuts. He could live with that.

To Jack's surprise, the bartender nodded and pointed to a man about Jack's size, broad shoulders and wearing a ball cap with his back to them, sitting comfortably alone at a small table overlooking the rolling sea. Jack recognized the arrogant posture of the man immediately.

Jack's heart pounded, and he unintentionally tightened his fist, ready to walk up and just punch the man. He controlled the urge by taking a few deep breaths and reducing his heart rate.

"Long time no see. *Mr. Jack.*" Jack spoke clearly as he sat down next to Will.

Will glanced over in a nonchalant kind of way. "It took you longer than I expected."

Jack leaned toward his old friend. "What the hell, Will? Do you know what a mess you left at home? How bad you broke her heart?"

"I'm sure you had no problem piecing it all back together. Tell me. How long did you wait, huh, to swoop in?" Will's tone was laced with indignation.

And jealousy?

Whatever.

"How dare you! I never disrespected your marriage—at least not while you were still in it," Jack fired back.

"I wasn't blind. I saw how you looked at her from day one." Will focused on the ocean.

Jack ignored the comment. "She's been through hell, Will. Investigated, implicated...because of you."

"I know. Unintended fallout." Will sounded detached.

"I should punch you right here and now, drag you back to the States, and turn you over," Jack snarled in a low voice.

"I wouldn't blame you if you did. But it wouldn't matter." Will leaned back in his chair, still looking at the sea and still seemingly not rattled at all by Jack's presence.

"What the hell am I supposed to do, Will? She won't move on because she feels loyal to you. To your marriage." Jack's voice cracked, and he winced at the inadvertent reveal.

"Oh, poor you. She won't say yes to you because she still loves me. And I should feel bad for you?" Will laughed, and this time, he looked directly at Jack.

"No. You should feel bad for *her*. You left her stuck. She's tormented. She's trying to be someone else. She's alone." Jack paused. "She has the government and the cartel watching her every move. And those Colombian thugs are getting bolder. This isn't a game, man." Jack could barely fight the impulse to grab Will and shake him to his senses.

"The cartel? What?" Will seemed caught off guard and muttered something inaudible. Then Jack heard him say under his breath, "That wasn't part of the deal."

Finally, Jack detected some emotion in Will's eyes. Fear? *Well, he might just be human, after all.*

"Yes. The cartel. There have been a few guys snooping around. I caught one of them at her house. At. Her. House. Will, listen to me. You left her in serious danger. And...what deal?"

Will stared blankly at Jack.

"You said 'wasn't part of the deal.' How deep has this gotten?" Jack probed.

"Shit." Will straightened in his chair, and for the first time since Jack had sat down, Will looked visibly uncomfortable.

Just then, a woman sauntered over and leaned in to kiss Will, which he avoided, but their familiarity couldn't be denied. Unsure, she eyed Jack and then looked back at Will. She said, "Jack, it's time to go." Will asked her for a few minutes, and she retreated to the bar area, out of earshot.

"What's with you using my name? You're a real bastard, you know that?" Jack could practically feel the daggers shooting out of his eyes as he faced the man he'd once called "best friend."

Will calmly answered, "I'm aware."

"Clean this mess up. Give Porter her life back—you owe her that."
Jack set his fist down on the table, silently, but firmly.

Will nodded. "Okay."

"You need to do it fast."

"Okay. I hear you. I'll put out a call." Will looked at his watch.

Jack wouldn't let it go at that. "To who?"

"Look, Jack. The fact is they don't want her. They want me." Will
shot him a knowing glance.

Jack's patience had worn thin. "Really, Will. Tell me something I
don't know."

Will took a deep breath and surveyed the other patrons nearby
before speaking in a hushed manner. "Listen. Things aren't always
black and white. But I don't have to tell you that. Come on. Think. Ever
ask yourself why the trail of evidence never amounted to pressed
charges or why the two agents watching her don't seem to know much
about the case?"

How does he know there are two agents?

Before Jack could interrupt, Will continued. "Use that Ivy League
brain that your granddaddy paid for. What about the bigger questions?
Ask yourself... how come no one was found? Seven of us on that plane—
just disappeared. Poof. No national news. Think, Jack. It doesn't add
up, right? But you know what does add up? Having a solid reason to
enlist a couple of federal watchdogs on her while everything goes
down...built-in protection, the kind that doubles as a red herring.
Everybody wins."

Jack retorted, "Nobody's winning, in case you haven't noticed.
That's just bad math, and you know it. Don't try to turn yourself into
some kind of unrequited hero."

"I'm not looking for a medal. I'm trying to make you aware that
this is bigger than any of us. Oh, forget it." He tilted his head and
squinted his eyes. "You know what? Now I remember."

"Remember what?"

Will looked smug. "Why you were always second in line. Why she
chose me."

Jack almost lost it. "You know what, Will?" He stopped himself.
This was going nowhere. Then he said, "Whose side are you on,
anyway?"

Will leaned in close as he spoke, "Do sides really matter?"

Jack ignored the implied deeper meaning and responded with a definitive. "Yes."

Heavy silence fell upon them.

Then, shifting in his chair, Will asked, "Are you going to tell her about me?"

Stewing inside, Jack hoped his words would cut razor-sharp. "I have to. I can't lie to her. I'm not like you, remember."

Will seemed unaffected, letting out a simple sigh. "You know, if you tell her, she's going to want to see me."

Was that a threat? Jack couldn't be sure. "Out of the question."

"Don't worry, Romeo. No need to plan a homecoming party." Will looked away. "Truth be told, she was always too good for me—always more suited for a silver-spoon type like you. Just a damn shame for you that I met her first." Spite dripped from Will's words.

Jack grabbed him by the collar and spoke close to his face, staring into his soulless eyes. "You won't hurt her again."

"Then tell her I'm dead." Will said it like a dare, then he pulled away and straightened his shirt. "It's the truth, isn't it? From what I hear, there's a tombstone with *Willem H. Stone* written across it."

Jack's heart actually ached as he recalled that gloomy day when Porter laid to rest Will's empty casket. "Yeah. And that almost killed her, for real."

Will reached into the pocket of his shorts. He threw something across the table to Jack. It slid...in what seemed like slow motion. Jack focused on the object, and as it became clear, he recognized the black-metal wings attached to a necklace that Porter had given Will. "Give her this," Will said flippantly.

Jack's heart stopped. He knew the impact the necklace would have on Porter. "What do I tell her? She gave this to you."

Will seemed wounded. "Tell her nothing. Tell her you found them. Tell her...I don't need them anymore. Tell her whatever you want."

Jack still didn't touch the necklace.

"Take it!" Will yelled.

"You don't have to do this. You don't have to pretend that you don't care. You don't have to be cruel." It killed him to say that, but

Porter didn't deserve this, either. Jack watched as the emotion that had been in Will's eyes faded and coldness took hold.

"Look, Jack. I knew Porter was a better catch than I'll ever have a chance at again. She's beautiful, smart and..." Will stopped.

"And?" Jack prodded as anger continued welling up inside.

"And, well, I don't have to remind you, I'm sure—you're both trust-fund babies." Will's nostrils flared as he said the last few words.

"You married her for money? I don't believe you." Jack slammed his fist down on the table, making a noise this time.

"Calm down, old pal. No. I'm just saying she was the total package. Too good to pass up."

"And you gave up the total package...for this? Life on the run, to be a traitor hiding in Costa Rica?" Jack's words struck like venom. "You framed her, you bastard. You know what? You're right; you never deserved her. You certainly don't now. I'll give her this necklace back. Happy to. I hope she throws it in the bottom of a lake."

Will spoke not a word. He stood and began walking away, before stopping and turning back. "I'll make that call."

Then he was gone.

Jack's jaw clenched as he stuffed the necklace Will had thrown across the table into his own pocket. He needed a moment to process. He waved to the waiter and ordered a beer.

Jack thought about everything he'd just heard. No doubt, he'd found himself in a tough spot. Unfortunately, one question kept coming up, the one he knew would keep him up at night: would he, should he, tell Porter about Will? There were so many layers. First, Porter would have to accept Will being alive, free not captured, and that he hadn't contacted her—by choice. Second, she would have to reconcile all of the time and resources she had put into trying to find someone who ultimately didn't want to be found. Jack knew the list of hurts wouldn't stop there. What about accepting that Will had been living a new life with someone else on an exotic beach while Porter lived under the thumb of government spies and, even worse, the threat of the cartel?

Jack winced. He knew what Will had done wasn't that simple. If only it were. "Dammit, Will." As much as it pained Jack, he had to

~ **63** ~

Cecil and I waited for Patsy in a back booth at Hatch. Counter seating wouldn't provide enough privacy for the conversations the three of us needed to have. We sipped our coffees, and I shifted in my seat, checking the door a third time for Patsy.

"Porter, she'll be here soon," Cecil said reassuringly.

"I know. But it's only a couple days until the gala, and this is kind of big news."

"Well, hello there, Sherlock and Watson." Patsy's jovial voice rang out from a few feet away.

I gave her a look that said *shhhh.*

She smirked and put a finger to her lips.

Cecil chuckled.

Patsy sat. "Okay. Let's have it, Porter. What's the important discovery?"

I gave a quick glance to Cecil, who nodded encouragingly. I took a deep breath and began explaining to Patsy about the diagrams I had found and how they implied that Mr. Mitchell had orchestrated the heist, including having the fake stones commissioned.

Patsy listened, wide-eyed. "But why? He didn't need money. The crown belonged to his wife."

Cecil interrupted. "No. Who knows? We have theories, but that's it. Maybe he needed to buy silence for other business dealings that were not on the up-and-up."

I nodded, knowing Cecil meant the bootlegging.

Patsy didn't catch on to Cecil's reference. Instead, she beamed. She could not have looked more excited.

"Porter, you solved the biggest mystery this town's ever had to offer. You are a hero."

"That's ridiculous. I found lost items in an old house that I inherited. That's all."

"This news is just grand. Perfect. This will be the icing—no, even better—the cherry on top for the gala." Patsy stood.

"Where are you going?" I asked.

"To work. I have to be at the library." With that, Patsy said her goodbyes and floated out the door.

I stared at Cecil. "What have I done?"

Cecil grinned.

~~~

Joe looked up when he heard the motorcycle approaching. Max let out a *humph*.

Sweltering in the summer heat, the two remained under the shade next to the guesthouse.

Jack walked up, leaving his helmet on his bike. The two listened as Jack updated them on Will and the cartel.

"Not great news," Joe said.

"Nope," Jack agreed.

"Okay. So, what's the plan?" Max asked.

"I'm working on one." Jack looked down as he spoke.

"So, basically, you don't have one." Max couldn't help himself.

Jack slowly raised his gaze to meet Max's.

Sensing the tension, Joe said, "Look, for now, let's just keep watch. Think on this information. We've got time."

Jack and Max remained just feet away, staring at each other. Then Max looked away.

Jack relaxed his shoulders and sighed. "Okay."

Max rolled his eyes.

"You guys keep a close eye," Jack said. "I'll be back soon. The tux shop closes in a couple hours."

As Jack started the bike, Max called after him, "Hey, big shot, think you could bring us some cold drinks while you're at it?"

Joe gave Max a side-glance.

"What?" Max feigned an innocent shrug. "Seriously, we're just supposed to wait it out for the traitor husband to make some call that will magically stop the cartel? Give me a break."

Joe looked at the ground. "I don't know. This whole thing isn't cut-and-dry."

Max kicked his foot in the dirt. "I know what I'd have done to that jerk, and it wouldn't have included asking him to make a phone call."

Joe let the comment go—he'd didn't fully disagree.

~ **64** ~

Rose sat in her comfy chair eyeing the gala invitation that rested on the table beside her. "Hmph." Reluctantly, she reached over and snagged it. She skipped over the fund-raising details and went straight to the propaganda section, as she had nicknamed it. *Turnberry 1925 Jewel Heist. Come celebrate the return of the crown jewels.*

Rose remembered something about the heist from her mother's journal. "Let's see. The heist...yes, it was in April, I think. The night Sophie passed away."

She struggled to get up from her chair. She made her way to the guest-room closet where she kept her mother's journals. After a bit of searching, she opened to April 27, 1925. There, in her mother's own handwriting, was an account of the evening's happenings.

Everything got all balled up, and Graham and I had it out after the gala tonight. I arrived on time to meet him, but he still needed to escort Sophie home. So, there I stood alone and watched the two of them, all dolled up, leave together. I felt less than him, less than her. He told me he'd be right back. I waited, but only to tell him once and for all that I was done. That he had been the biggest mistake of my life. The only reason I wouldn't go back and change it all is because of my darling little Rose.

He's gone too far this time with this caper. Making me the one to be the go-between for him and that shady jeweler with those fake stones. I don't want to be a part of his secrets anymore. And I told him as much.

Rose continued reading. She skimmed the whirlwind of days

following Sophie's death. Then something stopped her. A few sentences tucked in the midst of it all.

That lucky egg. Those jewel thieves never had a chance. They were stealing the fakes. Of course, now Graham thinks he's really the Big Cheese.

Rose started piecing it altogether. Porter must have found the real jewels in the house. "It's no wonder, with Patsy and Cecil coming over all the time, helping her snoop." And now, at the gala, everyone in Turnberry would find out. Rose gasped. It could appear as if Mr. Mitchell had actually stolen them. *Well, he kind of did.* She thought about telling Porter what she had read in the journal, maybe pleading to protect her birth father's name. "No," she spoke aloud, looking at her sleeping cat. Maybe he deserved a bit of tarnish. He never did anything for her, or for her mother. Rose checked "Will not attend" and sealed the RSVP, along with her father's long overdue fate.

~ 65 ~

The day had finally arrived. The 1920s-inspired charity gala—which only Patsy and I knew may have truly been planned for the green dress—radiated a magical aura throughout the hallway of the Grand Hotel. Patsy really had pulled it off, and so beautifully. Upon entering the ballroom, I felt instantly overwhelmed, as if I had entered a glorious portal into the past. The room overflowed with impeccably dressed people seemingly from a more sophisticated ripple in time. The room sparkled from every angle. Crystal chandeliers dripping from the ceiling. Candles glimmering in mercury glass vases. Even the tables seemed to exude auras of their very own with the metallic-threaded white tablecloths glistening under the enchanting lights. Patsy had thought of everything—even historic photos of Turnberry had been scattered about like jewels left for the guests to take as mementos. Completely enamored with the room itself, it took me a minute to acknowledge the maître de who tried politely several times to offer me a glass of bubbly. As I took my first sip of the decadent libation, I felt a soft touch on my arm.

"Oh, hi, Patsy. Everything is stunning. Like a dream. You've hit it out of the park, my friend."

Patsy smiled and thanked me. As I surveyed the room, I saw Stan and Peg. They walked over.

"You look very dapper, Stan...and Peg, you are a vision in that dress." Peg blushed a little, but I meant it. She looked amazing. We chatted for a few moments. We giggled about the paintings from my basement, which we had deemed only sentimental value at best...well, except for the one that maybe didn't even have that. Then I saw Cedric Barton from the bank. I raised my glass from afar, and he did the same.

I felt another hand on my shoulder and turned. "Mr. and Mrs. Tillman," I said with enthusiasm.

"Good evening, Porter. This is an amazing event for our little town." Mr. Tillman spoke more formally than usual.

Mrs. Tillman chimed in with, "Love your dress, honey. It brings out those emerald eyes of yours."

"Thank you both. I'm so glad you could be here tonight. Who's watching the restaurant?"

"The staff is just fine without us, I'm sure." Mrs. Tillman patted her husband's arm in a reassuring manner.

After speaking to a few more people, I noticed Patsy scampering back my way. She appeared to be on a mission. *Oh no.*

Patsy grabbed my hand. "Come with me."

We moved in slow motion, as if treading water through the intoxicating glow of the space. Patsy led me toward the small stage at the center of the room, and all eyes fell upon us.

Did the music stop, or is the weight of 150 sets of eyes deafening?

I grasped Patsy's arm just as we were about to ascend the steps to the stage.

"Patsy, I cannot go on that stage." My face definitely betrayed the terror that afflicted me. In that moment, I wished that I had tried a little harder to convince Cecil to come with me. He had said, "Porter, my days of late-night soirees passed many moons ago." In true Cecil form, he had more than made up for his absence with a generous donation.

Patsy gently put her hands on my shoulders and looked me eye to eye. "Porter, of course you can. The jewels you found and returned are the intrigue of this gala. You have to say something. Just speak from the heart."

"No. The historian renovation project is the reason, not my discovery. You planned this whole event. *You* should say something," I said in a strained whisper.

"The renovation is the reason, but you are the star of this show. Everyone wants to hear about the jewels. Now, come with me." She held my hand firmly and pulled me along as we climbed the steps to the dreaded stage.

I clung to the glass of champagne I held it like my life depended on it. *Breathe.*

Patsy gave a brief introduction...and now it was my turn. I smiled at the crowd, wondering if they could see my heart trying to escape my chest.

Here goes nothin'.

I shared the story of finding the jewels and how I realized where they belonged. I did what Patsy said and spoke from my heart. When I finished, everyone clapped enthusiastically, heads nodding, smiles beaming.

I looked over to see Patsy, aglow with pride. I did a little head-nod to the side, meaning, *Now get me off this stage.*

Patsy understood and rescued me.

~~~

From the corner of the ballroom—hidden by a sea of Turnberry's best-dressed, tipsy from glasses filled with barrel-aged liquors or wine from private reserve collections—stood a clear-minded Jack, watching Porter as if no one else even existed at all. She floated across the room with the poise and grace that one can only be born with. Dozens of eyes followed her every move as she made her way about the room, chatting with guests, each of whom lit up as they basked in hearing additional tidbits of her jewel story. Two younger men disguised their bold stares with forced sips from their glasses. He couldn't help but chuckle a little as he watched others overtly turning their heads, even slowly spinning on their heels, to gaze a little longer at the elusive beauty in the flowing, green dress. She had never known the power of her own presence, and that had not changed. Porter had no idea.

But Jack could see one thing that the others couldn't. Porter looked uncomfortable, nervous actually, and seemed to be doing everything she could to escape being the center of attention. He knew she counted the minutes until she could leave. Jack fought the urge to go to her, to gently interlace his arm with hers, whisper in her ear that she's not alone and that she didn't have to do any of this. But he couldn't, not yet, and his heart felt real pain, a physical ache, because he might never be able to do any of those things for her again.

Late into the evening, Jack found himself face to face with Patsy. He had been careful not to run into Porter, but he had forgotten about Patsy. His focus had been to make sure the cartel didn't slip a tuxedo-clad goon into the party. Joe had thought it sounded a bit Hollywood, but Max had agreed—*and volunteered*—that someone should be at the party as a lookout for trouble. Jack had not heard a thing from Will, complete radio silence since the meet up—not that he really expected to, but be that as it may, Jack had no way to know if the cartel really would call off the spies or not. Will's word meant less than nothing at this point.

Caught off guard, Jack looked down toward the kind voice.

"Oh, hello. I'm Patsy, one of tonight's hostesses. I don't think I've had the pleasure of meeting you."

Jack felt anxiety rising within him, but on the outside, his demeanor remained calm and, he hoped, exuded at least some sophistication. He graciously took Patsy's outstretched hand. "Why, hello. No, we haven't met. And thank you for this evening. This is a wonderful cause. Would you mind terribly...please see that Porter receives this."

He handed her a sealed black envelope embossed with wings. As Patsy gazed upon the curious envelope, he made a quick exit through the side doorway of the ballroom.

~ 66 ~

Patsy opened her mouth to speak, but found herself silent and stunned to see that the man had vanished. She felt a little flushed and put a hand to her throat, thinking, *Who in the world was that devastatingly handsome man with the intense blue eyes?* She rapidly scanned the room for any sign of him. Instead, her eyes only found Porter, standing alone and looking at one of the historical photos.

Making a beeline straight to Porter, Patsy actually knocked a glass out of one gentleman's hand. "So sorry!" Patsy halfheartedly called out without slowing her pace.

~~~

When I saw Patsy making a not-so-smooth dash in my direction, I wondered, *What now?*

"Porter, Porter." Patsy spoke breathlessly, her hands wringing.

I couldn't get a word in as an overexcited Patsy gushed in front of me. I even had trouble keeping up with what she was saying.

"There was this man, uh, not just any man. A tall, handsome one. Oh, and yes, he had the most intense blue eyes. Did I say he was handsome, like from a movie? And he gave this to me. Well, to you, for me to give to you. He said your name, Porter, specifically. Look at this envelope! Isn't it mysterious? Who has stationary like this? Much less, what *man* has stationary like this..."

And on and on she went, but her words had become white noise as my eyes fixed on the envelope.

"Porter, did you hear me? Did you hear what I just said?" She snapped her fingers in front of my face, and I slowly looked up at her, trying to maintain my composure. Not because of her finger-snapping, but because of what that envelope signified.

"Yes, I heard you, Patsy." It was all I could manage as I stared at the black envelope with embossed wings in my hand. *It's my very own stationery.* I had left a stack of it at Jack's house. This had to be from Jack. I scanned the room, spinning in a full circle. *Where is he?*

Patsy interrupted my thoughts. "Do you know who he is? Did you see him, too?"

I grabbed her arm. "Patsy, where is he now?"

"I don't know. I looked for him. He just sort of, uh, disappeared." She flapped her hands. "Well, open it! Probably another fabulous donation, huh?"

I stood almost paralyzed, except that my eyes continued to study the thinning crowd for him, for Jack. Patsy had the wrong idea. I knew this letter did not relate to the Historian Room or the library. This letter had only one purpose, and I don't think I'd ever been more afraid to read something in my life. I clutched the envelope, hoping that the words inside mirrored my feelings for Jack. *He must have received my gift. He knows I still care.* So, why hadn't he given it to me in person, though? I felt like laughing and crying at the same time when I thought about one possibility: I wouldn't have let him speak otherwise.

I stalled a moment, hoping Jack really hadn't left. I looked past Patsy and beyond the group of guests who still dawdled, staying as late as they could without getting shooed out by the wait staff, who were not so inconspicuous with the cleanup of the ballroom. No Jack.

Intending to downplay the whole thing, I finally found the courage to speak. "I think I'll open this at home. I can barely see straight right now. It's been a long night, a great night, but it's late." I recognized disappointment on Patsy's face. "Don't worry. I'll call you right away once I open it." I managed a small smile, and Patsy finally nodded.

"Okay, okay. Might be personal, huh?" She winked. "Good enough. Now, let's get this soirée wrapped up." She clapped her hands and inserted herself in the lingering group.

I made my exit.

~ 67 ~

Jack reached inside his jacket and pulled out a white rose he had swiped from an arrangement at the gala. He placed it gently against the bottom of Porter's side door, standing it upright. He wanted Porter to know that he was still here for her, still waiting, and still in love with her. If only a single white rose could say all of those things.

He felt nervous, wondering if she had read the letter yet. With Porter, it was hard to know. It would not be unlike her to keep the letter unopened for days while overthinking what was inside. Jack had seen her stockpile unopened mail for weeks at a time and allow unheard voicemails to collect on her phone. Porter did not like facing the unknown. She kept her heart so guarded after Will's disappearance. Jack had known how to coax her, but he had also learned the hard way not to coax too much. In fact, pushing too hard proved his biggest mistake with Porter. He'd pushed too hard for her to believe the worst about her husband. And now, he would have to open her wounded heart again with the news that Will hadn't died, but instead left by choice.

Jack sighed as his shoulders sank. "Damn you, Will." The mess that Will had left behind fell squarely on Jack's shoulders now. The only reason Jack didn't want to tell Porter what a monster Will had become stemmed only from him wanting to save her from another walk through hell. Selfishly, he wanted to rescue her, love her, and build a life with her...and never mention Will again.

Jack took a last look toward Rose's house. No sign of her in the windows. Too late for him to go over there now.

After a quick update to Joe and Max in the shadows by the guesthouse, he hopped on his bike and drove away.

~~~

"Who does he think he is, James Bond?" Max sputtered under his breath.

"What?" A frustrated Joe looked over at a pouting Max.

"The tux, the motorcycle... Oh, forget it." Max looked out the car window.

Joe shook his head in a "oh brother" way and then sat up straight, tapping Max on the arm as he saw Porter's car turning into the driveway. "There she is."

Max stayed silent. They watched as Porter parked and walked up to the door of her house. Her dress sparkling in the dim light, her hair blowing ever so gently in the night air as she leaned down to retrieve the single white rose. She paused and held the flower to her lips, then looked around as if hoping the tuxedo-clad Jack would be right there behind her. Of course, he wasn't. She stood a bit longer, alone under the stars, holding the rose—time seemed to stand still. Then she let herself inside, taking with her the enchanting moment.

Max made a *hmph* sound.

Joe reached for the pack of gum in the center console. "She's taken, buddy. There's a whole ocean out there—plenty of other fish."

"Well, if she's taken, then why does she look so lonely?" Max sniped.

Joe let Max's comment slide. She did look lonely. "Let's watch for a bit longer. Then head back to the motel. I want to take a look at that file again. It's late. Things have been quiet today." He yawned.

Max nodded and then yawned, too.

~ 68 ~

As I approached the side door, I saw a flower—a single white rose. "Jack." His name crossed my lips as a whisper. I held the rose close. Breathed in the scent. My heart ached. I needed to read his letter. Tonight.

I went inside to the study, heart racing, hands trembling, tears welling up, as I held the sealed envelope that Jack had delivered. My soul pleaded to read Jack's words. Gently, I placed Jack's rose on the coffee table, curled up on the leather sofa, and pushed my finger under the flap of the envelope. Something inside the envelope shifted. I poured the item into my hand—it was a delicate gold necklace with petite gold wings. I had never seen this necklace before, but the design matched exactly the embossed wings on the stationery. I clutched the necklace to my heart, knowing the deeper meaning behind the gesture. Jack knew that the wings symbolized loyalty, strength, and safety to me—all the things intrinsic to love. Opening the folded letter, I immediately recognized his beautiful handwriting, his penmanship resembling a lost art of the past.

My Darling Porter,

I miss you every day. Please don't be angry. I tried to stay away. I swear I did. But my heart has been broken since the day you left. Trust me, I know that you needed space. I understand that you needed to take control of your own life and that you, more than anyone, needed a new beginning. It's just that my life has no purpose without you. All of my dreams, my desires, they don't exist without you. Everything simply leads back to you. Every day, my heart aches, and I need you to know how sorry I am for that day, for expecting too much too soon, for not giving you the time and space you needed to heal.

The irony of all of this is that everything I was pushing for you to understand, about what you went through, was to help you find freedom from your past. I never meant that freedom to include leaving me. If you can find it anywhere inside your heart, inside your beautiful soul, to forgive me for that day, to let me back into your life, I promise you that I'll do everything in my power to make each day better than the one before.

Take your time. I'll be here. Waiting for you is no burden; it is a privilege. You stole my heart years ago, from the moment we met, but you know that, don't you? Let's leave the past behind together and build a new life so bright that it outshines all pain. Just say yes...I will do everything else.

Love always,

Jack

"I want to know you moved and breathed in the same world with me." F. Scott Fitzgerald

As I read, my eyes clouded with tears. Of course, Jack readily shouldered the blame. The truth remained, though, that I owed him a bigger apology than he ever had owed me. The even more brutal truth poked and prodded its way to my mind, and I knew that everything I wanted in my marriage to Will did not even come close to everything that Jack could actually give to me. I wanted a partner, a lover, someone who wanted to spend every day living and breathing in the same world. Jack knew that, and that was why he'd quoted my favorite author. And how fitting it was from the "Benediction"—the ending.

Long overdue, I needed to close my chapter with Will. I had every right to. Not that my choice needed justification, but I couldn't help but think how my husband never even knew what I liked to read. He didn't notice my passions; he never asked what filled the hours in my day. He focused on his career—Will was his own muse.

Looking back, I didn't know why I ever accepted that type of relationship. I needed to forgive myself and let it all go. I belonged with

Jack. Maybe in some twisted way, everything that had happened needed to for me to find Jack.

Carefully, I refolded the letter and put it back into the black envelope. I removed the necklace monogramed with the M that I had been wearing and put it in the dish on the coffee table. That necklace never belonged to me anyway. I put on the necklace from Jack—this one meant only for me. I grabbed the rose and filled the little bud vase from the bookshelf with water. Placing the small vase on the coffee table, I sat again, this time thinking about Jack and wondering again if the gift I had sent him had made the difference—if he had felt that maybe I would be open to seeing him again. Maybe that was why he had reached out.

And I couldn't have been happier. I felt so light, I thought I might fly.

~ 69 ~

Rose watched out her dark window as Porter arrived home from the gala just after 11 p.m. The flowing, green dress looked as amazing on her, as it had on Sophie Mitchell so many years ago. Not long after Porter went inside, the lights slowly went out in her windows. She must have gone to bed, surely exhausted from the big event.

Rose yawned and almost closed the curtain when she saw someone move in the shadows near Porter's garage. Then the man boldly crossed Porter's driveway and headed straight toward the guesthouse. He crowbarred the door open, causing Rose's jaw to drop, leaving her mouth agape, her hand clutching her throat.

What in the world...?

She first thought to call the police, but she quickly changed her mind and instead called Jack, like he had told her to do. His phone rang and rang. Rose hung up and tried again. All the while, she watched as a beam of light, presumably from the man's flashlight, crossed the cottage's window a couple times. She rang Jack again. *Please pick up. Please pick up.*

And he did.

She quickly told him what she'd just observed.

"I'll be right there," was all he said, and the line disconnected.

Rose bit her lip, her eyes gazing through the darkness at the guesthouse.

~~~

Jack called Joe for backup. A groggy Joe answered and explained that he and Max had gone back to the motel after Porter had safely arrived home from the gala and presumably gone to bed. There hadn't been any action all day, and with Porter out, Joe decided his time could be used more wisely going over the files he had unofficially slipped out of the office. He needed to get them back before anyone noticed. Tonight gave him an opportunity to work against that time pressure.

"I don't care about all that," Jack barked. "Get over to Porter's. Now. Something's going down." He told him what Rose had shared just moments ago.

"On our way."

They disconnected.

~~~

Joe threw on his clothes and jogged toward Max's room. It wasn't going to be easy waking the kid; he slept like a rock. He banged mercilessly until Max finally opened the door, bleary-eyed.

"Get dressed. The cartel guy just broke into Porter's guesthouse."

Max nodded and moved rapidly, stumbling and grabbing his clothes from the foot of the bed, then heading straight to the bathroom to change.

While Joe waited, he mentally reviewed the information he had read earlier in the night.

Max exited the bathroom and did a quick cock of his head. "Let's roll." As Max drove, Joe said, "The cartel got nervous. The file I had tonight said Jack's trip to Costa Rica and Porter's ticket to Colombia lit a bit of a fire. If I had to guess, they're preparing to smoke Will out of hiding by ramping up on Porter. I haven't figured out exactly how, but I think I'm on the right track."

Max nodded, but added, "Or...the guy just wanted to use a restroom or take a nap. He's bound to know by now that the guesthouse is basically unused."

Joe slapped him on the arm with the file folder.

Max jerked his head back and glanced sideways at his partner. "What?"

"I don't think he'd risk exposing himself and pissing off the cartel to use a restroom or take a nap," Joe said, irritated. "Besides, Jack told me there's a tunnel from the guesthouse to Porter's basement."

"Say what?" Max turned to Joe with wide eyes.

Joe pointed toward the road. "Focus."

Max flipped his sights between the road in front of him and his partner. "Umm. You didn't think that was something you should have mentioned before now?"

"Calm down. I just found out, too."

Max sped up.

~~~

Jack arrived at Porter's and parked next to the guesthouse. He didn't worry about the engine sound—time was of the essence. The front door to the little cottage stood ajar. It looked dark inside, and he didn't hear any noise.

He entered the cottage. Directly in front of him, a hatch in the floor stood open. "The tunnel," he murmured.

He shined his flashlight into the opening illuminating the steep staircase. No sign of anyone inside. Then, he listened for a moment and heard what sounded like distant footsteps coming from below. He tucked his gun at the small of his back and descended the staircase.

He moved swiftly, making sure not to create a telling echo with his footsteps like the guy in front of him.

~~~

Rose monitored the scene as Jack rode up, and she wanted to help, so she headed to her back bedroom to get the ancient revolver. She knew the gun had been left loaded for decades. "I hope this thing still works." Revolver in hand and still in her bathrobe, she only took a moment to put on her shoes before starting out her front door.

~~~

The car jolted as Max drove too fast over the railroad track crossing. *Thump, thump.*

"What's that?" Max shouted.

Joe muttered a few choice words, shaking his head. "Pull over. It's a flat."

"Do we have a spare?"

"We are about to find out."

~~~

Jack made quick time through the tunnel and could already see an opening ahead. The tunnel had made a couple sharp turns, so it had been hard to know how far he actually walked. He carefully exited, finding himself in a room with a bank vault. *What the hell?* Jack wondered if he had accidentally ended up somewhere other than Porter's basement. Then he saw another door, more like a panel. It was slightly ajar already. Jack pushed it open slowly, revealing that he had, in fact, landed in the basement. He looked around; ahead of him was a staircase that made a bend a few steps up from the bottom. Still no sign of the guy. A tinge of panic struck Jack at the thought of the man being in the house where Porter slept alone.

Upstairs, dogs barked. He hurried up the steps, taking them two at a time. As he rounded the bend, he saw that the door at the top had been forced open, the frame splintered and the door still swinging on its hinges.

~ 70 ~

The dogs barked and pawed at the bedroom door. I sprung up—"What is it Gatsby, Ripley?" I paused, trying to listen. Then, through the noise, I thought I heard the doorbell ring. Yes, incessantly. I looked at the clock. After midnight. This couldn't be good. My mind raced, and my heart hammered against my chest. Or maybe it was good. Maybe it was Jack. With the dogs in tow, I raced down the stairs, skipping a few in my hurry to fall into my beloved's arms.

I switched on the front porch light, and without looking through the peephole, I flung the door open wide.

I froze, and my breath caught in my throat. *What?* Everything moved in slow motion, as if I had entered another dimension.

I stared at the gun pointed directly at me. It was low, aimed at my stomach. My eyes climbed to reach those of the potential shooter.

"Rose?"

I could tell she barely had any idea how to handle a gun, but at this close range, if she pulled the trigger even accidentally, she probably wouldn't miss.

"Rose, are you okay? Can I help you?" I assumed she had not come here to shoot me and that maybe something had frightened her. I stood gripping the door, wondering if I should reach out and try to take the gun.

Her eyes bugging out, she spoke rapidly, saying things to me I didn't understand...about a man in my house, or under it, rather.

I didn't know what to do except try to talk to her, calm her. She sounded confused.

"Rose, it's okay. No one is here. Just give me the gun." I saw clearly that the revolver had a full round. *Wait.* The gun looked almost exactly like the Smith & Wesson in my safe. *Or is it my gun?* My mind was a blur.

"No. I need to help you," Rose blurted out, nearly breathless. "There's a man...man coming into your house."

Then I remembered the tunnel and the light in the basement. I could feel the blood drain from my face.

"The tunnel. Yes. Okay. Just give me the gun." I reached my hand out toward her.

"No," she yelled. "You go and lock the basement door. Now."

I shook my head. "It's locked. I keep it that way. We need to call the police. Rose. Let me have the gun," I pleaded with her. My eyes moved to the gun.

Rose's hands shook. "I called—" She stopped midsentence.

"You called the police?" I asked, still reaching out for the gun.

She stepped back, almost tripping over Ripley. "No." Her eyes focused on something behind me.

I didn't want to, but I turned my head, and there in the hallway stood a wavy-haired, olive-skinned man with a gun pointed directly at me. The only barrier between us—Gatsby. Growling, hair bristling. I found myself trapped between two loaded guns, not knowing what to do.

I recognized quickly the only opportunity to survive rested in my ability to overpower one of them before either could pull the trigger. But which one? If I went for Rose's gun, he'd undoubtedly fire his. If I went for his gun, he may overpower me and shoot both me and Rose. And Rose actually being able to aim at him seemed a far stretch. She couldn't help. I had to go for him.

Before I could make my move, a gunshot rang out and then another. Already grabbing the edge of the door, I crouched and tucked my head as low as possible while moving into the little bit of cover I could find behind the door. *Am I hit?* I patted my body, checking for wet blood. The smell of gunpowder filled the air. *I'm okay.* I stood a little straighter now. There couldn't have been two shots that quickly from the old revolver.

The shots must have come from the intruder. *Oh no...* "Rose!"

The split seconds of silence felt like minutes. I began to move slowly, trying to peer into the foyer to see. "Rose?" I said again. She lay on the floor in a heap. Then I looked in the opposite direction, down the hallway toward the basement door. There on the floor, in a pool of dark red, lay the intruder, face down. The blood looked like the kind that came from deep inside, the kind that meant death.

My heart raced, my chest cramped, and I clutched my fist in front of my heart. I looked around, attempting to get a clear assessment of my situation. What had happened, exactly?

Then I saw. I saw him, the handsome, blue-eyed stranger—no, not a stranger.

"Jack?" I stared in disbelief and relief at the same time. "Oh my God." I dropped to my knees, unable to stand any longer.

"Porter." Something about how he said my name made my heart skip a beat. His voice had power over me, and I just wanted to fall into the safety of his arms. Focused only on Jack's eyes, I tried to draw in his strength. I felt comfort in his face, the same face that had comforted me for three years and followed me to the ends of the earth. The same face that had told me I needed to free myself. The same face that I had screamed at because I couldn't accept the truth, a truth that didn't even belong to Jack. And, that same perfect face that had filled with a deep sadness the day I had left.

I remembered Cecil's words: *"You are a survivor. Your wings won't stay broken forever...you will fly again."*

"Jack." My voice amounted to barely a whisper as I leaned against the wall behind me. My strength fading fast. Had I been hit? Was I having a breakdown? Then my eyes landed on Rose's small motionless body. "Jack, help her," I managed to squeak out. Only a few feet away, but I couldn't seem to get to her.

With military precision, Jack stowed his gun and bolted toward Rose. His experience with combat ran deep. He checked Rose's pulse and looked her over. "She's breathing. Her leg is hurt. Help is on the way." Jack spoke calmly, and all I wanted to do was scream. Out of sheer relief.

He didn't say more, his eyes simply held my gaze as a thousand silent words seemed to flow between us. I actually believed I could see the missing piece of my own broken soul in his eyes.

I slowly tilted from my knees to my side, finally resting my head on the floor. The room spun. The lights blurred.

"You're wearing a tux?" I said before closing my eyes.

"Porter." Jack's voice penetrated the disappearing world, and I slowly opened my eyes to see the steely blue of his.

I rambled, my thoughts bouncing around. "I don't love him anymore. He never really existed—not the way I knew him."

Jack pulled me close, told me not to speak. I could feel his face pressing against mine.

Of course, I did anyway. "Jack. What happens now? Is she...?" My words drifted off into nothingness.

"Rose is okay. She will be fine." The first paramedics arrived, wasting no time putting her in an ambulance.

"Who was that man? I should have done more to stop him. I'm not..." I tried to push myself up, but Jack held me tight.

"Don't move, please."

"Who was he?" My voice rose on those three words. I needed to know.

"We'll find out soon enough. Just...please, shhh." He put a gentle finger over my lips. Then he began to stand, cradling me in his arms.

"Okay. Okay. Just make it all be okay. I want," I paused and added, "to be with you. I'm tired of running."

"No more running. I've got you. Always have, always will."

Jack placed me on the couch in the study and then held my face in his hands. He gently kissed my lips. Then I saw fear in his eyes as I locked onto his gaze. I felt strange, disconnected. My eyes went foggy, and my hands numb. We continued to look at each other, only drawn out of this private moment by the sound of more sirens coming down the street.

The horror of what had just happened in my front hallway hit me. "Jack, stay with me."

"I will never leave you, Porter. But for now, I need to talk to the officers."

"Officers," I said weakly.

Brakes screeched in the driveway, and the rapid footsteps of even more responders grew closer. Their radios carried with them a constant static, broken only by messages about the scene as they were reported back and forth. Somehow, reality did not seem believable—as if a cop movie played too loudly in my house. My vision became tunnel-like as I struggled to look to the front hallway. I could only see a blur of uniforms. Then I saw Jack. He stood talking to two officers with notepads in their hands. A woman in a light-blue shirt with a hospital patch and a stethoscope around her neck looked at me rushed to my side.

"Miss, are you okay?"

I managed a response. "Yes, I think so. I feel a little cold, and my heart is racing. That's all."

"Okay, you're going to be just fine. Is it okay if I check a few things?"

I nodded. "I'm so tired." I heard myself say the words, but it all felt dreamlike. *Why can't I open my eyes? Why can't I move?*

I heard a commotion mixed with lots of erratic talking. Then, I heard Jack's voice. He sounded unlike himself, frantic: "What's wrong? What's happening to her? Porter. Porter!"

The last words to fall upon my ears came from the female paramedic as she applied pressure to my neck. "The patient is in tachycardia. Performing carotid sinus massage." *Is she talking about me?*

~ ~ ~

When I awoke, I felt pleasantly warm and comfortable. *Where am I?* I could tell even through closed eyelids that the sun shone brightly. A hand wrapped around my own squeezed down just a bit, and I squeezed back. I tried like crazy to blink my eyes open, but couldn't—I felt drugged. Finally, I managed a few quick blinks and caught glimpses of the room. *I'm in a hospital.*

My memory came flooding back all at once. The gunshots, the strange man in my hallway. Oh my God, Rose. And Jack. Jack had been there. My dogs.

I heard beeping from a machine and a nurse saying, "The heart rate is elevated. Sir, please, I need to check her."

Then another voice, Jack's voice. "Porter, Porter. I'm here." I thought I felt his breath on my face. His voice grew louder as he called out, "She's waking up."

My eyes opened and stayed open. I squinted into the bright room, *so* bright. Jack looked down at me, then up at the nurse, who spoke again, "Heart rate is normal now." His handsome face came into focus as I tried to sit up. He leaned in, his face full of emotion, tears in his eyes. "Porter, thank God. Don't ever scare me like that again."

I managed a small smile. I tried but couldn't find my voice just yet.

Jack noticed my attempt to speak. "Don't talk. For once, don't talk." He smiled at his joke. "We made it through. Everyone, everything is okay. I am never leaving you. You will never be alone. Let me take care of you. I love you, Porter. Just let me love you. That's all you have to do. I'll do everything else." His voice broke as he spoke the last few sentences.

I mouthed, *I love you.*

His head fell gently onto mine. Our foreheads pressed together. Our lips brushed together, the sensation so tender. So...everything.

Staring out the car window, I watched the trees blur together as we drove. "What a beautiful day." I looked over at Jack. I loved watching him drive. My fingers reached up to my neck and touched the delicate gold wings he had given me. I could sit in the car for hours just like this. He was always so calm, so steady when he drove. He looked exactly how I'd always wanted to feel inside and how, finally, I felt in that moment.

I giggled.

Jack looked over at me, curious. "What has you so giddy?"

"It's just that...well, we both sent each other gifts when we were apart. Yours, however, stole the show. Whiskey glasses, no matter how nice, can't hold a candle to this necklace." My words were sincere.

"What?" Jack looked confused.

"I sent you a set—whiskey glasses and chilling stones in an engraved wooden box."

"I never—" He paused. "Well, I haven't been home in a while."

"You were busy, huh?" I jested.

He winked. I touched his hand. We had already discussed his watching me all that time. I thought it gallant; he thought it a bit on the line of creepy.

We finally arrived at my house. Excited to be home, I unlatched my seatbelt before we'd even stopped. I could not wait to put this all behind me, behind us, and start our lives together.

"Wait. Don't move, Porter. Let me help you." Jack sprung out of the car in a hurry to get to my side.

"I'm fine, really. I've had enough of people helping me." I started to stand. He reached for my arm.

"You were in the hospital for days, my little warrior. You still need time to gain your strength." He spoke kindly, but sternly.

I waved him off. "Exactly, I was there entirely too long. The only way to rebuild my strength is to get moving again. I can get myself out of the car, Jack." I slowly made my way to standing, though I did allow him to steady me a little.

He smiled and shook his head. "Porter, you will never change. You're so strong-willed."

Jack stayed next to me as I walked toward the house. He gave me just enough space to feel dignified.

"Okay, then. Jack, darling," I spoke with a touch of playful sarcasm, "please let the dogs out. I want to see them out here in the sunshine." I gazed up at the house and late afternoon sky, taking it all in.

"Uh, they may knock you down."

"Jack, they're my dogs. They won't knock me down." *No way.*

"Okay, but let's compromise. Go sit on the front steps. I'll bring them out to you." Jack waited for me to agree.

I gave him a pressing look but decided to comply. Out the dogs came. I thought they might explode from happiness at seeing me, and I felt the same way about them.

"Look, Jack, the dogs missed me."

Jack pointed to Rose's house. "They aren't the only ones." Rose sat in a wheelchair, in her front yard, waving. I smiled big and waved back.

Jack and I watched as the dogs tumbled and made little yelps like puppies.

I loved those two brutes so much. They made me happy.

Jack made me happy.

I was...happy.

I looked up at Jack, who stared kindly at me.

"What is it?"

"You. You look beautiful."

"Why, thank you. You're quite the looker yourself, mister."

"Shall we take this inside?" he said, helping me to my feet.

"Yes, please. I'm longing for my couch and a nice fire."

"Your wish is my command. But it's summer, so how about some candles instead?" He winked.

Once we had settled on the couch together, the dogs at our feet, we enjoyed the silence, the quiet togetherness of knowing each of us was there for the other.

I leaned up and kissed him on the nose. "I'm sorry for everything I put you through," I said. "I should never have left."

He held up a hand. "Hey. No more of that. Water under the bridge. No more apologies, please."

"Okaayyyy." I nestled closer.

"But I do have some things to share with you."

"Oh yeah?"

He took in a deep breath, then let it out. "Yeah."

His tone sounded off, so I looked up at him. "Jack, what is it? What's wrong?"

"Porter, I'll start at the beginning."

Jack explained the parts of his story that I'd not yet known. He told me the details about befriending Rose, which made me chuckle. He talked about how Joe and Max had switched sides basically and slipped him information about the crash and Will's disappearance. Then he explained how the guy in my house had been connected to the cartel.

We sat silent for a few moments, and then Jack took both of my hands in his. "Now is not the time, but really, Porter, there will never be a good time to say this."

The look on his face scared me. What could possibly happen now? My fear must have reached my eyes, because he squeezed my hand, reassuring me. Then, his words...

"Will is alive."

A dreadful hollowness overcame the room. Jack cleared his throat and added softly, in almost a whisper, "And he didn't want to be found, not by us."

My heart raced as I tried to understand. "He's alive? Where? When did you find out? What is going on, Jack?"

He opened his hand slowly. "Will told me to give this to you."

My eyes watched as his fingers released their grip from around the black metal wings that had once belonged to Will. Tears flowed down my cheeks. My hands went cold as I reached out to touch the familiar relic from my past. Then I sat straight up, putting distance between us.

"I'm sorry," Jack said. "I wish I had good news, but we weren't wrong. This wasn't just a crash. He wasn't innocent in all this, but it is more complicated than we thought."

I clenched the necklace, the edges of the wings biting into my palm, as my face grew expressionless. "Tell me everything. I need to know."

"Okay." Jack took a deep breath. "Well, to start, he looked like hell—probably aged ten years more than he should have."

I cracked a small grin. "Good."

As he talked, Jack became more animated, detailing how the government seemed to know exactly where Will had been the whole time. He shared his theory that Will had chosen to be a double agent, playing the role of US counter-drug enforcement gone rogue, smuggling drugs and cash for one of the Colombian cartels. Jack explained how he suspected the CIA asked him to play this role on their behalf—a covert operation. However, implicating me, using my name—that was something else. Jack struggled to say the words: "Will said he did it to protect you in some twisted sort of way." His eyes fell to his lap.

"This sounds like a movie. A bad one." I could feel the heat rising in my face. "But what about the cartel following me? Coming into this house?" I couldn't help myself, so I said it. "Did he try to have me killed to protect me, too?"

Jack ignored my vindictive remark and continued, "I'm just not sure, Porter. About any of it. Will didn't answer the hard questions, of course. But from what I could gather, I think he messed up, owes somebody, maybe the cartel. I don't know. But I think his orchestrated death was supposed to close the case. No one counted on us still searching. Did that tip off the cartel that he was still out there? Who knows?" He pounded his thigh.

I shook my head, thinking how if this was all true then Will could have, should have, contacted me, or Jack. Told us himself he was alive and to stop searching.

Jack continued. He surmised that the crash probably wasn't

planned, and that it may have compromised Will's operation, exposing him, his crew. "The bottom line, Porter, is that I don't know all of the details. And I don't think we will ever know the full truth. But what I do know is that Will left an intentional trail back to you for reasons he deemed justified. Whether this whole thing was a master plan by the CIA or not, I don't know. But, Porter, he's living off of money from somewhere in a non-extradite country, by the beach, watching sunsets..."

I interrupted him. "Yes. While you and I dodged bullets from the cartel in my hallway." I fumed.

Jack looked pained. "The one thing I know for sure...I can never forgive him for what he did to you." He choked on his words. "Whether he meant to or not."

"Does his paradise island have telephones?" My sarcasm ran thick. But deep inside, I wondered. What had it been? Greed, ambition? *Was he really just a bad guy?*

My mind swimming, I tried to make heads or tails out of it all. There were a lot of holes. I had a million questions.

Jack stared, his eyes tender. "I'm sorry."

"No. This isn't on you. It isn't on me, either. Does he realize what he put us through? He framed me. I could have *gone to jail!*" I yelled the last words.

"He knows." Jack's jaw clenched, and I could see him holding back.

"What? Jack. Tell me." I tried to overpower the shakiness in my voice.

He looked at me, took a deep breath. Then he spoke. "He knew about the funeral...well, that he had a headstone, at least." He looked away.

I could feel my eyes grow wide, my mouth dry. Then the words came. My voice cracked. "Oh, of course he did. If I could get my hands on him... No. No. I won't stoop to his level. But you know what? I hate him. Really, I do. I hate him more now than I ever thought possible to hate anyone." The tears started to well, but I held them back. Anger flashed through me instead. "You know what? Will is dead. He doesn't exist. Not to me. Not anymore." My hands started to shake. I clasped them together, hoping Jack wouldn't see. "In fact, if he were brave enough to stand here, I'd tell him so."

Jack hugged me close, and my next words cut through the thick gloom. "You know what hurts the most? We both were loyal to him. You and me. We would have done anything for him. Why would he do this to me, or to you, Jack?" *We could have died.*

"I don't know why." He stared across the room.

"Are we safe now? Or will we, or will I...will I be a target forever?"

Jack's eyes slowly met mine. I could see a reflection of my pain in his. "You will be safe. You have me. No one is getting past me."

I smirked at his intensity.

Then I watched as the blue behind the pain in his eyes began to brighten a little. "Porter, if you let me, I'll keep you safe for the rest of your life."

I was already there. Will existed as nothing more than a ghost to me in that moment. I turned and leaned into Jack, my back against his chest. We sat staring at the flickering flames of the candles Jack had lit. My soul danced between the love I felt for Jack and the coldness I felt for Will. I tried not to judge myself for the paradox.

Let it go. I had nothing to lose when it came to Will—no love lost. His disappearance—a gift. A path to freedom.

Suddenly, clarity grasped me as I looked to Jack, the beautiful soul there in front of me. "I'm so glad you came back to rescue me." I winked to lighten the mood, but meant it completely.

"I never left you. Porter. You know that I never will." His eyes, bright and serious, saw right through me. He lightly moved my hair away from my face. I leaned into him and rested the side of my face on his strong jaw. His fingers gently fell through my hair again, and he whispered in my ear, so close, "Let me carry this burden. I can handle it for us both. Just love me."

I took a deep breath and nodded. I reached for the courage to say what we both needed to hear. "I have loved you, Jack, for a long time. I love you now. And I'll love you always."

His eyes showed relief, and his shoulders relaxed. Watching him absorb my words, I could feel the past that haunted us fading away. Everything seemed raw, exposed, as his eyes locked onto mine. Hardly any space between us now, the heat of his body intoxicated me. His lips met mine, soft and warm. I felt the prickle of his unshaven face. Time stood still in that moment.

Then he slowly pulled off his shirt, revealing the ink dark on his flesh—new. When? There on the back of his shoulder I saw my name intertwined in wings, written into his very being—a permanent mark. My fingers moved slowly, tracing the crisp outline. My body filled with heat from the inside out, and my breathing became shallow. The feeling swept me away. He was all I wanted. *Don't let this moment end.* His warm lips, gentle touch, the glow of his skin from the flicker of the flames. I realized I had never known true love until this moment.

~ 72 ~

"Jack, let's go to the shore. Let's see the ocean." It had been over a month since everything had come to a head, my involvement in Will's calamity had been cleared once and for all. And I chose to believe the government this time. With the load of my past lifted, my words rang out weightless, like a song, across the lawn on that sunny afternoon. I stood assessing the garden, deciding what I should plant for the impending fall, while Jack threw the ball for the dogs. He looked back at me, and I caught just a little smile.

~~~

The next morning, Jack and I sipped our coffee at the kitchen table, with the dogs at our feet. Casually, Jack lowered his mug, stood, and brushed his hands together. "We need to start packing."

"Huh?" I stared at him, thinking I must have misunderstood his words.

"I'm taking you to see those crashing waves."

"So, you did hear me yesterday." I giggled.

Jack winked. "How does Morro Bay sound?"

"Perfect. Absolutely perfect."

I laughed and wasted no time throwing essentials in a bag. We left that evening.

~~~

Jack tossed his keys to the valet on his way to the front desk. Porter headed off to explore the beautiful hotel.

"Welcome to the Henley, sir. Checking in?"

The clerk behind the desk offered Jack a glass of champagne. Jack instinctively waved it away, but then accepted as he recalled how Porter loved the look of a glass of bubbly. Sometimes she'd drink it, and sometimes she'd just revel in the beauty of the liquid gold and trace the bubbles up the side of the glass with her delicate fingers.

"Could you point me in the direction of the best view of the Pacific?" Jack knew exactly where he would find her.

With a confused look, the desk clerk signaled to a bellboy. "Steph, please take...uh, Mr. Wade, to the main veranda."

"My pleasure. Follow me, sir."

Jack followed the young, slickly groomed bellboy through the lobby toward a large set of French doors.

As Jack entered the terrace, his eyes surveyed the area. There. His breath hitched in his throat, and his heart began to beat a little faster as he watched her long, white, strapless dress catch the wind. She stared off into the distance, seemingly deep in thought.

Nothing could compete with the sight of her, not the cascades of wisteria, not the humming sea, or even the elegant backdrop of the grand hotel itself.

He took a step, clutching the sparkling glass, his aviator sunglasses reflecting the sun. At six-one, lean, strong, and rugged, he didn't blend well into the elegant atmosphere, and he could feel the casual glances coming his way. Not that he cared, really. He knew he looked as if he'd just walked off a ranch, dressed in his dark jeans and sporting broken-in ropers. In fact, Porter had told him so, many times—and she adored it. No, he didn't care about any of that now, so he strode with natural confidence like he had some serious business to tend to. Which he did, of course.

Then she saw him.

Immediately, she squealed, "This is like a dream."

Jack grinned and opened his arms as she fell into them—her face shining up at him as he leaned in to kiss her on the lips. She nestled her head into that spot on his chest where she fit perfectly. After a moment, she stepped back and tugged him toward a couple of cozy chairs.

"Whoa," he said, nearly spilling the champagne. "Here, this is for you."

She giggled, took the glass of bubbly and sipped delicately, her eyes twinkling with happiness as she peered at him over the rim of the glass. He practically melted right there and then.

"I'm so happy," Porter whispered as she laid her head back on the chair and closed her eyes...

~~~

"It's time. You can do this." I took a deep breath and braced myself as I stood on the majestic rock above the gleaming sea with its powerful crashing waves, my hair lashing at my face as the racing wind blew in from the vast ocean in front of me. All at once, I felt free and powerful and loved. This world belonged to no one and everyone. The time had come for me to live again and to trust again. And I readied myself to dive in.

I did not have to carry the burden of my husband's fall from grace. *I never had to.* Marrying Will had been my biggest mistake, and one that belonged to only me, and so I set him and every memory of him free. I imagined all of it, the good times, the regrets, the guilt, and every fear flying away as I threw the necklace, his dark wings, over the edge of the jagged cliff into the mighty abyss of waves below. And just like that, my heart felt whole again. I felt free, grateful for everything. He had never belonged in my life, and now I stood reborn to live this beautiful life with Jack—for the first time the thought of the unknown didn't scare me; instead, it sparkled, tempted me.

I turned back toward the shore. Jack waited for me. I ran as fast as I could toward him—we had a lot to do, and I didn't want to waste any more time. He reached out to me and grabbed my hand, smiled and winked as he recited one of my favorite lines of all time. "Are you ready, Porter, because I want to do and see everything on this earth with you."

I squeezed his hand and smiled. "I'm ready, my love."

~ 73 ~

Her injured leg almost back to normal, Rose decided to park the wheelchair and walk with her cane over to Porter's house. Cecil had the dogs, Patsy had plant-watering duty, and Rose intended to hold up her self-assigned duty of picking up the mail while the two lovebirds undoubtedly frolicked in the ocean air on the other side of the continent. Rose proudly let herself inside the house with the key Porter had given her. As she neatly stacked the letters and sales brochures that had gathered on the floor just beneath the mail slot, a distinct black envelope adorned with embossed wings slid out of her hands, falling as if in slow motion to the polished wood planks beneath her feet.

Rose retrieved the familiar envelope and examined it closely. It looked exactly like the stationery Porter had given to her when, as Porter had put it, she returned the M necklace and sapphire ring to their rightful heir. Rose looked more carefully and noticed that the postage seemed strange, foreign. She searched for a return address but found only a name engraved on the back seal. Her voice eerily broke the silence in the empty house as she read aloud, "Willem H. Stone."

~~~

"And in the end, we were all just humans...drunk on the idea that love, only love, could heal our brokenness." F. Scott Fitzgerald.

ACKNOWLEDGEMENTS

I would like to thank the following:

My husband—without his support and unfaltering belief in me, this would not have happened.

My mother, who inspired my love of reading.

My author friend, John Nuckel, who told me to write it down.

My friend Candace, who inspired courage when I needed it most.

My editor and publisher, Janet Fix, for her unending patience and guidance.

And to all those friends and family members who cheered me on—I am grateful.

ABOUT THE AUTHOR

J. Leigh Jackson finds her niche in the romantic suspense category. In her debut novel, *Dark Wings*, she draws inspiration from her southern roots, which she seamlessly weaves together with her military experiences—thanks to her husband's former career as an intelligence pilot.

She holds a bachelor's in English with a minor in journalism, as well as a master's in communication. She taught undergraduate courses in business and professional writing for several years. Currently, she lives in Southern California with her husband, two children, and a rambunctious mini Aussie.

CPSIA information can be obtained
at www.ICGtesting.com
Printed in the USA
FSHW010145180820

9 781948 225861